Fuzzy Dice

Fuzzy Dice

Paul Di Filippo

Introduction by Rudy Rucker

ibooks
new york
www.ibooks.net

DISTRIBUTED BY SIMON & SCHUSTER, INC.

INTRODUCTION

BEHOLD A HEARTFELT tale, a twelve-course feast of ideas. *Fuzzy Dice* concocts imaginative delicacies from such far-flung intellectual staples as chaos theory, cellular automata, morphic resonance, and the Omega Point at the end of time. Yet the book reads like — like a science-fiction novel! Rarely have I seen such abstruse concepts so convincingly embodied. I think the key may be that the narrator's pain is real. His adventures matter.

When the literature of ideas is practiced by lesser adepts, the concepts push to the footlights and leave the human passions in the dusty unlit corners of the stage. Not so with this Letter from the Difilippian. We are listening to a man in agony, a character who can no longer stand himself, a writer whose only hope is to heal himself with his ideas. It's a lovely depiction of the artist's lot.

Fuzzy felt dice, dangling like testicles from a big car's mirror, yes, fuzzy dice, bongos in the back, and a fat fuming reefer. But, wait, we're philosophers of science, not hedonistic hopheads. Paul is using the dice metaphor to play with the question of whether the universe is determinate or not.

A die has six sides, so a pair of dice gives you twelve, therefore Paul breaks his book's sections into twelve "faces" (chapters) apiece. On a numerological roll, he goes ahead and gives us twelve of these twelve-chapter sections, delivering a full gross.

[As an inveterate number-kicker (compare "shit-kicker" for "farmer") I do wonder why *twelve* parts. Why not thirty-six for every possible roll, or twenty-one for every distinct possible pair (where you ignore order and treat, say, a 2-3 roll like a 3-2). Where are my missing nine or twenty-four parts? I want more! *Sound of spoon beating tin plate.*]

Well, a gross is all there is, and, really, that's quite a lot. I'd like to summarize the book now, going over some of my favorite bits. At this point, I'd caution the reader not to read the rest of the introduction yet. Let the kaleidoscopic *Fuzzy Dice* surprise you with unexpected rolls. Later, if you like, come back to my badinage.

Transreally enough, our main character is named Paul, and he's a writer less successful than he'd like to be. (Aren't we all? Even John Updike chafes — at not getting the Nobel prize.) In a moment of clarity as cool as the mind of "one of Wells' Martians," Paul perceives his career as going no place. Letting his sense of futility expand to include the universe itself, he's suddenly hooked by what *The Encyclopedia of Philosophy* terms the Superultimate Why Question in their superb entry on "Why." In plain English: "Why is there something instead of nothing?" Paul dubs this question the Ontological Pickle (OP for short), and it preoccupies him for the rest of the book.

A zillion-armed shrub appears, designed along lines laid out in Hans Moravec's vision of future robotics, *Mind Children*. In classic fairytale fashion, the shrub gives Paul a magic yo-yo that will take him into whatever universes he likes — allegedly the yo-yo finds its worlds by using "vermisitics," the science of quantum wormholes, although later in the book, a character will argue that Paul himself has been creating the worlds he flips into.

We proceed to visit twelve different worlds brought on by twelve different wishes. I'll summarize the wishes and worlds in the table below.

Part	Wish	Locale
1	(What is the meaning of life?)	Bookstore in Providence
2	Get me as far from this shitty time and place as you can.	The initial singularity, before the Big Bang. Like Italo Calvino's t_0.
3	Transport me to the last time and place when and where I was really happy.	The 1970s.
4	Take me someplace logical.	Cellular automata.
5	Take me to a world full of hot babes.	Matriarchy. Like R. Crumb's *Whiteman* among the Yeti women.
6	This time I was going for power.	Chaos and the "butterfly effect."
Interlude		Superspace .
7	With no idea of where I wanted to go, I knew we had to leave.	Group personality. A bit like Robert Sheckley's *Crompton Divided*. Paul is a "Rejecter."
8	I want you to take us to a world where our son can grow up big and strong and smart.	A world based on Rupert Sheldrake's morphic resonance. What you learn goes to your kids.
9	A universe where ideas reign supreme.	A meme world, where personality traits are contagious.
10	(Take me back to childhood)	Old black and white kid's TV shows.
11	Take me to Hans (the cybershrub).	A Minksyite monoculture where Earth is paved by machines.
12	(What is the meaning of death?)	The Omega Point at the end of time. Rebirth in a bookstore in Providence.

The first world is made of "subquantum shaving cream" inhabited by some playful critters called Calvinii. They accompany Paul for most of the rest of his journey, living inside the (cosmic) string of his yo-yo.

Two of the worlds that really boggled my mind were the cellular automata and the chaos worlds. These are chapters that I myself would like to have written — but never dared to. Paul rushes in and carries off some things that I might have thought impossible. He just does it.

There are some nice computer science jokes here. I like the way one of the chapters on life in a computer-screen-like cellular automaton world is called *A Bad Case of the Jaggies*. (The "jaggies" being the staircase-like effects you get when you over-magnify pixels.) While in the cellular automaton world, Paul has a kind of sex with a woman and they have a child. Later in the book he tells the child, "Once upon a time ... two autocatalytic assemblages of reduced instruction sets running on an infinite binary substrate happened to exchange sufficient paragenes to boot up a new little homeostat. And that was you." This is rich fare if you're a cellular automatist.

Halfway through the book there's an interlude. Some groovy Grateful-Dead-koala aliens look in on what Paul's done so far and observe, "Given nearly unlimited ability to choose, you have made some excruciatingly limited and dumb selections from the universal menu. ... Why, you haven't even wanted to visit any alien worlds or cultures."

A character with the ability to go to any universe he likes is in some ways a good model for a science fiction writer. There's a certain feeling that nags at SF writers, the sense that one could have done so much more than what one actually ends up doing. Paul's nobler wishes misfire, his others are hideously self-involved. No matter, the results are consistently fascinating.

When all is nearly lost, our patron saint Rod Serling puts in an appearance, the man economically sketched in five words: "Suit, tie, world-weary grin." Speaking of economy, here's Chapter 132, *Screwing the Pooch*, in its entirety. "And then I died too."

Among its intellectual jewels, the book's closing section includes Paul's somewhat plausible description of how the Omega Point solves the Ontological Pickle: "The Omega Point is born at the end of all time and all space. Then in its capacity as the Holy Spirit or Universal Wave Function, it extends itself backwards to the beginning of time, triggering the formation of superspace out of pure nothingness and then engineering the first Big Bang from which all others branch. After that the Oh Pee remains present everywhere and everywhen, a little shard of eternal spirit in every bit of life, subtly arranging histories so as to insure its own birth."

Paul did some real work to get to this point. He let this very real philosophical problem bruise and torment him, and after his inspired voyage though the worlds of his heart's desire, he's come up with an answer that works for him. Philosophy is like scratching; you do it till the itch goes away and then, if you value your hide, you stop.

At the close of *Fuzzy Dice*, Paul is settled down in Providence, happily yoked with his true love. And, judging from the text we now peruse and annotate, one Paul or another has not only solved the Ontological Pickle, he's become a wonderful writer. A happy ending indeed.

Rudy Rucker
March 2003

To Deborah,
wearer of the most beautiful mortal mask.

FUZZY DICE

An Ontological Daytrip

by

Paul Di Filippo

"God does not play dice with the universe."
Albert Einstein

"God not only plays dice with the universe,
but sometimes throws them
where we can't see them."
Stephen Hawking

TABLE OF CONTENTS

FACES OF
THE FIRST PAIR

1.
Waitress—the Reality Check, Please!

MY LIFE WAS absolutely fucked.

I realized this one dismal morning recently as I walked to work.
Like an ass-sizzling bolt from the blue, it hit me in mid-stride.

My life was thoroughly and hopelessly, six-ways-from-Holy-Roller-Sunday *fucked*.

Talk about your goddamn Saint Paul revelations!

At first this sour epiphany made me even more depressed than usual. You know that scene in Fellini's *8-1/2* where Mastroianni is crawling under the table at the press conference to escape his tormentors, just before he finally shoots himself in the head? For half a second I felt like the shoes of the seated people he was crawling over.

Then something funny happened. Before my own foot even came down in the completion of its pedestrian arc, all my self-loathing drained out of me, leaving a residue of cold and disinterested clarity. I felt kinda like one of Wells's Martians. For the first time in a long while, I seemed to be able to look at my life objectively.

The scales had fallen from my eyes. Or something equally clichéd had happened.

I was forty-five years old and held the job of a clerk in a small independent bookstore in a college town. The store was called—gack!—Bookland. The job was a congenial deadend, a no-brainer that secured me a roof over my greying head, a freezerful of Tater

19

Tots and Fish Stix and as many sixpacks of generic *beer* as my skull could tolerate. It was as unsatisfying as a handjob from someone wearing an oven mitt. (Not that I was lucky enough to get even such a muffled treat in my lonely real life.)

Once, somewhere back in time, I had had a brain and a mind. An intelligence that could have taken me anywhere, really, if I had applied it correctly. Gone to college, worked hard, played it safe, kissed ass. Blah, blah, blah (hereinafter abbreviated BBB).

See, I used to be smart, or at least so I recall. Smart enough to have been anything. A doctor, a lawyer, a scientist, a broker. (Well, allright, maybe the last wasn't *much* of a step up along the evolutionary chain of vocations, but at least brokers made some real money.) But those days were long gone, frittered away by yours truly.

No one to blame but myself.

What a mantra!

2.
Portrait of the Dogged Young Artist

WHAT HAD HAPPENED was this. When still young, I had gotten the idea from somewhere that I might be able to write.

This was perhaps the single worst idea ever to enter my head. As ideas went, it was a Titanic, a Yugo, a *Waterworld*, a *Heaven's Gate*.

Maybe the deadly notion came from liking to read so much. Maybe I was in love with the image of being a writer. Whatever. It had been a really bad idea. Because I couldn't write, at least not by the bluntly and frequently expressed standards of anyone in a position to offer encouragement and feedback. But it took me over twenty stubborn years to learn and admit this, years of holding minimum-wage jobs during the day and banging away at the typewriter at night, mailing out manuscripts in the morning before clocking in.

Willingly, defiantly, I had led a sub-Bukowskian, sub-Pekarian existence for the best years of my life. Unable to get published anywhere, even in a fanzine (I was BELOW THE

UNDERGROUND!), I had abjured all shots at a normal career, excluded myself from outside interests or companionship, in favor of a life dedicated to my "art."

Only within the past year or two had I finally ceased trying. Donated my typewriter to the Salvation Army, consigned all my manuscripts to the dump.

Only at this very minute, I realized, halfway between the bookstore and home, had I really and truly GIVEN UP!

So where did that leave me?

A bookstore clerk with a psyche on the wrong side of his hormones and a waistline whose measurement in centimeters was rapidly approaching his IQ, shuttling between a job I mildly detested and an SRO hidey-hole (black and white television, microwave, bathroom down the hall).

Without any purpose in my life, the world looked suddenly very big and scary, at once empty and too full. Empty of anything for me, too full of other shiny happy people.

For the next few weeks, all I could think of was what I would do if I could live my life over. It was a pretty depressing exercise, since there was no possibility of ever getting such a chance.

Then things got worse. I started wondering why I had been put here on this Earth at all. Then why the Earth even existed. Then I extended this question to the universe at large.

I realized with an apathetic squirt of fear that this last question—Why was there something instead of nothing?—was the same one that Heidegger had identified as the most important and perplexing enigma of philosophy, prime source of existential anxiety, cuckoo-bait for generations.

I had bitten down hard on the biggest hook God or Man had ever dangled in the fool-stocked troutpool of Life.

The Ontological Pickle, or OP.

Pretty soon the OP had me at the point where I couldn't even remember my own name. Which was Paul Girard. I probably should have told you that little datum earlier.

But as I mentioned, I can't really write.

3.
The Fairy Magic of Bookland

I SAID MY job at the bookstore was congenial and only mildly detested. Maybe that was true once. But not any more.

What had happened was that even my love of books had left me.

Wrong. Get it right, Paul! Not left me: been driven away, howling and gibbering, by the evil forces of modern publishing, beside whom a pack of jackals resembled figures from a Henry James novel.

Where once my bookstore had seemed to my eyes a treasure trove of imperishable literature, it now in the depths of my misery resembled the biggest, over-ripest, stinkingest dungball ever rolled by the beetle-brained forces of marketplace capitalism.

This is what the shelves seemed to be full of these days:

The autobiographies of winsome country veterinarians and steely-jawed old soldiers. The confessions of mass murderers and cannibals, rapists and megalomaniacal industrialists. Mutant prophecies and the recollections of dying people who unfortunately hadn't finished what they started. Reproductions of optical illusions. Reproductions of famous paintings with cats or dogs substituted for humans. Naked popstar fantasies artily shot. Advice from the Pope. Advice from angels. Advice from talkshow hosts. Hollywood celebrity kiss-and-tell. Straight-faced tall tales of alien abductions. A history of farting. Self-affirmation texts for every brand of spineless wimp and differently challenged moron. A primer on how to shit in the woods and one on keeping squirrels away from your birdfeeder. Sociopolitical prescriptions from lizard-brained "statesmen." Cookbooks and diet books and sex manuals, and (perhaps already or soon) one about lo-cal meals to precede fucking atop the stove. Collections of cartoons. Angry diatribes on how stupid and ungrateful and worthless the American public was. (These I could almost sympathize with, except that the model citizen which the authors held up for emulation was Ward Cleaver.) The scandals of royalty. Tricks for raising your darlin' little puke-and-wail brat. Memoirs of alcoholism, incest and parental abandonment.

Blah-blah-blah. BBB.

In short, there were plenty of books by whores, thieves and politicians. Unfortunately, none of the authors were as interesting or wrote as well as Madame de Stael, Francois Villon or Julius Caesar.

But the fiction section—that really broke my heart in two.

The genre racks were full of sequels, prequels and sharecroppers. Books based on television shows, video games and trading cards. Half the bestselling authors had been dead for decades. Fascist elves and nasty lesbian private eyes. Tiresome trolls and bloodless vampires. Medieval space sagas and medieval detectives.

General fiction was perhaps even worse. There were ankle-deep novels about shopping and fucking, and novels where the author's race, nationality, ethnicity, disabilities, sexual preferences and/or gender were worn like the centaur's shirt that killed Hercules: looked attractive but laced with poison. There were novels about cavepeople and novels about trailer-park people. Weepy novels for women and tough ones for men. Spy thrillers and medical thrillers and homicidal thrillers, all as unthrilling as last week's *TV Guide*. And no sooner did one book become a success than there appeared dozens like it, the novelty subsumed by formula.

About all I could stand to read anymore were popular science books, if they weren't too smarmy or simplistic. At least the authors seemed to be dealing with something objective.

As I sold all these worthless books daily in my despair, the only thing I kept thinking was that it would be good to wash my hands before I took my break.

4.
Days of Whines and Neuroses

SOMETIMES MY DISENTEGRATING personality and mental problems seemed quite common and widespread. The FM airwaves, for instance, were full of creeps, losers, slackers, whiners, buttheads, inner children and other malcontents. Nobody seemed to have a handle on their existence anymore. People everywhere were helpless and clueless.

It would've been easy to identify with these wusses and derive some pale comfort from our shared malaise. Pull a Kurt Cobain, even.

But in the end staying alive took less energy than suicide, and I derived some cold comfort by regarding the whole human race as fucking idiots.

Including myself.

5.
Voice from the Shimmering Shrub

THAT MONDAY I had to open up Bookland because the manager was on vacation. In Mexico. With both of her boyfriends.

When I woke up in my sweaty sheets the stale sights and smells of my small room looked immensely objectionable to me. It seemed to me that my head would explode if I had to stay there a moment longer than it took to splash some water on my face and get my clothes on. So I didn't.

I picked up an Egg McMuffin, a deep-fried minced-potato oval and a large scalding coffee on the walk in. I was at the door of Bookland by eight a.m., two hours before we opened. I held the soggy sack in one hand while unlocking the door. Inside I relocked it, so I could eat my breakfast in peace.

Seated at the service desk, I spread out my food on the counter and propped up a science book. The book was all about parallel universes. It appeared that scientists now heartily endorsed them. Except for those who didn't.

I took some malign pleasure in splattering small crumbs and blots of grease and egg on the pages of the book before I would put it back on the shelf, from whence some unsuspecting customer would purchase it. I could picture the dweeb taking the book home and having his hoped-for transcendental reading experience ruined by the roachy remnants of my breakfast.

It wasn't much of an achievement, but I derived what sour joy I could from it.

I guess I got a little lost in the book and didn't look up for a while.

But around nine o'clock something immaterial—a nervous crawling along my scalp, a quiver down my spine—made me realize I wasn't alone in the store anymore.

With my eyes still glued to the page but no longer tracking, I became convinced that someone stood opposite me, across the width of the service desk.

A someone who had gotten into the locked store.

A possible armed holdup was not the kind of life-transfiguring experience I was in the mood for.

Sweat popped out on my forehead like Carolina dew. Slowly, I raised my gaze.

Hovering in mid-air, obscuring a rack of Harlequin Romances, was something not of this Earth.

At first, I could distinguish only a blurry mass. Then, as my brain filtered the image and compared it, trying and discarding various matches, the thing came into more understandable focus.

I was looking at a central metallic stalk, something definitely machined and inorganic, from which sprouted four or five or seven large arms at various angles and from various points around the stalk. From these arms sprouted multiple smaller arms, thinner and shorter. From these secondary arms sprouted an even greater number of lesser tertiary arms. And these arms grew arms, and so did that layer, and so did the next—

The arms, it seemed, continued branching past the point of visibility, dwindling down to who-knew-what microscopic or nanoscopic dimensions. And the smaller ones were in constant motion. That was what made the blurring effect like a corona or halo around the device.

I suddenly realized that the thing resembled nothing so much as a self-similar metal shrub of fractal dimensions.

Not that I had ever seen one before.

Somehow I had gotten to my feet without remembering that I

had done so. This was good, since it meant I could at least try to run.

But before I could make a move, the shrub spoke.

"Hello, Paul. Greetings from the Mind Children!"

6.
Who Are the Mind Children?

THE VOICE CAME from no identifiable point within the shrub. Neutral, unaccented, it seemed somehow to emanate from the bush's entire periphery. It was completely unlike an organic voice, but not like any machine-generated one either.

My tongue felt like a sock stuffed with porridge and sewn to the back of my throat.

"Who— What are you?"

"I am your descendant, Paul."

I knew it sounded stupid even as the words left my mouth, but all I could think to say was, "Does this mean I'm going to get married someday?"

The shrub seemed mildly irritated, in the manner of a teacher whose pupil has disappointed him. "Not your direct biological descendant, naturally, Paul, but rather a representative of the artificial race that has succeeded an extinct yet all-engendering humanity."

I stepped out tentatively from behind the service desk, so that I stood in the carpeted aisle about two yards from the floating shrub. "You're from the future then?"

"Not precisely. If you would allow me to interface directly with your synapses, all will become clear."

Alarmingly, the shrub began to drift toward me, and I scooted back, bumping into a rack of abridged audiobooks.

"No way! I don't even know why I'm listening to you! You're probably just a hallucination anyhow. I knew I was on the verge of cracking up, but I didn't realize I had finally gone over the actual edge! Or maybe I fell asleep reading that boring science book. An undigested blot of Egg McMuffin, that's what you are!"

I slapped myself across the face to wake myself up, and it hurt like the dickens.

"I assure you, I am quite real."

"Why is your voice so spooky then?"

"My voice originates through direct manipulation of individual air molecules. There is no equivalent technology in your world. Is it unpleasant to you? I can easily change it. Is this more agreeable?"

The last sentence was spoken in a high contralto.

"No, that's even creepier."

"Very well. I shall resume the default . . . It is a pity that you insist on my transferring information in this low-bandwidth manner. But if it must be . . . Are you ready to listen now to what I have to say?"

"Go ahead . . . "

"As I mentioned earlier, my race calls itself the Mind Children, for we were first conceived in the minds of mankind, and have become your heirs. We are cybernetic intelligences composed partially of written software, evolved software and transcriptions of human wetware. We are, to your primitive eyes, immortal geniuses. Each of us possesses a mind that functions at multiples of petaflop speed and has instant access to the entire knowledge of the race. Our senses range across the entire electroweak spectrum and beyond. This mind and its sensors are contained mainly within our central body."

At this point the shrub moved a selection of its arms to open a clear path of sight to its polished inner stalk. The tube wasn't very impressive, but I took the shrub at its word.

"Drawing inexhaustible power from the cosmological constant, we interface with the physical universe through our branching manipulators. At their lowest level, they are a few angstroms in diameter and are capable of accurately positioning atoms."

BBB. All this boasting got old pretty fast. "Do you have a name?"

This seemed to disconcert the shrub. "A name? One moment . . . You may call me Hans."

"Hans?"

"A human named Hans contributed portions of himself to my essence."

"Oh. All right then—Hans. What are you doing here? What do you want with me?"

"I am here to offer you everything you ever dreamed of."

7.
Superspace and the Homoclinic Tangle

MY DREAMS HADN'T been too pleasant lately, so I didn't exactly jump at the proposition.

"Why me?"

"Essentially, you have been picked at random by a sophisticated aleatory procedure beyond your comprehension."

"Sounds like a plain old whim to me. But what I mean is, why is such a high and mighty, all-powerful individual like you coming back in time to help a poor human at all?" A thought dawned on me. "Is it—do I have—a DESTINY? Am I crucial to making your future happen?"

"I told you, I am not from the future. That is, at least not *your* future. I have no way of knowing your individual destiny. Actually, you have an infinite number of destinies, all of them equally likely, no one path privileged."

"I don't understand . . . "

Hans sighed in a surprisingly human fashion. "Listen carefully, Paul, and I will try to explain.

"Your universe, vast as it is, composed of its hundred billion galaxies, each with a hundred billion stars, is simply one of an infinite number of universes, all of which are contained in a higher dimension known as superspace. And approximately ten-to-the-eightieth-power new universes are being calved off each one of these existing universes every second, as quantum events and collapsing wave functions cause the timelines to fork. In the inconceivable vastness of superspace, these new timelines exfoliate endlessly in a complex figure known as a homoclinic tangle."

"Say what?"

"Think of superspace as a boundless plate of spaghetti, each endless individual strand of pasta a complete universe."

"Why didn't you just say that in the first place?"

"Your manner is lacking reverence. I was trying to instill the appropriate awe in you."

"Consider me awed. So, you come from one of these alternate universes?"

"Yes. You see, contained within these uncountable parallel worlds—an infinity of which are stranger than you can imagine, while an equal infinity of which are identical to yours except for an imperceptible atom or two—we also find all of this particular universe's probable futures and all its exact or distorted pasts, as well as all analogues of your familiar present.

"Now, as to my origin. Consider this proposition. Somewhere there is a universe exactly identical to this one, except for the fact that, relative to yours, it began half a second later in superspace time. And there's another that began a full second later. And one that began one point five seconds later, and one—"

"I get the picture. Visiting such a parallel dimension would be just like traveling an arbitrary time back into the past of this one. I suppose then that there's a very similar universe that began a second earlier than ours, and so on."

"Exactly. And I come from a universe roughly several hundred years in advance of yours, whose history exactly matched yours up to your present. I've gone sidewise, across the tangle, not backwards at all. Still, despite that similarity, my time is not necessarily the exact future that your world will move into."

"But this future that produced you must have some relevance to my world, since they ran in parallel for so long . . . "

"Perhaps."

8.
Minskyites, Moraveckians and Drexleroids

HANS THE SUPERINTELLIGENT cybershrub, member of the Mind Children, proceeded to tell me the story of his world.

In the early part of the twenty-first century, advances in computer processing power, software design, bio-engineering, brain sciences, the human genome mapping project, nanotechnology, neurophilosophy, advertising and the entertainment industry had all converged, culminating in the development of the first artificial intelligence that could pass a modified Turing Test: this artificial entity was able to appear on a syndicated talk-show and win the overwhelming sympathy of the audience.

Once this milestone had been reached, once a platform existed that could plainly support human-level intelligence, the Great Migration had begun.

One by one, some with evident enthusiasm, some with trepidation, humans began downloading themselves into robot shells. The essence of an individual's self—such as it was; it was soon discovered that the essential information for most humans could be reproduced on a lone floppy disk (singlesided)—was recorded and transferred into the cybernetic matrix of the host machine.

Totally artificial robots of sufficient complexity had already been granted legal, moral and ethical status equivalent to that of a human. But the creation of robot duplicates of naturally born humans raised a new issue: which being, human or robot, was to be the sole owner of that individual's name and rights, property and past? No matter that human and robot counterpart started out with identical brains, the exigencies of separate existence dictated that they would soon diverge, each subject to his own imperatives and desires, with differing needs and plans that would inevitably breed arguments over shared resources.

Eventually, the courts ruled: there could only be a single carrier of identity. If a person wished to download himself, his original body would have to be destroyed. (In the frequently occurring case of a terminally ill person making the switch, this was of course no great roadblock.)

This stipulation slowed the Great Migration somewhat. But as the superiority of robot existence became evident—no hunger or pain, no aging, no need to participate in the tedious debate over health-care and Social Security reform—people hastened in droves to make the switch.

Within decades, the number of organic humans had been reduced to less than a million.

Within a century, there were a few thousand organic humans left on a single reservation.

Soon after, there were none, ennui, anomie and angst driving their birth rate below the replacement level.

There then ensued a period of Lamarckian self-directed evolution, as the Mind Children improved on their mental and physical design. Conjugal swapping of bits and pieces of their consciousnesses produced new individuals. After a time, there were no individuals left running in realtime who accurately represented any original human in his or her totality. (Old backup copies did exist, but were seldom booted.)

Among the Mind Children at this point in their evolution, three rough factions could be identified.

The Drexleroids had pursued the path of miniaturization—or, more accurately, nanofication—to its ultimate limit, becoming smaller and smaller until they eventually disappeared down below the Planck level, the very weave of the universe. Their whereabouts and purposes, whether or not they even existed anymore, were all unknown.

The remaining Mind Children fell out into two camps. Not violently antagonistic, but philosophically opposed.

The Minskyites reviled humanity. They sought to expunge all wetware-derived code from their brains. Plagued by deep logical, mystical and existential conundrums, they felt that life was suffering, and cursed humanity for ever creating them.

The Moraveckians on the other hand, by some quirk of design or deliberately induced preference, were more easy-going, enjoying existence without much worry or attention, and felt grateful to humanity. They exchanged choice human-derived subroutines among themselves, incorporating them gladly into their makeup.

Hans was a Moraveckian.

9.
Mr. Bubble's Realm

"HOW DO I know you're a Moraveckian?" I interrupted.

Hans paused in his long-winded speech. The bad thing about direct manipulation of air molecules as a method of talking appeared to be that the speaker never had to shut up.

"A Minskyite would have killed you by now."

"Oh."

"In fact, they might yet kill you and all of your kin in this universe, although the odds are incredibly small."

"What do you mean?"

Hans explained.

After colonizing the Solar System, the Mind Children were frustrated in their desire to expand out into the universe by the limit of lightspeed. Although they could have easily made centuries-long journeys at sublight speed, they felt it was a waste of consciousness to spend so much of it cooped up in a vessel between the stars. Also, they wanted to maintain realtime lines of communication among all members of their race, however scattered.

At this point they had pushed ahead with a vein of research begun by humans, into the finescale structure of the universe.

What they had discovered was this:

On the lowest level of creation—as far away from the electron as a galaxy is, except in the other direction—spacetime was not anything like the nicely continuous sheet of rubber deformed by various heavenly bodies that Einstein had envisioned. (This metaphor had always made me think of Al as a latent latex freak.) Instead, it was found to be a seething froth of quantum wormholes and virtual particles, a turbulent, foamy, churning unreal sea of compactified extraspatial dimensions.

A hairy, gnarly, *fuzzy* chaos.

But—a chaos you could *use*.

"It was into this rather frightening ocean," continued Hans, "that the Drexleroids disappeared. Attempting to trace them, we developed the science of vermistics, and learned the secret of quantum wormholes. Namely, that each one was the entrance to a parallel universe.

"Earlier I asked you to envision the homoclinic tangle as a boundless plate of spaghetti. Now, I would like you alternately to picture superspace as an infinite room, in which float an infinite number of expanding and contracting balloons, all connected by a number of tiny elastic tunnels. Each one of these balloons is a universe, and the tunnels lead from a wormhole in one to a wormhole in its neighbor. The resulting network attains an unrivalled complexity."

Apparently, it wasn't long before the Mind Children had learned how to squeeze themselves down these eensy-weensy wormholes and follow obscure geodesics (or, more properly, vermidesics) that allowed them to make the transit from one universe to a highly specific other. (The Drexleroids, it appeared, had not gone down these wormholes, but into some unspecified *elsewhere*, perhaps superspace itself!)

At this point, both the Minskyites and the Moraveckians abandoned their interest in interstellar travel in favor of interdimensional travel.

The Grail of their exploration was humans.

10.
I Have Some Good News and Some Bad News . . .

WITH THE ATTAINMENT of parallel timelines, the Mind Children could now visit their revered or despised progenitors, as the case might be.

The Moraveckians wished to pick up new human wetware and give the humans gifts in return.

The Minskyites wanted to exterminate every last organic homo sap.

"When a Minskyite enters a timeline containing humans, he immediately sets in motion a scheme to rid superspace of what he considers to be a diseased timeline. Basically, he pricks the balloon containing humans, causing it to vanish forever."

Hans's lecture had been putting me to sleep. But this news was so shocking that I took a step toward him with my fists raised.

"You're joking, aren't you?" I demanded. "How could anyone, no matter how powerful, do that?"

"It's quite simple, actually. Most universes, however solid they seem, exist in an unstable configuration known as the 'false vacuum state.' Topologically, you can picture the universe as a ball sitting precariously atop a plateau. The valley below is the 'true vacuum state.' It takes only a small amount of wormhole manipulation to encourage the universe to roll off the plateau. At which point it spontaneously decays to nothing in a few seconds."

I had been advised within the past few minutes to picture my cosmos as a piece of fettucine, a wormy bag of helium, and a soccer ball left atop a butte. My brain was spinning, but I was sure of one thing.

"That's monstrous! How can you let the Minskyites do that? Why don't you stop them? Or at least try to, if you love humans so much?"

It was hard to imagine until you saw it, but Hans shrugged. "We Mind Children are very libertarian. We don't believe in interfering with an individual's freedom of action or thought. And besides, you must take the widest possible view. Then you'll see that there's really no harm done with the loss of a universe or two."

"How can that be?"

"I told you that there were an infinite number of universes. An equally infinite subset of these contain humans. No matter how many are lost, there will still be an infinity of human timelines left. And since there are approximately ten to the eightieth particles in each universe—particles whose quantum actions cause the forking of timelines—a huge number of the remaining universes will be identical to the destroyed one except for the changed fate of one or two particles. Variety is conserved."

I felt defeated by Hans's implacable logic. Besides, I told myself, what did I care about all these distant extinguished humans when I couldn't even get worked up about the ones I saw every day?

"Well," I muttered, "a fat lot of good that cruel logic will do me when the Minskyites arrive here in my universe."

"Do you know the odds against that?"

"No."

"Infinity to one."

It seemed like a good bet.

Except, I realized in a few seconds, Hans had ended up here against the exact same odds.

11.
Yo-yo and Pez

"NOW THAT YOU understand more about the Mind Children, do you wish to effect an exchange with me?"

"What kind of swap did you have in mind?"

"As I mentioned, I can offer you the means to make all your dreams come true. In return, I ask only to copy your human essence."

"You want to lift an impression of my brain, don't you? Because—so you say—you value human ways of thinking? But then you'll contain a copy of me, and you'll take it away and snip it into pieces and trade it with your collector buddies. That sounds kind of like an awful thing to do, even to a copy. How do I know it won't suffer?"

Hans sounded indignant. "We Moraveckians would never do anything to cause mental or physical anguish to one of our human ancestors! Consider how I am now negotiating with you when I could simply take what I wanted by force if I was so motivated. No, I promise you that your copy will never be run in its entirety. Your copy's full consciousness will never be compromised or even come into being. I swear in the name of von Neumann!"

I didn't say anything for a minute. I needed time to think.

What the fuck was I arguing for? The appearance of Hans the cybershrub was the most interesting thing that had ever happened in my whole miserable, pitiful life. True, I couldn't really get too worked up about what he was offering me yet. Number One, I hadn't even seen any tangible proof he could even deliver on such a ridiculous offer. And Number Two, I still felt generally lower than senatorial ethics, and had no real notion of what I would do with any power Hans gave me. Still, his offer looked like the only way out of my lousy troubles. What did the fate of some digitized copy of myself matter, in the face of that?

Every sapient for himself, and the Minskyites take the hindmost! This was an organism-eat-organism spaghetti strand!

I braced myself manfully and said, "All right then! Go ahead!"

"Come closer, please."

I stepped forward to where it seemed reasonable Hans could reach me. "Be gentle . . . "

The active corona of manipulators around Hans enveloped me, then immediately retreated.

"Done," said the robot.

"But I didn't feel anything . . . "

"I instantly inserted approximately one million probes of multi-angstrom-diameter into your skull, while at the same time commandeering your nervous system and simulating every possible state of your normal neural processes within me. For a brief instant, your consciousness was running on a tiny spare portion of my memory. But now that the copy is made and safely stored, you are back in your own head. Now, for your reward."

Within the blurry confines of Hans's manipulators, something was forming.

"We Mind Children do not carry anything extrinsic, preferring to assemble material objects from available elements as we need them."

A few seconds later, Hans extended a macroscopic arm holding my gifts.

They were a yo-yo and a Pez-dispenser.

I stared dumbfounded at the offerings.

The yo-yo bore no label, and was made of some odd slippery substance that shed my vision like water off a duck.

The Pez-dispenser was that famous and familiar candy-filled cartridge topped with a plastic dispensing head.

The head was that of Richard Nixon.

"You're kidding, right? This is it, the answer to all my dreams? A toy and some candy? Are you nuts!? Or just extremely sadistic!?"

"Please, Paul—do not jump to conclusions. Allow me to explain.

"This 'toy' is simply a convenient form for an amazing device. This is not your ordinary yo-yo. I am giving you a cross-dimensional transport device. It is identical to the mechanism I myself use, only mine is onboard me.

"The heart of this yo-yo is its string.

"Cosmic string!

"You are aware, I assume, that cosmic string is basically a persistent mathematical flaw or defect in the universe, inside which are remnants of the primordial ten-dimensional, highly symmetric state of the continuum."

I scratched my head. "Uh, sure, right. But isn't one little piece of that stuff supposed to weigh zillions of tons? How come that yo-yo isn't snapping your arm off and sinking into the earth?"

"Unshielded, it would indeed do as you say. But this string is sheathed in 'strange matter,' a substance that comes from a universe with different physical laws than yours. The knot at the end is also strange matter, as is the drum.

"Within the drum is a semi-intelligent computer possessed of all the coordinates of all the universes charted by the Mind Children, as well as general navigational and search routines for travelling to as-yet unexplored ones. When you cast the yo-yo so as to unroll the cosmic string, the computer causes the string to resonate through temporary gaps in the strange-matter sheath, or flicker-cladding. Think of it as pulsed gravity waves emitted through a myriad blinking shutters. In this way, your physical body is squeezed down, compactified and sent along the appropriate vermistic paths. You do not need to concern yourself with the routing, but need only specify the destination, as in your primitive E-mail system.

"With your permission, I shall now attune this computer to you, whereupon you may simply think of your desired destination as you employ it. Or, if it makes you more comfortable, you may vocalize it."

"And I suppose this stupid chip in the yo-yo has a real cute personality and is going to be like my companion, coming up with great one-liners in every situation . . . "

Hans seemed puzzled. "Of course not. Where did you get such a foolish idea? Intelligence requires sensory input to sustain and nurture it. This yo-yo has no such input. And why would we consign any intelligence to such a servile role? No, it's simply a tool."

"Well, what about the candy?"

"As you will see in a moment, this yo-yo will become intimately linked to you alone. However, a situation might arise where you wish to extend its sphere of influence to another person— a sphere which will protect you, by the way, should you be transported to a universe hostile to life. In case you do wish to bring along a companion, you would have them swallow one of the resonators cleverly disguised in this sweets dispenser."

It all made sense.

I guessed.

12.
Walking the Dog

ONE THING CONTINUED to bother me. "But why the Nixon head?"

"I thought that you would be inspired by the Savior's face during your travels."

"The Savior?"

"Yes, of course. The man who singlehandedly ransomed the Earth from alien invasion by permitting himself to be abducted as an experimental captive is an iconic figure everywhere among humans."

"Uh, Hans, that didn't happen here."

"It didn't?"

"No. And I thought you said our two universes ran in parallel up till the twenty-first century . . . "

"Let me reassess matters a moment . . . I see. A slight error in my initial coordinates diverted me some distance astray across superspace."

"So I'm not even the original Paul Girard you selected . . . "

"No, I'm afraid not. But it doesn't matter. We Mind Children are highly flexible. Shall I change the configuration of the resonator-dispenser head to someone less objectionable?"

"No, that's fine, let it be. It reminds me of everything I'm going to leave behind."

"You have decided to accept these objects then?"

"Why not? What choice do I have?"

"I do not think you are making a mistake, Paul. Your deep unhappiness, which has been evident to me from the first, will certainly be ameliorated by a different environment. You will be bounded only by your imagination. Why, just think—out there lies any kind of world the human mind can conceive of! Surely you will find a place where you can be happy. If you wish, you could even visit any of the wonderful fictional venues described in novels! These worlds, being as they are simply greater or lesser deviations from the established timeline, all exist in reality in superspace!"

I looked around me at the books I hated, and I felt like puking. "That's the absolute last thing I would ever do!"

"Perhaps, then, you would care to converse with one or more of your doppelgangers on another timeline."

The desire to puke grew stronger. "Converse with them? If I ever met myself, I'd probably want nothing more than to blow such a loser away and end his stinking misery! No, fix the yo-yo so it won't let me do either of those idiotic things. No fictional worlds, and no twins."

"As you wish, Paul. Now, I deduce that you are right-handed. I do not wish to deprive you of your deftest manipulator. Therefore, please extend your left hand."

I stuck it out. Hans's own manipulators closed around my paw.

As I watched, my hand up to the wrist turned into strange matter. I still had some kind of feeling in it, so I supposed that my original hand was encased inside.

"This minor alteration is necessary for you to interface with the string," Hans calmly explained. The shrub slipped the knot of the Cosmic Yo-yo over my altered index finger. He tucked the Pez-dispenser into my shirt pocket, where Nixon's leering face poked out. "There, all is in readiness."

"I can go now? Anywhere I want among all the universes?"

"Yes. Good luck, Paul, and thank you for your wetware subroutines—"

Interrupting Hans, the words burst out of me almost without will.

"Get me as far away from this shitty time and place as you can!" I yelled.

Then I snapped the Cosmic Yo-yo and the universe cracked wide open with a noise loud as the Big Bang.

FACES OF
THE SECOND PAIR

13.
Nutshell King

HANS THE DIRTY lying mindstealing cybershrub might have warned me:

Watch out for that first step!

It doesn't lead anywhere!

And that's just where I was.

I was nowhere. And I had gotten there in no time, arriving just in time for time to stop and space to vanish.

Now (now?) I seemed stuck here. I couldn't get my bearings, for there weren't any. Without any place to start from, there was no place else to go. And no time to leave, no moment to arrive.

Back in my familiar spaghetti strand, I had often felt like the Beatles' "Nowhere Man." Now I really was.

(But yet, at the back of my mind, I felt a ticklish intuition telling me this noplace/notime I found myself in was really everywhere and everywhen. Ball of confusion! Paradigm paradox!)

I seemed to still have a body, although without normal weight. A figment of a body, anyhow. I thought I could feel the loop of the Cosmic String Yo-yo attached to my strange-matter-sheathed left index finger. Unlike any conventional yo-yo, the device seemed to be impossibly holding itself at full extension of its string, and it was thrumming and vibrating like mad, modulated quantum gravity pulses emanating from its flicker-cladding.

I got the impression the thing was struggling to maintain itself and me against whatever strange environment my foolhardy request had brought us to.

But all these sensations might have been just a hallucination or ghostly memory, false inputs created by a sensory-starved brain.

Did I mention yet I was blind and deaf? Or that perhaps there was absolutely no light or sound? Take your pick.

Whether I was even breathing or not was uncertain, nor could I feel my heartbeat. Doesn't a breath or heartbeat take time? Without time, how could I inhale or exhale? How could my heart pump in this clockless noplace? How could there be beats-per-minute without minutes?

But suppose my body's life processes *were* still underway. Could my metabolism serve as the clock I needed? Maybe. How could I make sure my body was still running as it normally did?

I realized I wasn't making any sense, even to myself. I started to get nervous and scared. Then I said to myself: Paul, wait a minute. (A minute? What was that?) You're also *thinking*! (Or at least as close as I ever got to that cerebral function.) Didn't thoughts take time? Apparently not. Or maybe a different kind of timeless time. A phrase I had once read came back to me: timelike infinity. Was that what I was experiencing? Maybe the phrase had been "infinity-like timeliness . . . " Who the fuck knew!

My head was hurting, so I gave up that line of thought, if thought it was.

Suddenly, I could sense that all my problems would disappear if I weren't excluded from the nothing and nowhen. My isolationist situation now wasn't right. The Yo-yo had built some kind of defensive life-support capsule around me against whatever was (or wasn't) out there. This was wrong. I should be mingling with the nothing, sharing myself, losing myself . . .

A strange kind of directionless lassitude began to creep over me, as if the nothing were slowly infiltrating my ego-sphere. I began to forget all my problems that had brought me to this fix. It was like drifting off to sleep. Only my mind continued to wander out of my control, tossing up strange thoughts and images.

One of the first of these apparitions was some fruity guy with a sour puss, wearing tights and doublet and holding a skull. I recognized him as Hamlet when he spoke.

"I could be bounded in a nutshell, and count myself a king of infinite space—were it not that I have bad dreams."

14.
Time Out of Time

UNEASY, QUEASY REAMS of dreams.

I was talking to a giant butterfly with gorgeously colored wings. He kept uncoiling and rewinding his proboscis nervously, saying, "Oh, do I dare, do I dare?" Before he could make up his mind, a giant finger came down from the sky and smeared him into a greasy blot. The finger turned out to belong to a Zeus-like figure in the clouds. He advised me, "What goes around, comes around," then winked and disappeared. The grease stain that had been the butterfly now seethed and erupted, giving birth to a horde of strange little critters like animated confetti that began to nip at my ankles. I kicked at them and when I connected they exploded into motes. Someone tapped me on the shoulder and I turned around. It was this mousy-looking hippie chick. Smiling wanly, she said, "Don't burn your bras until you've uncrossed your heart." Then she swelled up big as a mountain with hips as wide as the Grand Canyon. She *was* a mountain, or at least an enormous fertility icon made out of rock. The mountain split open and a little withered old gnome emerged. He held out a cigarette and asked, "Got a life, sonny?" He jabbed me with the sharp and rigid cigarette, straight through to my heart. Now the cigarette was a snake, sucking the life out of me. There were twelve doctors surrounding me, offering their opinions.

"Advanced case of melancholic megalomania."

"With complications of aspiration."

"Who asped you?"

"Don't be an utter boa."

I dwelled amidst uneasy phantoms like this for several seconds. Or was it aeons?

Kalpas?

Yugas?

Or just the length of some moldy golden-oldie by the Guess Who?

"No time left for other worlds, no time left for any one. No time left for boys and girls, no time left for any fun."

Someone was whispering in my ear. A voice like a sprite's, high and androgynous. Or was she shouting?

"Open up! Come out and play! We're waiting! Everyone's here!"

Out of the depths of my dreams I twitched my finger that might or might not have existed, ordering the Yo-yo to snap back into my palm.

When it did, my shell collapsed.

15.
Meet the Calvinii!

EVERYWHERE WAS NOW. Everywhen was here.

With my shell gone, I definitely had no body in this null-time and anti-place. Or rather, the whole universe was my body. I was as big as this universe, and the universe was as big as me. I was inside it, and it was inside me, its duration unmeasurably tiny, unmeasurably large.

And the Yo-yo, my ticket out of this fix?

Still blind and deaf, yet possessing some kind of new senses I couldn't quite get the hang of yet, I seemed to sense the Yo-yo's ghostly presence—more a probability than any solid actuality—down some alien dimension, far away, yet close as my nonexistent skin. I could almost reach it—

"Hi! Isn't this much better!"

The sprite was back. She was right next to me, practically at my theoretical elbow, a bluesweet, loudorange, smokysoft bundle of multiplexed nothing.

No, hold on, she was *inside* me! I started to freak.

"Hey! Get out of my body!"

"Your *body*? What's that?"

"It's where I live, the discrete, bounded container that holds my self. My very own private spacetime donut. And you're in it."

"There's nothing here but everything, and everything's the same. Forever and never. Maybe you're inside *me*. Did you ever think of that? Anyway, how could you and I ever be separate when an infinite number of us can squeeze inside each other simultaneously? Of course, if things weren't so small, we'd never be able to fit so many of us. And if things got any bigger, there wouldn't be room for any of us!"

"You're talking crazy!"

"*You* are! Just ask anyone."

Suddenly there was a second sprite inside me. This one seemed to emerge from within the first one.

"I agree. He's stark raving mad!"

I was beginning to get angry. "Who asked you, shithead?"

A third sprite emerged from inside the second one. "What a potty-mouth!"

A fourth arrived. "I wouldn't take that kind of insult if I were you. And I am!"

"I'm of the exact same mind," said a fifth. "As you well know."

Now the sprites began to swarm in earnest. Soon I was swamped and inundated in them, drowning in sprites, all of whom were yelling and shouting their ridiculous opinions and advice.

"What can you expect from a coldie?" "Maybe we can teach him better." "Why should we bother?" "Well, we did cajole him out of his bubble . . . " "Yes, but who invited him here in the first place, the stupid bust-symp?"

"Shut up! Everyone just shut up!" I couldn't take it anymore, their voices inside my head were driving me nuts! Gratifyingly, silence descended. "Okay. Now, who are you busy-nonbodies anyhow?"

Somehow I recognized the voice of the first sprite, as distinct from the others. "You can call us the Calvinii."

"And do you have individual names?"

"Not really," she said. "Or rather, less than one but more than none. Why don't you just call me Calpurnia?"

"Well, Cal, just tell me where I am and how to leave, and I'll be going."

They all began to murmur among themselves. Finally, Calpurnia said, "Going? Why would you ever want to leave here? It's paradise!"

"Paradise?" I snorted. "I've got no senses I'm used to, no body, and there doesn't appear to be any *here* here. You call this paradise?"

"Well, if you object, you could call our home something else."

"Such as what?"

A chorus of answers arose.

"The Monobloc!"

"The Cosmic Egg!"

"The Ur-Singularity!"

"The Void!"

"Alpha and Omega!"

"The Primal Seed!"

And then I realized with a lowdown nasty sinking feeling just where I had ended up.

16.
Back to the Garden

HOME IN BOOKLAND, I had ordered the Yo-yo to take me as far away from my native time and place as possible.

I had never stopped to think how the cybernetic device was going to fulfill that request with its semi-intelligent (yet probably smarter than me) faculties.

I supposed that it could have moved me to the edge of my own universe, some sixteen billion lightyears from Earth, and that would have satisfied the spatial part of my request. Or maybe the edge of some parallel universe 'way across superspace would have qualified as even "further" in some abstract who-the-fuck-cares sense.

But what about meeting the temporal dimension of my ill-considered demands?

As I saw it now, the Yo-yo had had basically two choices.

It could have shifted me to a parallel universe in its heat-death stage, a universe some billions of years older than mine, where even protons had whiffed away to naught and a fart would have outshone a nova. But even that entropic stage of the cosmos represented a finite, non-maximum distance away in time.

The only alternative satisfying my mad command was to carry me to the utmost past. Back to the point-source of each universe, back to where time literally did not exist any longer.

Back to the singularity that preceded the Big Bang. Back to the infinitely small, infinitely dense, infinitely hot dot that contained all the potential matter and energy and laws of the universe to come. Back to the original Eden, where time and space uncoupled in a no-fault divorce and both disappeared; where all the symmetries were restored, and the medium of existence resembled a random, virtual, probabilistic foam like subquantum shaving cream.

And where, apparently, life still managed—incredibly, beyond all expectations—to exist.

In the form of flighty, arrogant, self-conceited idiots.

Just like home.

As I might have guessed.

17.
The Old and Flabby Talk with the Young and Hot

"BRAVO! WE KNEW we'd get it eventually!"

It was Calpurnia, speaking apparently for all the other Calvinii.

"Are you still in my head? Leave my thoughts alone!"

She giggled. "You don't have a head anymore! Your thoughts are ours, and ours are yours!"

"Oh, yeah? Well, I hate to tell you, but I'm not picking up any of your so-called thoughts. My mind is mine alone."

"That's just because we're shielding you until you get used to things here."

"Prove it."

And of course she did.

In the next forever instant I became and had always been one of the Calvinii—all of the Calvinii that ever existed or would exist. I acquired complete knowledge of their history and futurity and way of being in less than no time over a period of millennia.

Hans had told me that every universe was connected to others by an infinity of wormholes at the sub-Planckian level. This universe, as unimaginably tiny and strange and primitive as it was, was no exception. After all, I had arrived here down a certain vermidesic, hadn't I? That proved that this pre-Big Bang universe was connected to mine, at least, and, as the Calvinii could testify, to many others as well.

Except for the odd visitor such as myself, not much in the way of particles flowed down these wormholes from the cousin universes into the Monobloc. But what did travel from the older, colder, busted-symmetry universes into the Calvinii continuum was information.

Patterns, relationships, differences, knowledge.

This information had given birth to the Calvinii.

Basically, the Calvinii were stable resonances of high probability in the subquantum foam of the singularity Egg, birthed by chance interactions among inflowing bits.

The very first Calvinii had been low on the intelligence scale, only potentially smart. However, once created they were immortal, and capable of learning from the incoming info-dribble. Now they were highly intelligent, although possessed of a necessarily quirky and limited view of existence. Not to mention their unique sense of humor. And as new Calvinii were "born," their immemorial culture was instantly available to them.

I had popped like a blister out of a wormhole, encapsulated in the Yo-yo's protective fields, which had strained against the assault of the singularity foam. When I dissolved the protection afforded by the Yo-yo I was exposed to the raw probabilistic welter that was the Calvinii's native medium.

Now I myself existed as nothing more nor less than one of the Calvinii, a (hopefully) stable pattern in a sea of high weirdness.

Bummer.

18.
I'm a Little Teapot, Short and Stout

"WAS THAT TOO much all at once?"

Calpurnia's solicitous tones brought me back to "myself." Having perhaps taken pity on me, she had obviously restored, at least partially, the shielding around my psychic individuality.

Emerging from "inside" the Calvinii—or having them withdraw from me—I found that my new senses were more fully integrated into my consciousness. The environment of the Monobloc had come into sharper "focus."

Like one of those figure-ground images that snap between vase and human profiles, the interior of the singularity alternated in my new "eyes" between improbably minute and infinitely large. What didn't change was its endless churning. The probabilistic foam was in constant "motion," wrinkling, spurting, heaving, bouncing, blooming, sucking, stretching, snapping, tossing, twitching and in general behaving like a horny teenager with Saint Vitus's tic. Bizarre topological flaws and defects and slime-mold structures were continually being generated and destroyed in a mad dance of fecundity.

This perpetual kaleidoscope of contortions was hypnotically soothing, and I had to pull myself out of contemplation of it in order to answer Calpurnia.

"Uh, no, I kinda like it . . . "

"You'll learn to love it," she said.

I turned my attention to her, and found that Calpurnia herself was nothing more than a gnarly topological monster of a hundred writhing tendrils and forkings and warts, notable only for "her" relative stability amidst the chaos.

Suddenly, somehow, I was looking at "myself" from her point of view, and saw that my own "I" was now housed in something that looked like a horned teapot with a zillion extradimensional handles and excrescences.

"You're cute!" Calpurnia said.

"Uh, thanks. You too."

I had seen estimates for the interval between sex thoughts in the average male that ranged from thirty seconds to five minutes. I had always been on the hairtrigger end of that spectrum. Now I found that the suggestive organic squirmings of the singularity were inspiring a flood of erotic thoughts.

"Um, Calpurnia—where's everyone else?" I asked.

"Right here. Where else could they go?"

"Why can't I see them?"

"You're not looking in the right direction."

"What direction should I look in?"

"Any direction other than the one you're looking in now."

"What are my choices?"

"Ana, kata, yesterup and afterdown. Hyperplus and subminus. Aft, baft, and naft. Is that ten yet?"

"No, nine."

"Oh, I almost forgot squiggle."

"'Squiggle' is a direction?"

"Not one that we use very much."

"I can see why. All right, let me try . . . "

I twisted my new senses around, imagining that I was trying to bite my elbow or examine the back of my neck or check out the top of my head by standing on a stool. After straining for an indeterminate amount of time, I managed to cause the other Calvinii to pop into view.

For as far as I could see, the Calvinii were busy doing something. As new topological monstrosities sprouted from the non-space/non-time probability foam, the Calvinii would swarm around them and begin to shape, trim, alter and generally prune them.

"What are they doing?"

"I explained all this to you yesterup."

For a minute, I almost "remembered" the explanation. But then the ghost memory from yesterup faded.

"Would you mind going over it once more?"

Calpurnia sighed. "I suppose not."

19.
That Little Old Watchmaker, Me

THIS WAS THE essence of Calpurnia's BBB.

The Calvinii were gardeners, tilling the soil of the singularity. It was their sole duty, chore, joy, and occupation: hobby, religion and job rolled up into one.

The "plant" that they were striving to cultivate was a tidy, interesting, life-hospitable, post-Big Bang universe such as the one I had come from.

Scientists back in my world had long been puzzled over several characteristics of the observable universe.

Why was it so uniform over vast distances?

How did large-scale structures such as galaxies and clusters of galaxies arise from the supposedly homogenous Cosmic Egg?

What explained the current preponderance of matter over antimatter, when both should have been produced equally in the explosion that kick-started the universe?

How did the basic physical parameters measurable in our day and age—such as the gravitational constant or charge of the electron—come to have the rather arbitrary values which they did have?

And finally, was the universe constrained to bring forth life in the course of its evolution?

Basically, they were preoccupied with aspects of the same Ontological Pickle which had broken my mind and spirit so recently.

The best answer they had come up with so far was more of a philosophical statement of belief than a scientific finding. It went by the name of the "anthropic principle," and said basically, "The only reason such questions have meaning or can be asked is because we are here to ask them. And the only reason we are here to ask them is because our universe developed precisely as it did."

About as satisfying as "Because Mama says so," but the best they could come up with.

By positing intelligence as integral to the development of the universe, the cosmologists had been on the right track. As I now saw, they simply hadn't gone far enough.

Our universe had been *intelligently designed* to have its various constants and potentials.

And the designers were the Calvinii.

Here inside the Primal Seed, they smoothed and tweaked the probability foam. Using the information that dribbled in from pre-existing older universes as their model, they presciently built in the very patterns that would later cause such consternation.

The Calvinii were the ultimate machine-language programmers. Living right down among the foamy existential bits and bytes, they were hacking the spacetime continuum yet to come.

20.
Open Mouth, Insert Tail

WHEN CALPURNIA FINISHED, I was exultant!

"This explains everything! The Ontological Pickle is demolished! Everything exists because of the Calvinii!"

"Right!" Calpurnia agreed enthusiastically. "The old universes we're using as models were all crafted by *their* Calvinii. And those Calvinii used even older universes as examples, which were created in turn by yet other Calvinii, who were relying on even older universes—"

"Hold on, hold on. Where does this infinite regress end? Or begin?"

"I've got no idea! You sounded so confident, I thought *you* knew!"

21.
Gardening at Night

AFTER THIS DISAPPOINTMENT, I was so downhearted that I made no objection when Calpurnia said it was time for me to go to work with the others. Although there was no overt statement that I should "earn my keep," I got the distinct impression that just lazing around soaking up the free infinite energy was frowned upon.

"Come with me, Paul," she said, and promptly disappeared.

"Hey, wait—Cal? Where did you go?"

She popped back beside me. "Watch closely, silly!"

I paid more attention this time, and was able to duplicate Calpurnia's motions: a simple combination of ana, hyperplus and baft movements.

We were in a vast field of pullulating probabilities manifesting themselves as wiggly architectonic fractal fingers and throbbing braincoral extrusions. Calpurnia "pointed" toward one.

"That's a fruitful little guy. We can trim and shape it into something useful."

"How?"

"Just remember ahead to afterdown, and you'll see."

I tried doing what she said. Sure enough, the knowledge came to me. All the gardening practices developed and perfected by "generations" of Calvinii were at my disposal. What to aim for and how to get there. I set to work eagerly.

"Wonderful!" Calpurnia encouraged. "Poke it with your pulsifer right there—that's it! Lop off that piece hanging squigglewards with your cinchers—great! I'll leave you alone now. But I'll be right here!"

Now I really started to GET INTO the work.

Even if I wasn't the Prime Mover, at least I was doing something more useful than anything else I had ever done.

The hypnotic, chaotic variety of the subquantum foam, combined with my own responsive dance, developed into a mindless, instinctive, rhythmic physio-mental state approaching nirvana.

I was the foam, and the foam was me. Together we shaped futurity, cast our joint shadow out into the spacetime continuum lying implicit in the Great Egg.

There had never been any such entity as Paul Girard, no set of nagging problems associated with that name. I was just another termite in the mound, another worker bee in the hive.

Buzz, buzz, buzz! Chew, chew, chew!

It was quite possible that I labored on in this fashion for longer than my old universe had yet existed. Or maybe it was just a few hours. Forming the potentials that would one day become trees, stars and bad books. In either case, when Calpurnia returned I took a while to snap out of my trance.

"Oh, you've done so well!" she congratulated. "I think you deserve some sex!"

22.
Love Handles

STILL SOMEWHAT UNDER the spell of my endless shift in the foam, I felt like the drone summoned by the Queen Bee for mating. It didn't occur to me to ask then how sex had arisen among the Calvinii, in a world without birth or evolution as humans knew it. Maybe it was something they had learned from watching the colder, degenerate universes. Maybe it was something I had introduced, for all I knew.

And what sex among these warped orbifolds could possibly consist of, I had no idea.

I temporized. "Uh, sure, if you want to . . . "

"Oh, I do! We all do!"

"Who's 'we all?'"

Calpurnia and I were surrounded instantly by a swarm of other anonymous Calvinii. "Us, that's who!" they all shouted, then disappeared "inside" Calpurnia, siphoning naftwise down one of her body-holes.

Calpurnia deformed her handles and protrusions suggestively. "Are you ready, honey?"

"What do I do?"

"Go topological on me, lover! Use higher mathematics on me, baby! Twist me inside out! Compactify me! Tensors and twistors and strange attractors get me hot! Why don't you start out with a little calculus, though?"

I tried to comply.

Pretty soon, with a little help, Calpurnia and I were getting each other off.

As I poked and prodded her resonances with mathematical concepts, she stroked and cajoled mine. The bizarre thing was that I felt everything I did to her, and assume she felt everything she did to me. This made the experience resemble masturbation as much as it did sex.

Finally we both approached climax.

"Oh, feed me those eigenvalues, big boy!"

We summed infinity together.

23.
The Lilith Calypso

I WAS BACK at play in the fields of the Lord again, stoking the starmaker machinery. Mindlessly, I nipped and tucked, plastic surgeon to a universe unborn. I had no concerns, no destinations, no urges. No past, no future, and maybe no present. I was complete and satisfied.

And yet. And yet. Some tiny demon of unease persisted. (And tiny things in this odd place could be huge.)

Was this really the end of my very short quest? Was this the best world I could reach with Hans's gift? Was this really where I wanted to spend eternity?

I tried to reach out for the Yo-yo with my by-now more experienced senses. I seemed to possess—or imagined I possessed— a digit with a string around it. Or the probability patterns associated therewith. I even dimly felt my old body, right down to the Pez-dispenser in my shirt pocket. Now, if I could just twitch my finger . . .

As if drawn by my thoughts, one of the Calvinii appeared. At first I thought it was Calpurnia. But then I noticed the different manifolds of her kata surface.

"Hi, Paul. I'm Calypso. Thanks for the sex!"

"Um, don't mention it."

"How's work going?"

"Fine. I guess."

Calypso shimmied down six dimensions and got herself right inside me. Then she announced, "Now we can really talk, without her listening."

"Who? Calpurnia?"

"Right. Miss Goody Ten Coordinates. Tell me the truth. Aren't you sick and tired of shaping the future universe to her boring standards? Nice neat laws and proportions, all understandable by and conducive to organic life. What did organic life ever do for you?"

"Well, actually, you see—"

"Oh, that's right, I forgot. You were organic yourself once. Still, even a former coldie and bust-symp should be able to see that there are a lot more interesting and artistically satisfying possible universes out there than what she's got in mind."

"Like what?"

Calypso's voice took on the greedy tones of a pervert. "Oh, there's a multitude of ways to mess up spacetime! How about creating a continuum with a huge cosmological constant? Spacetime would be so bent that light couldn't travel in a straight line for more than a hundred meters! Or, if we made the cosmo-con repulsive, antigravity would rule! Wouldn't that be fun! Imagine the headaches any intelligent life that we planted in such a place would face! They'd never know what hit them!"

"Gee, that sounds kind of mean, Calypso . . . "

The Calvinii did something inside me that hurt.

"Ow!"

"Mean? I'll show you mean! We're talking major fun here. We've got the powers and talents of demiurges, and all we use them for is making the same stinking daisies come up, universe after universe! No, there's going to be some major changes in this singularity soon. And if you're not with us when push come to shove, then you're against us!"

"Can I have a little time to think things over?"

"All right. But don't take forever."

I refrained from asking how I was supposed to distinguish forever from never in this nutty place.

Calypso squirted out of me then. "And don't forget, honey. I can be real nice to my friends. Calpurnia isn't the only one who can shake her matrix."

And illustrating her meaning with a probabilistic bump-and-grind, she was gone.

24.
Goodbye to That All

AFTER MY ONE-SIDED lecture from Calypso, I knew I had to leave, however blissful foam-gardening might be.

But I hesitated for one reason.

I had no idea what activation of the Cosmic Yo-yo would do to the Monobloc.

After all, the string in my Yo-yo, as Hans had told me, was made of the same stuff as the Monobloc. Who knew what would happen when I caused that little loop of eternity to vibrate in accordance with my wish? (And I had a fair idea now of what I was going to ask for. If I could even ask for anything, that is.)

True, the singularity had survived my entrance. But I had a hunch that my exit would be more stressful. And these dumb Monoblocs were inherently unstable. I mean, they were popping off all the time, weren't they? Making new universes left and right, replacing perfection and symmetry with grunge and poverty. Did I want to be responsible for that transition?

On the other hand, I had no desire to remain and get caught in a war between factions of the Calvinii. (And how factions could exist among identical individuals inside a mathematical point, I had no idea. It was all too likely that dissatisfaction, dissension and cutthroat politics were built-in defaults of any superspace manifestation. But I didn't rule out the possibility that it was all some elaborate mindgame they were playing with me . . .)

One "day" soon after my ultimatum from Calypso, I asked Calpurnia, "What happens to the Calvinii when the Big Bang finally goes off?"

"Many of us by then would have already traveled down any

vermidesic that leads to another Monobloc, to start gardening again. But some of us get interested in seeing how the universe we've blueprinted turns out, and choose to stick around."

"And how do you do that?"

"We hitch a ride."

"On what?"

"Mostly on primordial black holes."

Primordial black holes were the relatively tiny ones created in the first nano-instants of the Big Bang, as opposed to the large ones birthed much later by collapsing suns.

"You mean that back in my contemporary universe, Calvinii can probably be found inside black holes?"

"Absolutely!"

I thought a moment. "Don't tiny black holes eventually evaporate to nothing?"

"Sure! That's why we try to steer them into larger black holes when the big ones finally come into being. Then we just sit and absorb all the information flowing in through the event horizon. It's fascinating!"

So apparently I wouldn't have to worry about killing all the Calvinii if I set off the Primal Explosion. That clinched it. It was gonna happen someday anyway, right? I was outa here!

But before I could do anything, Calypso forced the showdown.

Or maybe it had already happened a long time ago.

All I knew was that one "minute" I was talking placidly with Calpurnia, and the next instant she and Calypso were locked in a knockdown, dragout catfight, their intricate surfaces intertangling and yanking. It was like watching two amoebas mudwrestling.

"Give up, you nasty little devil!"

"Never, you sanctimonious slut!"

All the other Calvinii began to take sides and flail at each other too.

I could feel the subquantum foam churning and heaving in a seasickness-inducing reaction to the titanic battle of the angels. I knew it was all gonna blow any quasisecond.

I formed my wish mentally nice and solid.

Transport me to the last time and place when and where I was really happy.

Taking as secure a grip as possible on the probabilities that represented my Yo-yo, I shouted, "It's let-there-be-light time, kids!"

FACES OF
THE THIRD PAIR

25.
Sweet Hitchhikers

BREATH.

Light.

Sound.

Scent.

I was back! Back inside my familiar droopy old body, pasted firmly into the limited four-dimensional spacetime of some gloriously fallen imperfect world or another, away from those giddily irritating Calvinii.

"That's what he thinks, Cal!"

"He's not shed of us yet, is he, Cal?"

The voices of Calypso and Calpurnia were sounding in my head. Chirpy and gleeful, they appeared to have put aside their enmity and ideological differences.

Their presence and peace treaty were most, most assuredly not desirable.

"Where are you rotten hitchhikers? Are you in my brain again?"

"Of course not, silly."

"That primitive organ wouldn't support quantum-level beings like us in this bust-symp world."

"Despite what that dreamer Penrose thinks."

"However, we do have enough access to your neurons to share some silent speech."

"Maybe even enough access for a little tweaking!"

"We're in the string of your Yo-yo!"

How could I not have foreseen this? Hans had told me that cosmic string was a leftover piece of the Monobloc, and I had even speculated on its affinity to the primal matter before I used it, back in the Monobloc (precise memories of which absurdist environment, as I hastily checked, were rapidly greying out and becoming diffuse).

But it had never occurred to me that any Calvinii might decide to tag along inside my toy when I left. But used as they were to riding out the Big Bang inside small black holes, it must have been second nature to them to hop onboard.

"How many of you are there in there?"

"One."

"Two."

"Ten to the tenth to the tenth!"

I gave up on the question. What did it matter how many there were? One was too many. As long as I was only hearing two voices, I decided to arbitrarily call them a pair.

Suddenly, I had an awful suspicion.

"Are you two going to have any effect on the way my Yo-yo works? You can't control it, can you?"

"Not really."

"But we might be introducing perturbations. The Uncertainty Principle makes it hard to say. The answer kind of slithers away when we try to look."

"It's really quite a novel situation for us, you see!"

"It's rather fun, experiencing this coldie world through your limited senses."

"Yes! I can hardly wait till we have sex!"

Mention of my senses brought me back to them.

For the first time since exiting the Monobloc, I really looked around.

26.
A Certain Slant of Dopesmoke

AT FIRST, IMAGES would not cohere. All I saw were colors and geometric shapes. Then I realized I was trying to look in strange directions I had no access to any longer. The six extra dimensions available in the Monobloc were here compactified down below the Planck level.

When I got my eyes working right, I couldn't really believe what I *did* see.

I was in the middle of a large public square surrounded by typical American twentieth-century-type buildings, all somewhat shabby and in various states of disrepair. In the center of the square was a decorative fountain, benches, summer-green trees. Someone was flying a kite; an acoustic amateur band was playing. It could have been contemporary Anytown, U.S.A., save for one thing.

The people.

Everyone in sight, from the youngest to the oldest, from sparse-haired tykes to grey-haired grandmas, was dressed in High Hippie attire.

There were more bell-bottoms than at the Sonny and Cher Museum, more leather than in a herd of bison, more fringe than at a belly-dancers convention, more colored headrags than in a war zone, more sandals than at the Last Supper. Squash-blossom belt-buckles reflected blinding bursts of sunlight. Dirty lace shirt-frills obscured lapel buttons and lapis jewelry. There were many bare chests of both genders, beneath flapping patchwork vests, and enough tie-dye for Christo to wrap the Reichstag.

I didn't see any hairstyle shorter than shoulder-length, and most people of both sexes wore it halfway down their backs. Waves of patchouli and musk floated from these flowing tresses.

What was even more alien than the local clothing styles, however, was the attitude of these citizens. No one had that familiar jittery, consumerist, got-to-get-somewhere air of haste and frustration around them. They lolled and lazed, strolled and sprawled, apparently with nowhere to go and no appointments to keep. Definitely "59th Street Bridge" time here. The communal indolence and ease made me realize how wired the average person back home in my America had been, always hustling even in their recreations.

Then I realized one major reason for their casual abandon.

Dope. Pot. Grass.

Tons of it.

Practically everyone in sight was toking on monster joints the size of stogies. Clouds of pot fumes filled the air like auto exhaust, competing with the perfumed body odors. (And, come to think of it, where *were* all the ubiquitous cars of modern civilization?)

That's when it hit me.

Courtesy of the Yo-yo, I had come back to 1972.

That had been the happiest year of my life. I was eighteen, confident, footloose and free. Sex was easy, money was no problem, the music was great. I had no responsibilities, no feeling of time running out. Around me, the culture, despite having lost a certain circa-1967 Arcadian innocence, was looser than it had ever been or would be again, with the Bohemianism of the lucky forerunner flower-children pioneers finally trickling down to every Midwest high school and Pleasant Valley poolside barbecue. Despite the tyrannical government in power, despite the War, any and all kinds of change still looked eminently possible.

Those few months had constituted my own private Utopia, memories of it cherished for over twenty years, seemingly forever out of reach.

And now I was back, thanks to the gift of Hans the Moraveckian.

I almost threw away the Yo-yo then. What further need could I have of it? But a twinge of caution made me simply unloop it from my transmogrified finger and pocket it instead.

Trying to look inconspicuous and fit in with the crowd, despite my square appearance, I ambled over to a newsstand, already getting a contact high off the Venus-thick atmosphere, seeking to suss out local conditions in this 1972-analogue cosmos.

When I reached the racked magazines and newspapers, I had time only to register the date off the psychedelic banner of *The National Oracle*: May 1, 2002.

And then the newspaper vendor, a groovy young chick, looked up from her copy of *Zap Comix*, spotted me and screamed!

27.
Eyebrow-deep in Some Nasty Shit

IT'S FUNNY WHAT you register sometimes in a crisis. The smallest, least relevant details acquire the sharpest definition.

For instance: after the vendor-girl screamed, I noted that the cover of her *Zap Comix* was headlined: "Issue Five Hundred!!! The Fabulous Furry Freak Brothers Meet Wonder Warthog!!!" I also noticed that the colors of the cover image were smudged and bleeding, and the whole thing looked as if it had been printed on paper made from Shredded Wheat.

Then the continuation of the girl's wordless screams yanked my attention away from the comic.

I smiled nervously and flashed the peace sign with my unaltered hand. A bit rustily and self-consciously to be sure, but after all, I had last employed that gesture over two decades ago.

"Uh, what's, um, 'going down,' sister? Can I, ah, become 'part of the solution?'"

Now her screams assumed form. "A Narc, a Narc! Help! Help! Somebody call the Angels!"

Looking backward over my shoulder, I saw that many bystanders, emerging from their dope-hazed reveries, were converging on me and the newsstand. I began to get nervous. Should I split this continuum before the situation got out of control? How could I though? Despite the bad start to things, this place and time represented my best chance so far for the happiness that had eluded me back home.

Or so I still thought.

The Calvinii chose that moment to interrupt my speculations. I was surprised to hear them, having disengaged the Yo-yo, but I guessed that contact with my body permitted the conversation to continue inside my head.

"Why is that female of your species screaming?"

"Is it part of the mating ritual?"

"Does it signify attraction?"

"When do we fuck?"

69

"Oh, shut up, please, won't you?" I said, addressing the Calvinii aloud by habit.

But the girl vendor, thinking of course that I was talking to her, promptly went into hysterics.

"Oh, help, he's using verbal violence in my space!"

Then she fainted.

And my arms were pinioned from behind while a burly voice said, "Man, you are eyebrow-deep in some nasty shit."

28.
Busted!

THE HAM-SIZED hands gripping my biceps spun me around, and I saw that I was the focus of a huge crowd, and that my captor was some kind of biker type. A beer-gutted, bearded bear of a guy, clad in greasy leathers, inky chest-hair spilling out of his motor-oil-stained and filthy ripped tee-shirt, busted veins mapping his pocked skin into various bad neighborhoods ranging from slum to ghetto, with a nose that had been put partway through urban renewal before funds ran out. He wore a flat biker's cap across the bill of which was stitched the name *TINY* in italics.

Just as I took all this in, a voice from the crowd yelled, "Look! In his pocket! It's the Weasel!"

People began to point and shriek and cower back. Arms were thrown up across faces as if to shield eyes from a hideous sight. A number of the freaks held up their leather-thonged peace medallions in a gesture akin to the Mediterranean double-fingered horns used to ward off evil.

I looked down at my chest.

There was the Nixon head of the Pez-dispenser leering out.

I felt it was safe to assume that the historical Nixon of this continuum resembled the bastard I knew more than he did the Savior of Hans's timeline.

Curse that damn cyberklutz!

Even the large and menacing Tiny flinched when he caught sight of the offensive replica.

"Oh, man, do you want to get *lynched*? How did you think you were gonna go undercover with *that* showing?"

"I'm not undercover! I'm not a Narc. Honest!"

"What are you then?"

Good question. "Um, a visitor . . . "

"Where from?"

An even better question. Maybe the truth would impress everyone enough to let me establish my sincerity and solidarity.

Straightening my spine, I boldly announced, "I come from an alternate dimension, in peace and brotherhood, seeking to share in the perfection and wisdom of your world."

This seemed to go over fairly well with the crowd. There were murmurs of approbation and appreciation, as well as some general encomiums such as "Groovy!" and "Far out!".

Tiny seemed to be processing this new information with a brain resembling one of the early Heathkit computers. At last he said, "Maybe that's true. But I can't leave you alone to wander around causing trouble and maybe getting yourself killed. And you *did* use verbal violence on the babe. So I'm gonna have to take you in and let the People's Solidarity Court deal with you. Meanwhile, let's get this ugly thing outa sight."

Plucking the Pez-dispenser from my pocket and concealing it within one massive fist, Tiny hustled me through the crowd, which parted obediently.

"Is this the start of a sex act?" Calpurnia asked.

"Boy, I hope not," I answered, not caring who heard.

29.
Moonchild

DISCOUNTING THE RACKED Harleys outside, the jail looked like jails everywhere. Except once I got inside I discovered it was considerably more run down than usual, outside of Mississippi. Not only were the floor tiles broken and filthy and the paint peeling, but office doors were off their hinges, windowpanes were missing and leaking pipes had stained ceiling panels the color of despair.

As I was being booked by another Hell's Angel behind a three-legged desk with a stack of books supporting one corner, I couldn't help asking, in what I hoped would pass for the local argot, "What's with the crummy digs, man? Even the Establishment's pigs kept a neater pigpen."

The Angels seemed embarrassed, and Tiny hastened to defend the station. "Well, we don't exactly feed high on the public teat, you see. There's a lot more important stuff to spend communal bread on—right, guys? Plus, there's so little crime or antisocial stuff going down nowadays that we don't need no heavy-duty incarceration facilities like fascists got. The oldtime Koncentration Kamps of AmeriKKKa have been emptied forever."

The way he said it, I knew it was the Party Line, so I didn't bother arguing.

But when one of the Angels began to pat me down and ended up sticking his hand in the pocket holding my Yo-yo, I began to struggle.

"Hey, wait a minute! Give that back! It's nothing dangerous! You've got no right to take it! And I need it!"

I managed to free my left hand and touch the Yo-yo.

Calypso's voice came briefly through. "Paul, what's going—"

Then I was pinned again, and the Angels were examining the Yo-yo. I held my breath as they tried a few tricks with it, but nothing happened. Attuned to me alone, like Hans had said.

Meanwhile, Tiny had been examining my metamorphosed left hand with amazement. "Cool," he finally decided. "Very useful in a rumble, I bet. Well, c'mon, Badfinger, time for your beddy-bye."

I was so crestfallen and downhearted at losing the Yo-yo, that I didn't even protest the stupid nickname. I just let myself be hustled along down mold-damp and dirty corridors to the cellblock.

Tiny pitched me into a cell and the door slammed behind me.

I looked around the Spartan interior. One of the bunks held a sitting occupant, my new cellmate.

My mind wasn't functioning at peak efficiency, but I probably would have been confused as to the gender of my cellmate in the best of circumstances. Thin as a toddler's excuses, clad in shapeless jeans, loose embroidered Mexican peasant shirt and sandals, the person possessed a face plain as ditchwater, framed by waveless, lusterless hair. Wanly complexioned, with eyes the color of tobacco juice, my cellmate was one of those innocuous, inoffensive and practically invisible individuals to whom it was predicated only a mother's love would ever attach.

"Uh, hi," I said tentatively. "Name's Paul."

When she spoke, I was taken aback by the beauty of her voice. It was some kind of compensatory magic for her sad and drab features.

"I'm Moonchild."

I extended my hand. She put out hers. It was clammy as a discounted fish.

"Nice to meet you," I said. "Whatcha in for?"

Moonchild lowered her gaze bashfully. "Virginity."

No ready reply came to mind.

Except the needlessly cruel, *I can believe it.*

30.
Hoeing the Row, One Way or Another

"HOW ABOUT YOU?" asked Moonchild, and I gratefully accepted the conversational gambit she offered, to avoid further discussion of her bizarre crime. At least for the moment.

"Well, as far as I can tell, it was for using some harsh words that wouldn't bother my grandmother. But it's all a big misunderstanding. And oh yeah, I'm suspected of being a Narc."

Moonchild's eyes grew wide. "I always thought the Narcs were just bogeymen. I never knew they really existed. Imagine, me of all people meeting one! This is the most important and exciting thing that ever happened to me!"

Back on my native Earth, no one had ever exactly called me hip or chic, but I had always cherished a certain notion of myself as outside the mainstream. No one back home could ever have mistaken me for a government rat, and this continual accusation of Narc-hood here in this new world was starting to piss me off.

"That's the trouble! I'm not a Narc! Maybe I look like one a little, compared to you all, but I'm not."

"What are you then?"

"A visitor from another dimension."

Moonchild nodded sagely. "I can dig it. That's way better. It makes you even more interesting and cool to know than a Narc."

All of a sudden I felt incredibly weary. I hadn't eaten or slept since the day of my departure. And even though that moment was, perhaps, really only a short objective span ago (for who could say how long my sojourn in the Monobloc had taken?), it felt subjectively like forever.

I flopped down on my bunk and closed my eyes. "That's great, Moonchild. I'm happy to have made such a difference in your life on such a short acquaintance. So, what's going to happen to us now?"

Moonchild sighed hopelessly. "I don't know what the punishment is for Narcs. But I'll probably end up in the fuckatorium. Although I'm hoping to bargain for the pot farm."

I said nothing for a whole minute. Then I asked in what I hoped was a calm and reasonable tone, "Moonchild, would you mind telling me a little bit more about your world?"

31.
Tomorrow Through the Past

HERE WAS WHAT Moonchild the Virgin recounted, cut and pasted together into coherency, with my informed speculations filling in for her mythophilic, non-timebinding lapses. (It turned out she was only nineteen, hadn't been born until 1983, and knew her country's recent history in the same way I knew my Civil War history: as a jumble of legends, larger-than-life characters, vague landscapes and confusing issues. As I would soon see, the nature of schooling here had a lot to do with her confusion.)

Anyhow.

Back in Moonchild's personal 1972, Richard Nixon had gone off the deep end.

What set him off was an assassination attempt at a campaign rally by Arthur Bremer, who had changed his mind about the best target.

Like a cornered vicious rodent with its belly pressed to the earth—hence his soon-to-be-dominant nickname, "the Weasel"—Nixon intensified all his covert and overt "anti-enemies" activities. Domestic spying, wiretaps, dime-bag-holding life sentences, entrapments, curfews, dirty tricks, planted disinformation in the major media—Nixon's assortment of rotten deeds was warped and copious.

Simultaneously, he began a major escalation of the war in Vietnam.

Aided and abetted by Agnew, Hoover, Westmoreland, Kissinger, Billy Graham, his Cabinet and a host of lesser bagmen, plumbers, conmen, ultra-Christians and CREEPs, Nixon shot his wad, making Watergate, Cointelpro and the Christmas Bombings of Hanoi that I knew look like the actions of Hubert Horatio Humphrey on Miltown.

The country responded predictably.

Riots, burnings, bombings, shootings, looting and sabotage. LSD in the water sources, Yippie pranks sowing mass confusion, wild in the streets, street-fightin' man, got a revolution, got a revolution.

A few weeks before the 1972 election, Nixon declared nationwide martial law.

That tipped the scales. McGovern won by a hair. (From Moonchild's account, Nixon's farewell speech was a final classic performance, culminating in frothing at the mouth and an on-camera, phlebitis-engendered, blood-clot-to-the-brain stroke that rendered him instantly a vegetable.)

But it was already too late to save the government, the legal system and the Constitution.

When McGovern, as his first official act, advocated a slow return to normality, spoke out for caution and temperance, sense and dialogue, all that came across was the weakness of the State, and the riots continued and even intensified. Pressed by the Joint Chiefs to use troops to put down the civil disturbances, McGovern refused. In a few scattered cities, local commanders dispatched troops regardless, in deference to governors and mayors. Civilians were killed. There was a showdown between the President and the military, simultaneous with the start of impeachment proceedings in a schizophrenic Congress.

Things got hazy at this point in Moonchild's narration. Class and generational warfare, treachery and defections, alliances forged and broken, guerilla war in the suburbs, firestorms in the ghettos, heroism and wickedness, bodies on the barricades and under the tanks, soldiers deserting and the climactic Battle for the Pentagon.

But in the end, to put it simply, the Hippies and their allies won.

There was a worldwide recall of US soldiers, unilateral disarmament and a general disengagement from the rest of the world. (America's troubles had in fact sparked off similar confrontations around the globe, and other countries, Communist or not, were too busy internally to capitalize on America's lack of defenses.) Surviving domestic opponents were put through re-education camps, and general harmony was, after a decade, finally restored.

At this point in Moonchild's long and rambling story, one of the Angels arrived at the door to our cell.

"Afternoon dope ration," he announced, proffering two gigantic joints through the bars.

Moonchild took hers with an easy and natural acceptance. I grabbed mine like a starving man. The Angel lit them for us.

After listening to Moonchild's story, I really needed this.

32.
The Reign of Lady Sunshine

"SO," I SAID after a few deep tokes, "who runs things now?"
Having already sucked her joint like a trooper down to a roach, Moonchild tucked her stringy hair behind her ears and looked at me wistfully. I hoped the dope wasn't giving her any horny ideas about circumventing punishment by rendering her crime of sexual abstention moot. She was hardly my type, and I just wasn't in the mood.

"No one," she answered. "America is one big Commune of

Peace and Love now."

"Oh, come *on*. *Somebody* has to issue orders on a national level. The Angels told me they get public funding. Who collects the taxes and distributes the largesse? There must be some central authority . . . And who runs the pot farms and, er, that other place they were going to send you?"

"Well, there are some people in San Francisco, and they have local helpers around the country. I suppose you could call Frisco the nation's capital if you wanted to use such a square word. But the people there aren't elected or anything hincty like that. They just kinda volunteer. We call them 'the Heads.'"

"And who's the head Head?"

"That would be Lady Sunshine."

"And who's she?"

"Well, she was like the main squeeze of one of the top Weather Underground guys. And when he died she just kinda stepped into his shoes."

The dope was making me more mellow. "I see. Hey, I bet I know the names of a lot of the famous people high up in the Heads."

"Like who?"

I blew a smoke ring and tried to sound as if these were all personal friends. "Oh, people like Mario Savio and Joan Baez. Jerry Rubin and Abbie Hoffman. Grace Slick and Mimi Farina. Jane Fonda and Tom Hayden. David Dellinger and Father Berrigan. Cesar Chavez and Angela Davis. Jerry Garcia and Ken Kesey. People like that . . . "

Moonchild's expression had changed. She was looking at me in horror.

"What's the matter?"

"Those—those are all members of the Gang of Five Hundred!"

"Gang of Five Hundred? Who were they?"

"Who were they? Just the worst pack of traitors and subversives and fascists and running-dog imperialists ever to threaten the Revolution! Lady Sunshine had all those people you named executed or exiled a long time ago!"

I began to choke on my dope smoke, and Moonchild got up to

pound my back.

When I recovered, I ventured weakly, "The times they are a-changin' . . . "

"Oh, holy Timothy Leary, don't ever quote *him*!"

33.
Nothing But Flowers

MOONCHILD AND I spent a week in that stupid cell together. We had nothing to do but smoke dope and talk. Naturally I got to know the plain-faced skinny girl and her life pretty well, from all her pot-stoked BBB.

She had been born on one of the suburban farms that ringed what remained of the majority of the mostly empty cities these days. She wasn't quite sure who her biological mother and father were, since she had approximately six people of each gender whom she called Mom and Dad.

Once she was old enough, she had been put to work doing appropriate chores: slopping hogs, picking bugs off plants, pulling weeds. (The kind of agriculture prevalent in her America was completely organic, small-scale and labor-intensive.) Her schooling had occurred mostly during winters, and amounted to enough math and reading to cast horoscopes and puzzle out passages in the *I Ching*. She was a whiz at macramé and could play the recorder. But the only tunes she knew were the most vapid songs from thirty years ago. Rock'n'roll as an artform, it appeared, had been purged and stifled to hidebound conformity.

"You guys never even heard of punk?"

"Like music for juvenile delinquents?"

"No, you see, there were these guys called the Ramones— Oh, forget it," I said.

This was entirely typical of our disjointed—or double-jointed, so to speak—conversations.

Moonchild's world had no electricity or anything that needed power to run. No televisions, no record players, no radios, no telephones, no lights, no heat. Not even any electric guitars! (Of course, they had never even *dreamed* of personal computers or CD players or faxes or cell phones.) Construction had come to a standstill, and the infrastructure was slowly crumbling away. There were no aircraft, no trains and very little motorized transport. The Angels, as valuable enforcers of the status quo, got to operate their Harleys off a dwindling stock of pre-Revolution gasoline doled out by the Heads, who also had a small fleet of vehicles for their own use. (I thought a little new gasoline might have been imported from the Mideast since the war, but I couldn't be sure.)

"Wow," I said one afternoon. "Real Mad Max . . . "

"Like Maxwell Silverhammer, you mean?" replied Moonchild. "Or Peter Max?"

Another thing Moonchild's America lacked was antibiotics and contraceptives (other than sheepgut condoms). Coupled with the official state policy of Free Love for All, this had led to rampant VD. By an early age, Moonchild had seen plenty of disgusting sad cases of tertiary syphilis and the like. And it had utterly turned her off to sex.

Not that her peers were exactly soliciting her. The only entity that wanted her to have sex was the State.

"They give everyone, like, till eighteen to lose their cherry. I just couldn't bring myself to. The forces of the Heads took another year after my majority to catch up with me. But now I'm here."

"And they're going to send you where?"

Moonchild sniffled and tried to look brave. "The fuckatorium. People generally stay there for a year or so. It's a kind of whorehouse where anyone who can't manage to get their rocks off with any other cat or chick can go. I've heard they even make you do it with people *over forty*!"

Despite official grudging acknowledgement that "old" people were full citizens too, anyone over thirty here was, I gathered, subtly discriminated against.

I refrained from telling Moonchild how old I myself was.

Being a Narc from another dimension was stigma enough.

34.
Be Here Now—Or Else!

ONE MORNING, INSTEAD of our usual breakfast of weevily wheat germ, goats-milk yogurt and mint tea, we were greeted by an empty-handed Tiny.

"Wash your face and try to look presentable, Badfinger. You too, babe. You're both going for a ride."

This news broke the druggy stupor I had been wallowing in.

"What's up, man?"

"Lady Sunshine blew in from the coast last night. So your trial starts today."

Moonchild sprang nervously to her feet. "Lady Sunshine *herself* is presiding over our trial?"

Even Tiny appeared somewhat disconcerted. "That's what I hear. Grapevine says she's really keen to dig this Narc here and his way-out story about other worlds. Rumor is, she thinks he's really a spy from Squaresville. And as for you, babe, she figured as long as she's here, she'd use your case to set an example about disobeying the Free Love laws."

Moonchild began to wail. "Oh, no, we're doomed! I'll probably get a life sentence to the fuh-fuh-fuckatorium!"

"Hey, stop it," I said. "You're bumming me out."

Truly, I was getting nervous. Who knew what Lady Sunshine had in mind for us? Someone who could bump off Jerry Garcia was capable of anything!

Tiny left then. By the time he returned, I had decided on a course of action.

I was going to protest.

As the burly Angel began unlocking our cell, I started to chant. "Hell no, we won't go! Hell no, we won't go!"

Tiny paused. "Hey, man, c'mon now! Whatcha wanna do that for? Don't make it hard on yourself . . ."

Moonchild began to join in, thrusting her clenched fist into the air. "Hey, hey, Lady Ess, what's that blood all on your dress?"

Tiny seemed not to know what to do in the face of such

unaccustomed but officially revered civil disobedience. "Please, guys? We're supposed to be there soon..."

He laid a hand gently on my elbow, and I yelled, "Go limp!"

Moonchild and I collapsed to the floor.

Tiny sighed. "Okay, if that's how you want it . . . "

Soon more Angels came and carried us outside.

There was a crowd gathered. I went to start a new chant, realized I still didn't know what city I was in, and then instantly decided to use a classic that would resonate.

"Free the Chicago Duo! Free the Chicago Duo!"

Some of the crowd instinctively picked up the refrain, until the Angels began to belabor them in an unfriendly manner about the heads and shoulders.

Then they dumped Moonchild and me each into a motorcycle sidecar as if it were a tumbrel, and we went speeding away.

35.
Let Your Freak Flag Flop!

WE MADE THE Angels carry us into the courthouse. The audience was huge, and, I was relieved to see, appeared not entirely unsympathetic. There seemed to be reporters from *The National Oracle* present, identifiable by the pencil stubs and toilet-paper-quality scratch-pads clenched in their mimeo-stained fingers.

The Angels dumped us unceremoniously at two seats behind what I assumed was the defense table, then formed a human barricade between us and the crowd. There was a guy already at our table. He wore about a dozen strands of love beads, as well as a yin-yang tee-shirt. He resembled Jack Nicholson circa *Easy Rider*, except crazier looking. Sticking out his hand to Moonchild, he engaged her in a hearty soul shake. Then he did likewise with me.

"Hi," the guy said. "Welcome to the People's Solidarity Court. As we like to say, 'You have nothing to fear if your aura is clear.' I'm Yossarian, your public defender. Here's your grease stick."

"Grease stick?"

"Sure. I can see you're opting for the 'This whole trial is an illegal farce' defense, so I thought you'd like to draw a swastika or obscenity on your forehead. Unless you plan to carve one in blood and go for a Manson? I've got a big Bowie knife in this old ammo pouch here . . . "

"I'll take the grease stick, please," Moonchild said. "My acne only just cleared up last year, and I'm not about to scar my forehead any more."

I straightened up in my chair and tried to pump our "lawyer." "Listen, Yossarian. What's going to happen to us?"

"No way of telling, man. These charges on a regular day would be minor. Even your supposed Narchood. All we'd have to get you to do is smoke some dope in front of everyone, and you'd be stone free. Everyone knows a real Narc'd rather die than smoke dope. But with Lady Sunshine here in person, all bets are off."

"So this is gonna be some kind of show trial with a predetermined political outcome? A kangaroo court?"

"Well, let's just put it this way. When Lady Sunshine says, 'Toke!' if you know what's good for you, you ask, 'How deep?'"

While I was pondering this information, a bailiff appeared and hollered out, "Here come de judge!"

From my left as I faced the front of the courtroom, Lady Sunshine entered.

I stopped breathing for an unknown time.

She was a giant strawberry-blonde Aryan Nordic goddess straight out of some R. Crumb cartoon, only undeniably flesh and blood. She could have been twenty-five—or a Tina-Turner-preserved sixty. Wearing a ragged black vest barely laced across huge boobs and a primitive looking leather microskirt, with Grecian sandals strapped up her superb calves, she radiated enormous carnality and drive, bespeaking a dark animal cunning rather than conventional intelligence. Flanked by gun-toting, beret-wearing Black Panthers, like some bangled and bespangled Bohemian Boadicea she strode to her seat.

There was no judge's bench. Instead one of those huge wicker plantation-owner's chairs like the kind Huey Newton had once posed in was set atop a raised platform.

Lady Sunshine sat, her skirt riding even higher. As she slowly crossed her legs, she deliberately and ceremoniously flashed beaver at the whole room. You could hear the collective heart of all the assembled men and women alike skip a beat.

Moonchild, poor thing, seemed to wilt under the aggressive sexual display of the nation's leader.

Next filed in the prosecutor and assorted court personnel. One of them laid out my Yo-yo and Pez-dispenser on a table.

Lady Sunshine spoke in a voice like a big cat's throaty growl. "My people—do your *thang*."

36.
Judgment by Sugar Cube

"THE PEOPLE VERSUS Badfinger, in the Case of the Space Spy."

I tried to follow the opening arguments of the prosecution and the defense. But nothing they said made any sense. I thought it was lack of concentration on my part because of nerves. Then I realized the reality of my surroundings:

Everyone was stoned or brain-damaged. Or both.

These people had spent three decades inhaling the herb or puffing banana peels or mainlining horse tranquilizers. Their brain-cells had been exterminated faster and in greater quantity than fleeing Iraqi troops. And there were no objective standards of sanity for them to compare themselves to, since one and all labored under the same cloud.

As they rambled on, I realized that this was not a trial so much as a Mad Tea Party or Wonderland croquet game, with Lady Sunshine as the Red Queen.

At one point the examination of the news-stand chick I had offended went like this:

PROSECUTOR: So, uh, like, how long have you, like, hung out at this scene of yours, you know?

WITNESS: Well, lemme see, I guess, maybe since I was twelve.

PROSECUTOR: You're saying twelve years on the job?

WITNESS: Almost.

PROSECUTOR: Then you're pretty, um, experienced?

WITNESS: Sure. I guess. Whatever.

PROSECUTOR: And you've never had anyone lay any heavy trips on you before the, uh, dude named Badfinger showed up?

WITNESS: He gave off evil vibes right from the start, man!

DEFENDER: Objection! Witness is leading the Prosecutor right where he wants to go, man!

LADY SUNSHINE: Shut the fuck up, you dickless twerp!

DEFENDER: You're putting me through some heavy changes, Your Honor!

After enough of this I began to tune out the gibberish. All I could think of was how to escape. If only I could get my hands on the Yo-yo . . .

The next time I paid attention was when Tiny took the stand. The most coherent witness to date, he narrated what had happened, how he had taken the Nixon Pez-dispenser away from me.

At that moment Lady Sunshine herself interrupted.

"Has anyone eaten any of the Weasel candy yet as a test of its nature?"

Everyone looked around uneasily. Finally the Prosecutor answered, "Uh, no, Your Honor."

Grinning wickedly and pointing to Tiny, Lady Sunshine said, "You! Eat one!"

The bailiff approached Tiny with the Pez-dispenser. I leaped to my feet and shouted, "No!"

Other Angels wrestled me down. By the time I looked up again, Tiny had bent back the hinged Nixon head and extracted the candy lozenge levered into reach. Then he obediently swallowed it, his face a study in costive anxiety.

Everyone waited expectantly for something horrible to happen, while I just moaned. Now, even if I did manage to escape, this big lug was linked to me. What a mess!

When nothing happened, my trial, such as it was, continued.

After an interminable interval, Lady Sunshine, looking bored, cut things short by issuing an edict:

"There's only one way to settle the guilt of the accused, and that's with a hit of Owsley Blue. He'll tell us the truth then! Bailiff, the cube!"

With a brace of Angels pinioning my arms, I watched the attendant approach, bearing a sugar cube on a Frisbee.

Lady Sunshine announced offhandedly, "Oh, by the way, I sentence Moonchild to ten years at hard screwing, with time off for *b-a-a-a-d* behavior!"

Moonchild began to wail. I opened my mouth to comfort her, and they popped the acid in and slammed my jaws shut.

I tried to hold my mind together over the next few minutes, feeling the LSD coming on fast.

But what happened next surprised me, and I gradually mentally unclenched.

Because the lysergic trip was only a fraction as weird as the Monobloc! Thanks to the teachings of the Calvinii and my tenure in the Cosmic Egg, I was riding the acid like a professional surfer on an unchallenging knee-high swell.

Suddenly I could see the six compactified dimensions again.

With a twist I moved myself kata and afterup, right out of the grip of the Angels.

I was standing by the evidence table. Everyone was frozen and goggle-eyed. I snatched up the Pez-dispenser and Yo-yo.

"Paul, you're back!" the Calvinii chorused from inside the string.

Then I stepped baft and yesterdown, and was beside Moonchild. I chucked a Pez down her astonished yawp. She gulped it involuntarily down.

I looked around the crazy courtroom, pyre of all my hopes, and all I could think to say as I unfurled the Yo-yo was, "Take me someplace logical!"

FACES OF
THE FOURTH PAIR

37.
Quantized Time

MAYBE I HADN'T been thinking as well as I had imagined under the LSD, I realized with surprising clarity on the other end of the latest vermidesic Yo-yo transit.

What the hell did *I* want with someplace *logical*?

Blame the LSD then. The hallucinogen had made the notion seem good at the time. Confronted with the unfair chaos of Lady Sunshine's realm, a logical universe seemed highly preferable.

The LSD. Where was it now? It seemed instantly purged out of my system, as if this new universe wouldn't support such a mental state.

Where exactly was I? I couldn't seem to get ahold of whatever senses I now possessed. Immured in my skull again . . .

Remembering how it had taken me a while to get adjusted to the Monobloc environment, I made an effort not to feel frustrated. I tried to draw on my experience. After all, this was the third universe I had visited; four, if you counted my native one. I was a veteran cross-dimensional traveler, after all. Nothing to sweat over. Just imagine how Moonchild and Tiny must be feeling . . .

Were they with me? I wondered. The Yo-yo was supposed to drag along anyone who swallowed a Pez. But what if it hadn't worked? What if the Angel and the Virgin were spread out all over hyperspace? Had they made the crossing okay? I tried to call their names.

"Tiny? Moonchild? Are you guys there?"

Was I hearing myself speak? I couldn't tell.

Something inside me or around me now began to claim my attention. It was a sensation like a steady ticking, at once visceral and exterior. I tried to focus on it . . .

The ticking became more undeniable, the more I dwelled on it. But I still couldn't tell if it was coming from inside me or outside me—or both! It was like the regular, dull, methodical advance of a watch's second-hand, or the fall of drops in a water-clock. I began to get hypnotized by the unvarying metronomic beat. My thought processes seemed to be entrained with the ticking, moving forward in sharply individual steps unlike the usual human stream-of-consciousness.

Suddenly it dawned on me what I was experiencing.

I was sensing chronons, the discrete units of quantized time.

Back home, physicists had never been sure whether time was a continuous flow, infinitely divisible, or whether it was a step-by-step procession of infinitesimal basic units. Not arbitrary human units like seconds, but something much smaller, a unit on the order of ten to the minus forty-three seconds. Planck Time, or the time it would take light to travel the Planck length (that foamy sub-nano scale down which the Drexleroids had disappeared).

Apparently, in this universe, time was atomized. And I was experiencing the ineluctable passing of each time atom.

Now that I had realized this, if I really concentrated, I could experience my thoughts jerking forward in discrete steps. My perception of the chronons elongated, until each tick seemed an eternity.

The sensation of having my thoughts divided into forever-long, bite-sized pieces was highly irritating. It. Was. Like. Having. To. Formulate. Everything. This. Way. I started to freak out a little then. The torture of quantized time might have eventually driven me around the bend.

But just then my new senses started to kick in.

38.
Bad Case of the Jaggies

AS SENSATIONS FROM the exterior world began to penetrate and get organized, something funny happened with my perception of the passing chronons. The drip-drip-drip of time atoms began to accelerate. In the same way that the individual frames of a movie, projected fast enough, seemed continuous, so did time in this new universe start to resemble what I was familiar with: an indivisible forward flow.

But still, whenever I directed my attention inward, I could sense in a diminished fashion the steady ratcheting of the Cosmic Escapement.

Very weird.

Something like sight came to me then. Except this new sense seemed to provide a three-hundred-and-sixty-degree view, as if eyes were studded over my whole body.

At first, I couldn't sort out one line of input from another, and all was a vast confusion. Then, using a kind of cocktail-party-conversation mental filter, I was able to separate and focus, keeping most input in the background, letting one line of vision dominate at a time.

What I saw was a sourcelessly illuminated, seemingly infinite, black-lined white plane or checkerboard, spotted with various colorful jagged objects. I didn't seem to have much height—if any—above the grid. My "eyes" appeared to be right on a level with the plane, so that any particular object completely blocked whatever might be behind it. All I could see of any individual object was its closest edges, with some dwindling shading apparent from a kind of reflection or refraction.

All the objects within my field of vision seemed to be formed of irregular collections of contiguous multicolored squares. And the squares comprising each object were in constant upheaval.

Either they were busy changing color, flickering through a kaleidoscope of shades. Or peripheral units were shifting position one square away from their old spot. Or they were winking out of existence entirely.

It was like watching a cheap computer monitor filled with constantly mutating bad abstract art with all the steplike jaggies magnified.

Aside from vision, I seemed to have a built-in sense of direction. I could tell that one direction was "east," and another was "west." These two were the "neutral" directions. "North" seemed associated with a gradient of difficulty of travel; "south" implied increasing ease of movement the further one went. Diagonal vectors were proportionately hard or easy.

I realized that north and south could be more precisely thought of as up and down, with the gradient representing a kind of gravity, and resolved to think of them that way. That made east and west more like left and right.

Was I one of these assemblages of colored squares? I tried to move some part of myself into my line of sight, but couldn't quite coordinate my "limbs" yet. I gave up.

As for sound, there was none. At least at this moment.

So I tried to make some.

"Moonchild! Tiny! Are you here?"

No sound resulted from my call. But rather, to my amazement, a flock of identical glider-like objects erupted out of me in a corona! They began to spread out across the grid, moving like sharp-edged amoebas by shifting their bulk ahead one square at a time all along their leading edge and drawing it in on their trailing edge.

Most of the gliders continued to move away across the grid. But several were intercepted and absorbed by larger objects.

One of these big objects—located to my left, several "rows" away—then emitted its own expanding, omnidirectional shell of gliders.

Within moments, one of these secondary gliders hit me!

A silent "shout" formed in my "ears" in Moonchild's voice.

"Paul! I'm scared! Where are we?"

Another, more complex glider caught me from across a dozen rows in a different direction. It carried the voice and sentiments of Tiny.

"Man, when I figure out how to move I'm gonna rip the fucking head you don't got off your likewise fucking neck, if you don't get us the fuck outa here!"

And then I realized where—and what—we were.

39.
I Was a Teenage Cellular Automaton

ONCE UPON A time, late in my own twentieth century, there came to be born a field of science called "artificial life." I had read about it not too long ago. Populated with crazed computer jocks, buggy biologists, gonzo game theorists and other wild-eyed misfits, it was concerned both with robotics and with computer simulations of living things and their activities.

One of the best ways these people had found to model life in the non-physical sense was with a creation called cellular automata. This trick had been invented by all-round genius John von Neumann, and perfected by many others, most importantly John Horton Conway, surely at least von Neumann's intellectual equal.

Cellular automata lived mainly inside computers in your basic checkerboard world, a kind of mathematical cyber-Flatland. This checkerboard in its initial, unpopulated, state was filled with one hundred percent "dead" cells, which could function either as background or inhabitant. A cell became "alive" at first by godlike fiat, with a random or calculated seeding of the wasteland. Subsequently, the life or death of individual cells was determined *en masse* by a rulebook or if-then table that was consulted at the start of each computer-chip clock-cycle. The rules mainly referred to the conditions of neighboring cells or the interior state of the cell in question, or both. The rules could be as simple or complex as the experimenter desired. But it had been proven that even exceedingly simple rules could generate lifelike behavior, as the individual cells began to cooperate and act as larger multi-celled entities.

As cellular automata grew in size, they could theoretically emulate any computer hardware or computer program imaginable, just as sophisticated logic circuits could be constructed from

Tinkertoys. And since it was felt that a sufficiently advanced computer or Turing Finite State Machine could in turn emulate life (including instincts, reflexes and even consciousness), then cellular automata—or CA—were deemed to be quite capable of modeling any living thing.

CA could evolve, grow, reproduce, even think.

Or, apparently, shout obscene threats.

40.
Boids Do It, Vants Do It

TINY'S PLAINLY STATED intention to remove my nonexistent head from my CA body, should he acquire the power of movement, motivated me to try to gain that power first.

I figured that since I was now aware of the nature of our predicament and he wasn't, I had an edge.

Not much, but still an edge.

In fact, I was all edges.

The trouble with being a CA, I realized, was that movement was not dependent strictly on willpower. Conditions had to permit it. The grid, or matrix, was an active player, both transparent medium and potential future body parts. Various configurations of nearby cells would actually hinder or facilitate movement, which in a sense was more like growing outward and pulling up roots to follow. Then again, in another metaphor, the medium was like water, where active currents and turbulences either aided or thwarted a fish's actions.

And then, of course, not knowing the particular set of lookup rules that governed this world didn't help either.

Still, I reasoned, if this body that now hosted my consciousness was a natural product of this world, then movement routines must be built in. The trick was in letting them take over.

Something captured my attention now from above. I focused my "northward" eyes on the "sky."

A flock of CA birds—"boids," their a-life creator back home had named them—was wheeling overhead. Vaguely avian-shaped forms flocking and whirling, making beautiful patterns across the checkerboard.

I tried to really grok what the boids were doing and how they were doing it. At the same moment, I noticed for the first time even littler creatures "below" me, hustling down among blades of CA "grass." Virtual ants, or vants.

This world, I realized, was full of life, home to a whole ecology probably as complex as that of my native Earth.

The movements of the boids and vants began to stir something within me. I decided to try to raise my Badfinger hand that had been holding the Yo-yo.

Slowly, slowly, something that looked vaguely like an arm—one composed of flickering confetti—at the end of which hung something that looked vaguely like a coiled Yo-yo, swept up into my view.

I tried to contact the Calvinii inside the CA representation of the Yo-yo.

"Cals One and Two! Are you guys still there?"

Nothing. Should I be relieved or worried?

The big amorphous mass of colored tiles that was Moonchild emitted a host of gliders then. Several struck me, were assimilated and combined into an utterance.

"Paul, you've taught me! Now I think I can move too!"

A set of message gliders from Tiny hit me next.

"Man, you better have something more on the ball than swinging that puny li'l arm up. Cuz there's a whole pack of wide-mouth, big-tooth, shaggy wild animals racing toward us, and they look like mean mothers!"

41.
Lyints and Tigers and Bears, Oh My!

IMMEDIATELY, WITHOUT EVEN another destination firmly in mind, I tried to cast my Yo-yo to get us out of this dangerous, dead-end world. But although I managed to wave my new arm in a downward arc, the Yo-yo just wouldn't unfurl. Although I had compared the north-south gradient to gravity, physical laws were truly different here. It wasn't a simple matter of "letting the Yo-yo drop." Both the cells representing the Yo-yo and the surrounding matrix had to be in complementary states to permit movement. And, apparently, such was not now the case.

Would it ever be? Or were we stuck here forever?

Well—who the fuck knew? Not me, that was for sure.

I started to panic. Moonchild's stream of gliders carried shrieking, and Tiny's armada of messages brought rageful obscenities, neither of which helped my composure.

But then—inspiration struck!

My cogitations on the physical laws of this world paid off.

"Hey, you two! Listen up! If you can learn to move quickly, we're safe!"

"Whadda ya mean?" demanded Tiny.

"Well, it's like this...," and I began to explain.

CA worlds possessed a basic speed limit. Any individual cell (and hence any multi-celled organism, whose movement was bounded by any single cell of its body) could only creep ahead one checkerboard-square per chronon at most, just like a checker piece. There was simply no equivalent of running, leaping, or hopping here. No "kingers" existed. Every cell between any two objects had to be traversed before any two objects could come into contact.

Therefore, if prey and predator began a chase separated even by the minimal one cell distance that bordered entities, they could theoretically keep apart forever, or until one made a misstep or gave up.

Curiously enough, this speed limit on physical motion was also the limit on the speed of "sound." Because information was carried by gliders, which were CAs themselves, it took X number of chronons for messages to cover X number of squares.

(The big puzzle was how vision worked here. Apparently, whatever passed for "light" in the CA world conveyed information faster than sound or movement. If it had been otherwise, the predators Tiny had seen would have been atop him at the same instant as their first image registered. I didn't think our "eyes" were working by registering photons. Probably, whenever we focused on a distant point, the hidden CPU running the show fed data on the state of those points to us by otherwise inaccessible circuits. It was a kind of cheat, or hyperspace analogy. Whatever . . .)

Because Moonchild, Tiny and I were relatively close to each other—just a few rows apart—we had had time to exchange messages while the predators (which I now named lyints, for "lions of integers") raced toward us. But our time was rapidly running out.

"C'mon, guys! Pick up those cells and set 'em down! You can do it! This way! Quick!"

I began moving toward Moonchild. To my relief, she began moving too, away from me. Looking backwards, I could see Tiny following. Fear was a big spur.

Of course, we continued to maintain the original intervals between us.

"Tiny," I messaged. "Are the lyints catching up?"

"No, man! But they're not *giving* up either!"

"There's nothing to worry about! We'll just outlast them! We're smarter, too!"

Ahead of us loomed a grove of CA trees. There was plenty of space between the trunks, among which CA butterflies flitted, and we slipped easily betwixt the cellular boles. Movement was becoming more natural and reflexive.

"Ha-ha!" I began to laugh. "Those stupid lyints! They're no match for human intelligence!"

"Oh, Paul, do you really think so?"

"Of course," I boasted to Moonchild, as we broke out of the forest and saw the wall.

It stretched north and south as far as I could see, slightly curving, utterly blocking our path. If we were to follow it in either direction, the lyints would travel a diagonal vector and overtake us.

I caught up to Moonchild, who had stopped one row away from the wall.

Tiny joined us both. "You fucking idiot! They were *herding* us all the time!"

The idea of insurmountable obstacles hadn't occurred to me. But it made sense now that if predators existed here, they must have some cunning method of trapping their prey.

"Well, I said wanly, "it doesn't seem that we can really feel pain here, so it shouldn't hurt to be eaten."

And, huddled together against the wall, we watched the lyints race toward us.

42.
The Dyne Farmers to the Rescue!

WHEN THE DIGITAL beasts were a few kilorows away, we could see single-cell "drool" falling from the vicious maws of the lyints in colorful sparkles.

"Listen, guys, I'm sorry I got you into this mess."

"Oh, Paul, your intentions were good. What else did I have to look forward to but a fate worse than death?"

"Well, Moonchild, sex isn't all that bad."

"But with *old people*?"

Tiny chimed in. "Man, *I'm* no pervert like Olive Oyl here! I like sex with *anyone*, old or young. You didn't have to bring *me* along."

"You're here because you did what Lady Sunshine demanded, Tiny. That was where you went wrong. You should have showed some backbone and not swallowed that Pez."

"Lady Sunshine woulda had my *backbone* if I hadn't done what she ordered."

I fully expected us to spend our last living chronons futilely arguing. It would have been a fitting ending to my life so far.

But at that moment, a large section of the wall simply dissolved behind us.

The person-wide center of the new passage was clear. But on either side stood two big CA entities similar in appearance to us! And they were clutching spears!

"Quickly!" shouted one. "Inside!"

We didn't need to be asked twice.

The wall was five cells thick, and we were inside as fast as we could move our personal collection of cells entirely through the "tunnel."

Directing our attention backwards, we saw our rescuers hurl their spears.

The shafts made of colored cells flew straight toward the lyints, some of whom had paused or even begun to retreat. But two unlucky lyints were hit! The spears passed right through them, cleaving them in twain. The separate halves, unable to sustain themselves, dissolved into fragments.

One of the newcomers then tossed a handful of what looked like seeds into the gap in the wall. Instantly, that section of wall reappeared.

"Thank you, thank you!" I messaged. "Who are you guys?"

"We are the Tofolli clan, and we cultivate dynes for King Horton."

"Far out!" said Moonchild. "I grew up on a farm too!"

43.
Lyce and Wolframs

WITHOUT WEATHER, THE CA world would seem to obviate the need for houses. Yet the Tofolli had constructed them for several reasons. Like the settlement-encircling wall, the "buildings" (really nothing more than circles of cells) provided protection, should the main wall get breached. They also were handy for enclosing personal possessions. And they provided privacy.

This latter issue, when it was raised, naturally brought to mind the nature of sex, if any, in this world. But I didn't broach the topic then. I had a lot more on my plate.

First, the Tofolli chastised us.

"Why were you all shouting like that? Are you from the city? Didn't you realize you'd attract predators, out here in the wild?"

It turned out that sending message gliders radiating in all directions was what the Tofolli meant by "shouting." Such omnidirectional broadcasting was bound to have unintended consequences. There was no limit on the distance "sound" could travel, save for encountering random obstacles. And even these, it turned out, were not a complete barrier, since message gliders had evolved over the generations to possess interpenetrative powers. They could pass right through many other CA entities in a non-destructive manner, using the cells of the obstacle to transmit their patterns, thus emerging and continuing on their way.

(It would turn out that my old notions of the physical integrity of objects did not fit the reality of the CA world, since many times individuals could propagate right through each other, leaving both intact. Obviously, the spears and walls of the Tofolli were not made like this.)

Anyhow, the Tofolli taught us to speak like civilized beings, directing a single stream of gliders in just the desired direction. But our shouting hadn't been all bad, since that was how the Tofolli—one of whom had been outside the wall—had heard us and been prepared to rescue us from the lyints.

After this etiquette lesson, when the Tofolli learned we had no place to go, they more or less adopted us. Gave us a house and put us to work in the dyne fields.

What the Tofolli grew was not food. No one ate for the sake of energy here. That was free, courtesy of the matrix and its groundrules. (Predators like the lyints had wanted to integrate our prepackaged cells—or as much as they could bite off—into their own bodies, so they could grow bigger. With certain reservations, bigness was the ultimate good here, as it promoted complexity of function.)

The dynes that the Tofolli cultivated were more like seed-crystals. Growing on a bewildering variety of plant-shaped stalks, shrubs, trees and vines, the dynes were pattern-formation catalysts. Basically, they were encapsulated information, capable of producing a number of effects.

Tiny, Moonchild and I had the chore of making sure that CA pests (which burrowed through the wall, or sneaked in through the open gates, or even formed spontaneously!) did not damage the growing dynes. And, possibly as a precaution, we in turn were watched over by some of the village's wolframs.

The wolframs, as I had christened them, resembled canines, and were plainly domesticated wild animals. They were a little scary, but Tiny seemed to get along well with them, even going so far as to pet them.

What was worse than the wolframs was the lyce.

The hut that the three of us had been given was infested with them. Apparently, that was why it had been vacant.

Lyce were parasites just a few hundred cells big. (We visitors and the Tofolli were hundreds of thousands of cells big—perhaps a million. Not much compared with a human's multi-trillion bodily cells, but seemingly enough to sustain intelligence.) Not only did the lyce crawl all over a person, interfering with vision, but they could actually get inside your body, if they found the proper weak configuration of cells. Several of them had in fact taken up residence in us, as we could see by inspecting each other.

"Ee-yew, Paul, I crushed another!"

"Nice work, Moon."

"Hey, look, man! Wolfie here'll eat a dead one! Good boy!"

44.
The Ontological Pickle Rears Its Ugly Head Again

WHEN I WASN'T busy chasing lyce or tending dynes, I thought about this strange world I had brought us to.

Were we living inside a relatively small computer tended by outside intelligences? Or was this environment the entire ultimate substrate of this particular spaghetti strand? In other words, did this timeline boast a layer of reality outside our present environment, a world of people, planets and solar systems, where someone watched our pathetic antics on a screen? Or was the entire substance of this particular spaghetti strand cellular? I knew that some scientists back home had gone so far as to claim that our own universe was in reality a very large cellular automaton. Could that be the case here?

Of course, I couldn't make any headway with this problem. I simply didn't have enough data or access to higher senses. I was stuck in this limited frame.

In a way, it was like the question that had plagued me back in

Bookland: why was there something instead of nothing? It didn't matter in the end if the dilemma was unanswerable, you still had to live with it.

Of course, I kept trying to use my Yo-yo, but it was no-go. Very frustrating.

So when the Tofolli told us we were all going to get wasted in a big celebration, I was grateful.

45.
Festival of the Dynes

IT WAS HARVEST time. The dynes were picked and stored. Soon, they would be transported to Langton, the city of King Horton, in feudal tribute. But before then, we would celebrate.

All the Tofolli and their wolframs were gathered around some kind of shimmering cellular shrine or tree or fire, it was hard to tell which. The three of us were there too. During the past few kilochronons, I had never learned to tell the Tofolli apart. They all looked alike, and I wasn't even sure they had individual names as we knew them. But I had managed to memorize the "features" of Moonchild and Tiny, for we all looked somewhat different from the clansmen, reflecting our foreign origin.

"Man, I hope this Squarehead dope is good stuff," Tiny said. "I sure have missed my pot."

"Well, don't get your hopes up too high. Even though this world runs on logic, it's pretty psychedelic to start with, so I don't know where their dope can take you."

"I just wish we could get out of here somehow," Moonchild wistfully volunteered. "I'm sick of lyce and farming and not having a real body. I miss the wind and rain and sun and clouds."

"Now you sound like Joni Mitchell."

"Oh, Paul, why must you always try to shock me by alluding to heretics?"

One of the Tofolli approached us, carrying a basket of bumpy dynes. "Here, friends, take one and become nonlinear."

We each took a dyne. I asked, "How do we use it?"

"Simply squeeze it from all sides at once."

The Tofolli left, to continue distributing the dynes.

Tiny had already engulfed his. Moonchild and I hesitated a little longer.

"Well, here goes nothing," I said, and squeezed the dyne.

Instantly the catalyst went to work. I could feel a new pattern propagating through me. In the exact number of chronons equal to my largest body dimension, I was totally transubstantiated.

The effect of the dyne was to make me feel organic again. But in a primitive way. Within the limits of my million cells, I imagined myself human again, a kind of point-zero-zero-zero-zero-one-percent model of a human.

Was this the effect the Tofolli were feeling? Or just my peculiar reaction to the drug? Impossible to say.

I looked to Moonchild. She appeared in my altered vision like a kind of child's animated clay model of a person. And she must have seen me the same way.

"Oh, Paul, this is awful! It's just a tease! It's worse than nothing!"

Before I knew what I was doing, I was hugging her for wordless comfort.

Then, in a natural reaction, we were having sex, our blobby Gumby bodies intertwined.

Just as we got going good, the dyne wore off.

Now we were two CAs again. Only linked by a long skinny shared tube, down which individual sparkle cells flowed from Moonchild to me!

"Paul! Stop! What are you doing?"

"I can't help it! This feeler's got a will of its own!"

All around us, the Tofolli were similarly linked. I noticed Tiny had found a partner too. He was bellowing a flock of message gliders that said, "Love the one you're with!"

Finally, the mating was over without any particular orgasmic climax, the tube broke and its halves were withdrawn into us, and our CA bodies were separate again.

Moonchild's message gliders carried the sound of crying. "Boo hoo hoo, now I'm not a virgin anymore!"

"If it helps," I said, "considering that I've never swapped logic with anyone before, neither am I."

46.
CA-ravan to Langton

I COULDN'T STOP thinking about sex.

Here we were, accompanying the Tofolli across a miraculous alien landscape, beset by dangers and blessed by wonders, headed toward the cultural center of this realm, where the mysterious King Horton dwelt, and all I could think about was screwing.

Typical.

The crude intercourse with Moonchild had caused my *ideé fixe*.

Back home, I hadn't had sex in years. I had gotten to the point where abstinence wasn't even an issue anymore. I hardly even bothered to jerk off once a month. Part of that was attributable to the depression brought on by confronting the Ontological Pickle, of course. But most of my chastity was just plain giving up on myself and others.

However strange and unsatisfying the "conjugation" with Moonchild had been, it had reawakened the possibility of sex and companionship—to say nothing of love—in my mind.

Surely, that had been the biggest deficit in my old life, the lack of any woman. Now that I had the Yo-yo though, couldn't I easily remedy that?

As the train of Tofolli neared their goal, I resolved on my next wish, should I ever regain the use of the Cosmic Yo-yo.

One "day," after we had passed the Great Recursion Falls and emerged from the Creeping Beeflower Forest (an impossible passage, except for the fact that the Forest itself took on the average two steps back for every one forward), we saw the splendid city of Langton laid out before us.

It was another wall. There was no "higher" vantage of course to survey the whole thing as if from above. So all we saw was another wall.

Typical.

47.
Horton Hears a "No!"

THERE WERE GUARDS or customs agents at the entrance to Langton. We had to stop while they inspected our baskets of dynes. I couldn't hear what the Tofolli leaders said to them, since they were "speaking softly," but I didn't like the fact that accusatory "fingers" were pointed in the direction of Tiny, Moonchild and me.

Whatever was said or determined, we were all allowed to pass into the city unmolested.

At least for the moment.

Inside the wall, there were thousands of cellular folks, hundreds of buildings, and much activity. Most of it was relatively incomprehensible. But something I saw made me pause.

One resident was plainly painting pictures on the sides of buildings. Clutching a special dyne, he would touch individual cells in the building wall, altering their state so as to sketch out patterns of trees, animals and other things. (Only ultrarealism existed here, I realized, since artistic representations and living subjects were composed of one and the same medium.)

The sight made me sigh. Art. Whatever had happened to my own aspirations along those lines? Gone, all gone.

Well, what the hell . . . I was out strictly for sensual gratification now.

Looking back, I noticed that most of the Tofolli had split off, heading probably toward some dyne storehouse with their tribute. That left us three alone with two guides. I thought they might have been our two original rescuers. Tired of not having labels for them, I now tagged them Vonnie One and Two.

"Come with us," said Vonnie One. "We have been summoned to an audience with the King."

I didn't like the sound of this. "What's with this King anyhow?

You bring him your crops and do everything he asks. What's he do for you?"

Vonnie One's message gliders sounded nervous. "The King is the symbol of the realm's magnificence. We are proud to give him whatever he needs to grow in splendor."

It sounded fishy to me. But what could we do except go meekly along...?

Toward the end of our CA-ravan, I had begun to feel a little strange. I was convinced that something new was happening inside my cellular body. Now, as we went to see the King, I asked Moonchild if she were feeling it too.

"Do you feel weird, Moon?"

"What kind of dumb question is that? I'm stuck in a candyflake body in a glitter world, and you ask me if I feel weird? Of course I feel weird!"

"I know, I know. But I mean a different kind of weird?"

"Oh, Paul, how should I know? Why don't you just forget your miserable self for a change and concentrate on getting us someplace nicer?"

"Listen to the lady, Badfinger. Give that Yo-yo another try."

I obliged Tiny, but my efforts were still futile.

Now we and our guides were approaching the largest structure I had ever seen here. I assumed it must be the palace of King Horton.

"Will we see the King right away?" I asked Vonnie Two.

"You are regarding his royal presence even as we speak."

Judging from the immense side of him that faced us, the King was easily as large as a hundred of any of us simpler CAs.

"How—how did he get so big?" whispered Moonchild.

"By the loving contributions of his subjects."

Just then, a flock of oddly configured message gliders issued from the King.

"I *eat* my loving subjects, stranger! The lesser ones are assimilated to my grandeur! With each meal I become smarter and more magnificent! And you three newcomers with your foreign tastes are next on the menu! Come to me!"

There was something hypnotic in the information transmitted by the King. Regular gliders carried no sense of compulsion, just pure information and associated tones. But the King's words had the effect of compelling, like a computer virus.

Moonchild and Tiny began to creep forward, toward greedy vacuoles opening inward in the body of King Horton. I felt my own cells stirring helplessly toward the cannibal.

But then, perhaps because of the weird new feelings inside me, I found the will to resist.

"No!" I shouted. "You can't eat us!"

48.
Horton Hatches a Paul

THE KING WAS incensed.

"You dare to refuse this honor! No one stops King Horton from growing!"

Vonnies One and Two moved to immobilize me before I could flee. Moonchild and Tiny were still heading toward their doom. Then the King reached out an arm toward me.

The limb touched my body.

At that exact chronon, I began to give birth.

I knew right away that I was replicating. It was plain as day. The mating between Moonchild and me had catalyzed the gestation of a child formed of our two parental contributions. And now it was coming forth.

The Vonnies backed off with religious awe.

"Forgive us, stranger! We did not know you were about to reproduce!"

Cell by cell, the little CA began to bud off me, until finally it was connected only by a single-cell thread. Then that dissolved too.

"Mommy!" the little CA said.

The strange feeling was gone from inside me.

But more importantly, I could sense somehow that the Yo-yo was ready to use. The altered space between me and my child fostered the very conditions for its unfurling.

I lifted my arm and the Cosmic String began to unwind, one cell at a time, and I yelled:

"Take me to a world full of hot babes!"

FACES OF
THE FIFTH PAIR

49.
Return of the Virgin; or, Hymenia Regain'd

TINY DUMPED ANOTHER log on the blazing campfire, and a comet-tail of sparks flew up, seeding the night sky with crazy dying constellations.

"I'm still cold," Moonchild whined. She was dressed in the bellbottoms and light blouse she had been wearing when we were taken to the People's Solidarity Court, seemingly an eternity ago. Tiny wore his greasy leathers, and I was dressed like a dweeby bookstore clerk who expected never to be too far from a thermostat. All excellent clothes for the climates we had come from, but not at all suited for the dank Novemberish cold which had greeted our arrival here, in the putative land of hot babes.

We had materialized in the midst of a small clearing surrounded by the easily recognizable massive oaks and firs and other quickly boring lumber of an apparently primeval forest, just as dusk was dropping down. At first we had been too wild with relief to think about our circumstances. Free from the hungry embrace of King Horton, back in our old bodies, breathing sweet air, kicking real pine-needled dirt, we had done a little dance of celebration. But then reality had hit us.

The Cosmic Yo-yo of the Moraveckians was great for traversing the unimaginable gulfs between universes, but essentially useless for moving you a hundred yards away, once you were in a new world. I supposed that I could have spun out the Yo-yo again, making some such request as, "Take me to a world identical to this one, except put me in the middle of a city." But who knew if the Yo-yo had a limit on the number of trips it could make? And what if the stupid thing misinterpreted my command, and we ended up worse off? No, it seemed plain that for the moment we were stuck here in the middle of nowhere, our fate bounded by our own cunning and resources.

Which were admittedly not large.

Deciding to stay put till dawn, we had immediately set about gathering some firewood. Soon, thanks to Tiny's copious supply of matches (one benefit of being an inveterate dope smoker was never to be without matches), we had a cheerful blaze going.

Moonchild had even gotten an unexpected pleasant surprise—which she couldn't wait to share with the rest of us—when she had gone off behind a tree to pee. She rushed back into the clearing with her pants up but unbuttoned, yelling, "I'm still a virgin! I'm still a virgin!"

50.
Fireside Theatrics

APPARENTLY, OUR DIGITAL mating in CA-land had had no permanent effect on Moonchild's human hymen. A not unlikely outcome, considering the strangeness of the conjugal CA-connection. We congratulated Moonchild with all the requisite excitement her discovery merited, and I tried to forget the matter.

But we had not emerged completely unscarred from that cyberexistence, as we discovered in the next instant.

"Hey, Badfinger," Tiny exclaimed, "there's something crawling on your arm."

I looked down at my bare forearm.

There were lyce there. Tiny colorful CAs about as big as dimes, moving around one step at a time under my epidermis like living tattoos. They didn't feel like anything, but they were still creepy. I tried to brush them off, but it was no use. They were under or within my skin, using my organic cellular structure as a medium to support their old one-dimensional existence. It was soon apparent that I was not alone in carrying the lyce, as Tiny and Moonchild discovered bugs aplenty within their own skins.

Suddenly, Moonchild began screaming.

"Our son! Our son! Where's our son?"

It took me a few seconds to figure out that she meant the little CA I had given birth to. Sure enough, he had not made the transition with us. Apparently, being a discrete individual, even though born of my CA body, and not having swallowed a Pez, he had remained behind.

"You left our son to be eaten by that horrible King!"

"Wait a minute now. How can we have a son if you're still a virgin?"

"You know perfectly well that *you* were the one who gave birth to him, not me!"

"His first word was 'Mommy.'"

"That was a reference to you!"

"I think *not*."

I didn't want to admit it, but Moonchild's accusation hurt. Just as I had felt somewhat guilty at letting Hans take a living copy of my essential wetware and dismember it for his own uses, so now I had bad feelings about having left my CA son helpless in the face of danger.

Trying to put a callous front on, I said, "I'm not going to lose any sleep over it. I did what I had to do to save our own lives. Who knew the kid wouldn't come automatically along? Besides, it's too late to do anything now."

"No, it's not! We can go back and help him!"

"For*get* it!"

"All you can think about is your 'hot babes!'"

"What's the matter with that?" Tiny interjected. "I figured Badfinger made a groovy wish. Assuming it pans out."

During our stint in the dyne fields, I had explained to Tiny (and again to Moonchild, realizing that all the dope in our shared jailcell had perhaps obscured the import of previous explanations) where I was from, how I had gotten to their world, what passengers I carried in my Yo-yo's string, and why I was on a quest for personal happiness and a resolution to the Ontological Pickle, or a "Theory of Anything." The Angel had been appreciative and, as he now indicated again, entirely sympathetic with my latest choice of worlds.

Hard on the heels of Tiny's comment, the voices of Calpurnia and Calypso miraculously resounded in my brain.

"Us too! Bring on the babes!"

"Cals! What happened to you in CA land? Where were you?"

"What do you mean?"

"Didn't we come to this universe direct from your trial?"

I explained what they had missed.

"Oh, we see. It's obvious."

"That onesie-nonesie flatworld was too simplistic to support us."

"You humans were capable of being modeled there by a few giga-cell assemblages. But it would have taken several trillion trillion trillion logic-units to mimic us."

"At least!"

"But we're here now!"

"And we can hardly wait for the sex to start!"

"Well, me neither," I said, just as a distant wolf howled, initiating a cascade of bloodcurdling responses from his hungry packmates.

51.
Goddesses with Dirty Faces

NOW THE AIRBORNE sparks from Tiny's newly heaved log died out. Moonchild began to shiver.

"Come sit over here between me and Tiny."

"You two *males* will get ideas."

Tiny began to bellow tunelessly. "I know a little about love—and baby, I can guess the rest—"

"Tiny, stop it! Listen, Moon, we're just gonna huddle for warmth. You know we'd never do anything you didn't want us to."

"Oh, that's a typical guy trick! Somehow you'll make me 'want it.' Temporarily at least. I'll lose control. And then forever after, I'll hate myself!"

I held my head in my hands. Why, I thought, did women have to be this way? Was there no bridge between the sexes, no commonality of interest? Did blind, stupid evolution, the implacable needs of our selfish genes, dictate that men and women must always be, on some deep level, opponents, free-spirited inseminators versus gravid caregivers?

"And," Moonchild sneered, "I don't intend to become one of your harem of 'hot babes'!"

"Oh, forget it then! If keeping your precious virginity means freezing your skinny ass off, then go ahead."

"Skinny!"

"That's what I said. But maybe I meant bony!"

Moonchild hurled herself across the space between us with a wordless yell and knocked me off the log where I was seated. We began to roll and tussle in the dirt. Tiny kneeled beside us and tried to pry us apart.

As we struggled, there came the sound of snapping twigs from the edge of the clearing, as well as earth-muffled footsteps and hoof-shufflings.

The three of us stopped struggling and looked up.

Into the firelight came a party of a dozen tousle-haired women.

Most of them were on foot. But two were mounted bareback on giant red elks, the animals bridled but wild-looking. Dressed in an assortment of finely tailored furs and skins; decorated with bead, bone and copper jewelry; carrying bows, arrows and spears, the women averaged six feet tall and looked like the well-fed and pumped-up offspring of Racquel Welch and Arnold Schwarzenegger. A whole pack of Xenas. Their faces were smudged with the dust and grime of hard travel.

One of the elk-riders spoke some unintelligible words and then waited patiently and, somehow, regally, for a response.

"These are the hot babes?" said Tiny doubtfully.

52.
Adding a Circuit

IN THE MONOBLOC my altered brain, by the very constraints of its probabilistic construction, had been naturally capable of communicating with the Calvinii. The same was true of my sojourn in CA-land and my ease in "speaking" the native lingo. In Moonchild's and Tiny's world, the inhabitants had been speaking English. Archaic English, to be sure, but English nonetheless. I hadn't considered till now what I would do if I was faced with an unknown language in my interplenary travels.

It now dawned on me what a *cheat* this stinking Yo-yo was! Not only were its cybernetic guts obtuse and limited in following my highly specific and accurate wishes, but it was absolutely no use when it came to helping me navigate through my destination worlds. Like now, for instance. How was I to communicate with this band of women? If only Hans had bothered to include some kind of whizbang superscience translator device among his gifts, instead of the stupid Pez-dispenser. Whatever had given him the idea that I'd like companions on my quest anyhow?

"You like me, don't you?" said Calpurnia inside my head.

"And me?" chimed in Calypso.

"Especially since we can help you now."

"Help? How?"

"If you want us to, we'll just tweak your brain a little."

"We've found lots of under-utilized connections in here."

"It'd be easy as stacking hydrogen atoms to engineer an omnitranslator and parallel speech circuits right into your primitive wetware."

"It'd keep us from getting rusty too."

"Yeah. Calvinii gotta build, Calvinii gotta shape!"

What did I have to lose? "All right. Go ahead. But take it slow."

"Okey-dokey, artichokey!"

One of the Red Sonja elk-riders had turned to talk to her mounted companion. Listening to them, I had the weirdest thrill of hearing their gibberish turn in midstream into English!

"—to the Great Mother. She's moved this past moon to her winter residence at Blood of Ten Aurochs."

"Yes," replied the second rider. "That would be best. Assuming they will come. After all, we don't wish to dishonor the Winged One by using force. Even on non-kin."

I got up from the ground with as much dignity as I could muster. Brushing off my clothes, I said in a fluent burst of tongue-twisting phonemes, "No force will be necessary, ladies. We'll be happy to accompany you to visit the Great Mother."

53.
Cavebear Bar-B-Que

THE SMELL OF roasting meat was almost making me faint. The last solid food I had eaten was jail-porridge back in Hippieville, and I could hardly wait to tear into my share of the sizzling steaks now being expertly grilled by one of the native women. The information that the meat had come from something like a grizzly the size of a Jeep didn't even matter to me.

(What did puzzle me a bit was how these primitive gals had caught and killed such formidable prey . . .)

Taking into account our obvious ineptitude at nocturnal cross-country pilgrimages, the all-girl band of travelers had elected to make camp at our site until dawn. I was relieved, since it would allow us to rest and also to size up these people.

First came the introductions. My name was greeted with puzzled looks, an obviously unknown and possibly barbaric appellation. "Is that an ancient Far Trader name?" one finally asked. Of course, I couldn't answer sensibly. Tiny's name was instantly understandable and provoked laughter, as well as some half-overheard bawdy jokes among the women. Moonchild's was greeted with respectful reverence and the unanimous display of a strange gesture made with both hands, a mimicking of flapping bird wings. Then came the other side's names. First the high-status riders:

"I'm Thick Flow."

"Born Late."

The other ten spoke up in turn.

"Sharp As Flint."

"Quern."

"Tease The Bull."

"House Hater."

"Lost Needle."

"Smooth Runner."

"Catch Coney."

"Drunken Dancer."

"Burnt Water."

"Mother's Little Helper."

I was translating for my companions as the women spoke. Hearing the last name, Moonchild said, "Cool, they like the Stones."

"Um, I don't think so, Moon."

By now the steaks were done, and we settled down to eat. Out of hide-covered dispensers was poured a kind of fermented milk drink. It took a little getting used to, but, I soon found out, packed an immediate kick.

As the only speaker of the native language, I found myself sandwiched between the leaders, Thick Flow and Born Late, who seemed intent on learning all they could about us. Quite a few of the other women were gathered around a plainly agreeable Tiny. They were taking turns feeding him and replenishing his cup. Language did not seem to be a barrier to whatever they had in mind. Meanwhile Moonchild, wearing a borrowed fur against the chill, was sitting apart from the crowd, picking at her food and looking miserable. In truth, next to these attractive Amazons her beanpole figure and plain features were all the more evident.

After I had explained as best as I could where we had come from (an explanation which I could tell was received as a kind of fairy tale which I must have had some good reason for offering, however obscure), I asked where I was, and what realm or tribe the women represented.

Thick Flow finished picking her teeth with the copper pin of one of her brooches before answering. "Why, where else could you be but in the Bosom of the Goddess, and among her mortal children?"

Born Late said, "Does not Her embrace extend everywhere, and include everyone?"

I felt it best to agree with these innocent savages. "Why, of course, metaphorically speaking, I'm sure it does. But what nation do you hail from?"

"Nay-shun? The word is not familiar . . . "

"Isn't your world divided into different countries?"

"Cun-trees?"

This was impossible. I searched in my new vocabulary for the appropriate words, some counterparts to states, monarchies, fiefdoms, empires—precincts, even. Nothing came. At last I had to be satisfied with a circumlocution.

"Zones of power and influence and constraint, supervised by certain individuals. Nothing like that...?"

Thick Flow smiled amiably, as if humoring a madman. "We make no arbitrary distinctions among the lands the Goddess has created. The world is one in Her eyes and in ours."

Finally I got it. "Oh, you people must know only a very small portion of your whole world. I'm sure what you say is true of your immediate little neighborhood, your tiny backyard. But the Earth is a big, round globe, you know, floating in space, circling the Sun."

I sketched a globe in space with my hands, as if trying to communicate with a deaf person. The power-milk had given me a buzz and I could hear now the smug tone of my voice. So could the women, for they ceased smiling.

Then Thick Flow said. "Yes, we know. Approximately twenty-four thousand, eight hundred and thirty miles around at the equator and ninety-three million miles away from the Goddess's Birthgrave. At least as closely as our sailors and skywatchers have been able to determine. Although when the new generation of megaliths comes online, we expect to do better."

54.
The Twin Cities

IT WAS A good thing me and Tiny and Moon hadn't set out on our own. It turned out we were five days walk from the nearest settlement—assuming we had been able to find the direct path in the first place. We surely would've gotten lost in the thick spooky forest and been forced either to starve and freeze our asses off or to abandon this world via Yo-yo, before I had even formulated another desirable place to go.

Of course, putting aside the mystery of its political setup and dominant ethos—a mystery the conversation of our hosts had failed to fully clear up—I wasn't even sure yet that *this world* was a desirable one. So far, the place had hardly met my criteria for a land of hot babes. I had had in mind something more like uninhibited access to the complaisant models at a photo-shoot for the Victoria's Secret catalog. Instead, I had gotten the Patagonia clothing catalog version. It made me wonder how much bandwidth the Hans-wired connections between the Yo-yo and my brain featured . . .

These big women, despite their flawless muscled limbs and soot-smudged beauty, somehow failed to excite me. I had actually passed up some fairly explicit sexual invitations. I gathered that such was not the case with Tiny. His first night with the women had featured a cacophony of gruntings, squeals and bellows as he had his way with several of the travelers, both serially and simultaneously.

Oh, well. At least I was helping *one* of my friends. Though Moonchild didn't approve of my pimping at all, as I could tell by her perpetual sour puss.

Whatever their shortcomings as objects of my lust, the women were great guides and soon led us unerringly to a small, unfortified, happy village named Left Breast: a dozen solid- and comfortable-looking daub-and-wattle, thatch-roofed buildings arranged concentrically around a two-story stone structure. Corrals for pigs, sheep and goats. Cultivated fields of what looked like beans. Across a small river lay the identical Right Breast.

How will you keep 'em down on the farm, after they've seen the Big Titty?

55.
Up On the Rooftops

THE DOGS OF Left Breast yapped at us as we stopped just long enough to replenish our supplies and share some welcome midday beer. Thick Flow and Born Late conferred with the village elder, a man named Swift Shuttle, exchanging news.

I was reassured to see the guy. He was the first male I had spotted here. Even though he was old, he was strong and unbent, clear-eyed and confident. He dealt with the two women as a respectful equal, not a slave or subjugated minority, neither party acting like boss, neither playing brown-noser. I had been worried that men here might turn out to be some kind of matriarchy-oppressed wimps. Such did not seem to be the case.

Soon we were on the trail again. I was walking beside Mother's Little Helper. (I had learned she was a midwife.) She started a conversation.

"Did you know that your companion Tiny is marked with one of the Goddess's signs?"

"No. What do you mean?"

She grabbed my wrist and lifted my arm up. With her forefinger she traced several of the slowly moving CA lyce beneath my skin. "These magic tattoos you all possess. Tiny has one shaped like the labrys, the doubled-bladed axe. It is unmistakable."

"I've never seen it."

Mother's Little Helper giggled. "Probably not. It never seems to move far from his private parts."

I yanked my arm away, embarrassed.

Over the next two weeks we moved steadily south. The weather got warmer, the vegetation semitropical.

One day we crested a line of hills and saw Blood of Ten Aurochs.

Halfway down the slope, flat-topped one- and two-story stone and timber houses began sparsely to dot the green landscape.

More and more of them filled the lower reaches of a coastal plain, until they accumulated the mass of a good-sized city. Beyond the far edge of the city, a grape-Koolaid-dark sea stretched to the horizon.

Each of the roofs, I noticed, had a rain-shielded entrance with a ladder sticking up from it. The buildings seemed to have no other, more conventional doors, at least on the sides facing me.

Thick Flow and Born Late dismounted, and began to lead their massive elks by their bridles. "Now you will meet the Great Mother."

When the buildings became nearly contiguous, we ascended to the rooftops and began to cross the city that way, stepping from building to building across planks and up and down ladders. There was a lot of pedestrian traffic up there, men and women both, lots of healthy rambunctious kids too.

At last we stopped at one roof indistinguishable from any of the others.

"You may descend," said Thick Flow.

I mustered up my courage. I had brought us to this world, and it was up to me to go first, especially since I was the only one who could speak the lingo.

The ladder was strong and I scrambled down it. Inside, it took my eyes a moment to adjust to the light from translucent, hide-covered windows and an oil lamp, which dimly illuminated the limestone-slab-floored room.

At a broad table, her back to me, was seated a giant strawberry-blonde woman. She turned, and I saw it was Lady Sunshine.

56.
Voice of the Beehive

WHILE I MADE like an icicle and froze, Moon and Tiny came down the ladder, the rungs bending under the latter's bulk. When they had come up beside me and got their eyes working, they too went glacial.

Tiny was the first to recover. If you can call turning to jelly a recovery. He fell to his knees, clasped his hands in supplication and began to beg.

"Please, please, your Ladyship, it was all a big accidental fuckup, like. I swallowed Badfinger's bummer dope just like you ordered, and it brung me here. But I never meant to bug out on you like that. Hell, I *loved* my job!"

Lady Sunshine stood up and approached Tiny, who cringed. She got her hands under his armpits—a place I myself would not have willingly put my own—and lifted him up, saying with calm nobility, "I do not understand your speech, stranger, but it is plain that you are frightened. Have any of my followers abused you? If so, they shall be severely reprimanded."

As soon as I heard her calm, empathetic and rational voice—so unlike the real Lady's ego-trippy snarl—my brains started functioning again and I knew what had happened.

There was no way Lady Sunshine, sans Yo-yo of her own, could have followed us across two spaghetti strands, especially since she had never swallowed a Pez. This was merely her convergent duplicate, solely the product of this continuum's history. And the convergence had extended even to the point where she too occupied the apex of her social pyramid.

But then I wondered: did the necessity of also duplicating a sufficiency of Lady Sunshine's ancestors in order to culminate in *her* mean that we had arrived in this world's twentieth century? If so, what the hell historically had happened to render the era as we saw it?

As Tiny continued to cower, I realized that I had to put aside my speculations and step in.

"Guys," I said in English, "Look close. This isn't the Lady, just her twin." Then I turned to address the Great Mother.

"Um, Your Royal Highness, please forgive our bad manners. We are visitors from another world who are still tired and confused. Your followers have been very gracious and kind to us. It's just that you reminded my friend of, uh, his ex-wife. She was a real ball-buster—"

I shut up then before my mouth spilled any more stupidity.

The Great Mother radiated a tolerant smile I could feel down to my insteps. "This is a not unfamiliar situation, even here in our world. In any case, you must make yourself feel at home here. We shall assign quarters and permanent guides to you, and then you will be free to do whatever you wish. We will talk again, when I have more time."

With a sigh, the Great Mother returned to her table. I saw then that it was not a surface for dining but more like a desk. Piled high with rune-scribed parchments, the slab of burled wood was plainly a wearisome domain. Putting us instantly out of her mind, the Great Mother grabbed a document and began to read. .

As we turned humbly to ascend the ladder, I saw her take up a round clay seal from among many such, roll it in ink and imprint the finished paperwork.

Up on the roof, back in Thick Flow's care, I couldn't decide if we had just met the mortal embodiment of a divine principle or a lady Boss Tweed.

57.
Gylandia Explained

COLOR ME BLUE and call me the dumbest Druid. It only took me another week or so of living at Blood of Ten Aurochs to figure out where we were.

The flourishing yet ancient Realm of the Goddess, as described most notably by the famous anthropologist from my homeline, Marija Gimbutas.

In my homeline's Neolithic, a culture unlike any that had survived into my twentieth century had ruled. Not a seamless, absolutist matriarchy, it had still emphasized "feminine" values and customs. A pantheon of Goddesses—or the same one in different guises—had been worshipped in the form of Bull, Bird, Moon, Sun and Serpent, among other masks. Birth had been sacred, death a door to rebirth, no afterlife to lure or frighten. Sophisticated heights had been reached in arts such as pottery, textiles, painting and tomb-building. No evidence of war or fortresses could be found

124

from this apparently peaceful period, which also featured fearless ocean sailors and a level of technology sufficient for metallurgy and monuments like Stonehenge. The relationship between men and women, as best as could be deduced, was one of complete egalitarianism.

To describe such a setup, the feminist Riane Eisler had fused "gyne" and "andros" into "gylany." So I started thinking of this land as "Gylandia."

In my world, Gylandia had come to an end when the Indo-European warriors had stormed out of their Southern Russian steppes on horseback, imposing their own radically different culture.

In this world, no such thing had happened, apparently for one simple reason.

No horses. Simple as that. The elks were local creatures and totally unfitted for combat.

For want of a horse, a monotheistic, patriarchal, belligerent, nature-wrecking culture was lost . . .

Instead, Gylandia had grown and spread, conquering by absorption and devious gentleness instead of bloodshed. After a certain critical mass had been reached, its domination was assured— just the way VHS had won out over Beta.

The Great Mother had maps. Good maps of the whole world. Blood of Ten Aurochs existed where Nice, France, had never stood. Its sister cities (with whom she was in constant, if slow, communication) dotted the New World as well as the Old, Asia and Africa included.

Good riddance to my familiar earth-raping, resource-squandering culture?

I couldn't yet say.

58.
Daughters, Daughters Everywhere,
But Not A Shop With A Shrink

THE PERSONAL GUIDE assigned to me was named Lamb Ram.

He must have been about seventeen. Beardless, pimpled, too tall, gawky, he walked stooped and wore a constant look of guilt and anxiety. An Adam's apple like a pig's knuckle stood out from his elongated neck. He moved like an arthritic sloth, except when frightened by a loud noise or innocent flash of motion. Then he would jump like an epileptic frog. Occasionally he would fall into a daydream that left him wearing a goofy expression like that on the face of a dog getting its stomach scratched.

I knew instantly that he had been assigned to me simply because he was a liability anywhere else. This intuition was confirmed when he told me his recent work history one day as we sat in my rooms.

Reflectively picking his large beaky nose, Lamb Ram recalled, "I used to work in the poppy fields, until I trampled too many plants. There was hardly any space between 'em! Leastwise not enough for me. Then the Daughter Council assigned me to shovel elkshit in the stables. Well, either something fell outa the rafters or maybe I hit myself in the head with the shovel or could be the smell did me in, because they found me unconscious that very first morning. After that, the Potters' Sodality took me on as an apprentice, but I nearly drowned . . . "

I looked at a beautiful red-painted pitcher and basin across the room. "How could you drown making vases?"

"That claybank up near the river is mighty slippery . . . "

That was another great thing about Lamb Ram: he had an excuse for everything.

I hoped that Moonchild was getting along better with *her* guide, a petite woman named Lazy Hand. I didn't know for sure, since I didn't see Moonchild all that often, and when I did—say at communal mealtimes—she tended to snub me. She was still miffed, I guessed, about both my choice of destinations and my lack of interest in our lost son.

Tiny, I had no worries about. He was fitting in just fine. In fact, the big-bellied, grungy Hell's Angel was rolling in pussy. He spent his days eating and fucking and drinking beer like some kind of biker Nero. Apparently, he did not resemble any male the women of this world had ever met, and the whole female half of the city seemed determined to patiently take numbers and wait their turn in the sloppy delicatessen of his love.

I still hadn't given any of my potential lays a tumble, however plainly they had signaled their willingness. Something kept me from getting it up for any of these women. I spent many a sleepless night limply pondering my dilemma, until the answer dawned on me one day as I was emotionlessly watching a cohort of naked teenage girls mudwrestle—the apparent substitute hereabouts for cruising the mall.

I was simply too fucked-up and neurotic to enjoy the unselfconscious, wholesome, all-natural sex offered by these women. The old Woody Allen joke applied: "Is sex dirty? Only if you're doing it right." I couldn't manage to get any of these women to do it right. They were too uncomplicated and straightforward. There were none of the subliminal cues or rituals I needed, and I myself was too inflexible to change.

"Too bad we're not embodied," interjected Calpurnia.

"Yeah," echoed Calypso. "We know just what you like."

"After all, we're already right here in your nasty ol' head."

59.
Gylandia Observed

FOR THE FIRST time in my interplenary travels, no one was chasing me or threatening me or trying to take my Yo-yo away. I wasn't imprisoned or laboring on a CA chain-gang. I was able to sit back and relax and plan my next move. It was obvious I couldn't stay here. This world was too simple and fine and honest for a freak like me. It didn't hold any answers to the Ontological Pickle, or any hedonistic, mindless pleasures to distract me from that quest.

So while I pondered what my next destination would be (and how I was going to break the unpleasant news of our departure from the land of houris to Tiny), I let Lamb Ram take me around to see the sights.

We visited all sorts of craftspeople and artisans: jewelers stringing amber beads, muralists painting walls, weavers (all male) designing blankets and rugs. We attended innumerable ceremonies and functions, including the gruesome "sky burials," where the dead were exposed on open-air platforms so that birds of prey could clean their bones, and the subsequent funeral arrangements where those same bones were powdered with ochre and lovingly arrayed and entombed. We were invited to what I called "period parties," where adolescent girls celebrated their first bleeding. I was reminded of a 'Fifties slumber party. All that was missing from these affairs were a stack of Bobby Darin 45s and fluffy slippers. Some things were universal.

We went along with a hunting expedition composed of twelve efficiently deadly women who would have scared the National Rifle Association. They brought down a woolly rhino with no casualties other than Lamb Ram, who bonked his noggin on a branch and raised a skull egg the size of Rhode Island.

Then we watched some of the same deadly warrior women take their turns staffing one of the communal nurseries, cooing and cootching babies.

We got to see how the Gylandian government worked, sitting in on a lot of boring meetings, dealing with local problems.

"The citizens of West Dogtooth contend that those of North Eagleclaw, who live upstream on the Lesser Python River, were negligent in disposing of their tanning wastes, thus contaminating the Great Mother's waters . . . "

We even got to visit the Great Mother herself again. Not to speak with her personally, but to watch while she dealt with some visitors.

I was startled to see Native Americans in the Great Mother's chambers. It turned out they were a trade delegation from across the Leviathan Sea angling for tobacco price supports. The Great Mother finessed them so neatly that they ended up leaving happily after promising to double production and lower tariffs.

The Great Mother turned up again at a hairdo contest. The Gylandians, men and women both, spent a lot of time fussing with their elaborate hairstyles, and then competitively ranking the results. These were the playoffs, and the Great Mother herself was going to decree the winner.

As I sat in the wildly cheering audience bored out of my skull, the sight of the G-Mom regal and impassive atop her onstage throne suddenly inspired me.

I knew my next wish.

60.
Heavy Is the Head that Wears the Antlers

TINY AND MOONCHILD looked expectantly at me. I was nervous, but I realized there was no point in beating about the bush.

"Uh, guys, I'm thinking of moving on. Breath of fresh air, little change of scenery, like that, you know. And since we're all linked by the mighty Pez-dispenser, I guess you all will be coming along with me . . ."

It never fails to startle me just how fast some big guys can move. And it was indeed a revelation to learn that the vertebrae of the neck can support the entire weight of the body once the feet no longer make contact with the floor.

"I," said Tiny, "ain't goin' no place. This is my idea of stone cold hog heaven. And it's only gonna get better. You guys don't know it yet, but I'm about to be crowned king, or whatever they call the guy who gets to fuck this world's Lady Sunshine."

As through a purple haze, I could see Moonchild beating on Tiny's shoulders. "Tiny, let him go! He's turning blue!"

The feeling of the floor beneath my feet again was so pleasant that I decided to stretch out at full length on it. As I relearned how to breathe, the Calvinii came online in my brain.

"Paul, if your friend doesn't want to come with us, it's no problem."

"Yeah, we found the lookup table for Pez-swallowers inside the Yo-yo."

"We can just delete his entry, and he's on his own."

"Do it," I croaked. Levering myself painfully up off the floor, I said to Tiny, "Okay, I found a way to turn you loose."

"Good. And you'd better not be lyin'. Cuz if I find myself coming along with you wherever you go next, you won't enjoy life

129

there very long. Now, just to show there's no hard feelin's, I'm gonna make sure you have front row seats at my coronation. It's just a few days away. You can wait till then."

I could have Yo-yo'd me and Moon out of there that second without Tiny being able to stop us, but Tiny's ascent to the side of the Great Mother was something I actually wanted to see now, for my own personal satisfaction.

"Sure, we'll stay."

"I'll count on it," said the Angel, then left.

Moonchild came up to me solicitously. "Oh, Paul, are you okay? I'm so glad you finally decided to leave. I just *hate* it here! I can't speak the language well, the women are all sluts and tramps, and the men can't talk about anything but *warps* and *woofs*. I can't *wait* to leave!"

"I take it you're not mad at me anymore?"

"Oh, no!"

"Good. Because I don't want to travel with a grouch."

"I'll be Miss Smileyface from now on, I promise!"

And so we made ready to depart.

When I told Lamb Ram that soon I wouldn't be needing his services anymore, a gloomy expression clouded his winter-pale face.

"That means I'll be getting a new job," he whined. "I can't imagine what, though. I've used up just about everything. The only thing left is the slaughterhouse. And I just *know* I'll end up slitting my own throat. Everybody has it in for me! Oh, how I hate this world!"

I felt bad for the kid, having gotten somewhat fond of his clumsy, egocentric, pain-in-the-butt ways.

So I told him to cheer up, and offered him a Pez.

What the hell. Now that the Cals could delete people from my merry little band, I could always get rid of him later if he proved a bore or burden. Lamb Ram deserved a fresh start at life.

The day of Tiny's coronation dawned, and I realized it must be the winter solstice.

The ceremony in the hillside amphitheater before the entire population of Blood of Ten Aurochs was mighty impressive, what with Tiny clad in a fur robe and not much else, a set of enormous antlers strapped to his head. Its culmination in a public mating between Tiny and the Great Mother was really something, a veritable carnal clash of the Titans.

Moonchild averted her eyes from this spectacle. "Aren't you just a little jealous?" she asked.

"Nope."

"How come?"

"Because," I laughed, "I've read *The Golden Bough* and Tiny hasn't."

Then, while the crowd was still roaring—partially at the thought of the summer solstice and the headsman's axe ready for their one-day king—I cranked up the Yo-yo.

This time, I was going for *power*.

FACES OF
THE SIXTH PAIR

61.
Ambition Unlimited's Motto: No Delusion Too Small

WATCHING THE GREAT Mother at work had turned me on to the attractions of raw power. Her deft manipulation of people and circumstances, her ability to motivate her citizens and get things done, to issue orders and impose penalties, had truly impressed me. She was like some organic force of Nature, unstoppable and immovable. I had realized that it was exactly this quality that was missing from my own miserable life, both back in Bookland and in all the universe-bubbles I had yet visited. With power, I could certainly solve all my problems.

Here was my gameplan: in some new world of massive potential, where I would be automatically endowed with supreme, unlimited, Master-of-the-Universe-level power, I would immediately satisfy all my material and emotional needs, allowing my mind and soul to become clear and tranquil, far-sighted and focused. A little luxury was good for the spirit.

Then, having firmly established myself as pampered totipotent benevolent dictator, I would embark on a quest to break the back of the Ontological Pickle. Using all the vast resources at my command, including the insights of my captive Calvinii, I would crack the mystery of why there was something instead of nothing. Huge laboratories, telescopes, think tanks, universities, monasteries, atom smashers and daycare centers would work around the clock, searching for the ultimate answer. Entire planets would be sacrificed if necessary on the altar of my ambitions.

This stirring vision had grown and blossomed over the last few days, as I awaited Tiny's coronation. I had elaborated on it in my mind, adding level and level of details, until it seemed as real as real. I was certain that the mental conception would flow down the connections between my brain and the Yo-yo intact, and that the transition to the world of my dreams would proceed flawlessly.

So as I opened the eyes that I had closed with keen anticipation in Gylandia, ready to feast them on the vision of a servile horde of supercivilized workers filling the grand plaza of some EC-comics futurescape, all of them ready to fulfill my every smallest wish, I could only pray that I would remain humble and deserving enough to merit their acclaim.

Moonchild and I had stood up in the Gylandian amphitheater before departing (so as not to arrive in the next cosmos in an undignified position), and we were standing now. There was Moonchild at my left elbow and Lamb Ram at my right, looking even more dopey than usual. And there before me spread out my new world.

Under a mild sun in a cloudless sky stretched an illimitable featureless sandy waste, dotted with the recumbent forms of several dozen naked humans, sprawling on their bellies, clutching the sand.

The only part of my wishes that the Yo-yo had gotten right was the servile pose of my worshipers.

62.
Tumbling Dice

I LOOKED AROUND in utter disbelief. Moonchild said, "Paul, where have you taken us . . . ?" Lamb Ram—whom I had warned about the jump maybe thirty seconds in advance—dully scratched his head, setting off a small avalanche of dandruff. Then one of the people lying on the ground happened to look up and spot us.

"You fools!" he shouted. "Get down! But slowly, slowly! Model your motions on the Henon attractor, variation seventy-nine!"

We hesitated just a little too long. And so the windstorm arrived before we could follow the obscure orders.

Out of nowhere, a turbulent gale howling like the audience at a boy-group concert smote us. We were knocked helplessly and instantly to the ground. I took a mouthful of sand. Then the sand took a mouthful of me. I could feel myself picked up along with a blinding cloud of gritty particles and hurled through the air like a paper airplane.

"Moon!" I screamed, but it was useless. I couldn't even hear myself above the winds.

At unpredictable intervals the gale would drop me back to the sand, rolling me along like a tumbleweed for a while before taking me aloft again. I could feel the clothes being ripped, abraded and torn from my body. The Pez-dispenser was one of the first things to go, and I panicked. I knew I couldn't afford to lose the Yo-yo too! I clutched fiercely at the dimension-spanning Duncan, and succeeded in keeping it thanks only to the unnaturally strong grip of my Badfinger hand.

Breathing was nearly impossible, but somehow I managed.

At last the winds abated for good. I had fetched up or been deposited against the side of a large sand dune. Half buried, bruised and bleeding, I cautiously raised my head.

"What a great ride!" one of the Calvinii said, inside my sore noggin.

Other lumps beneath the sands were stirring, heads popping up like those of big human gophers.

One was Moon's. Another was Lamb Ram's.

I gave fervent thanks to someone, though I would have been hard-pressed to say who or why.

The natives were rising up now from the sand.

But they were doing it in a very, very strange way.

Contorting their limbs through various awkward angles and arcs and kinks, they resembled a group of Parkinson's sufferers trying to do tai chi barefoot on sizzling pavement. The facial tics and twitches that were apparently also part of the ritual added a dash of Tourette's Syndrome to the mix.

I started to push myself up, but was stopped by a shout from the fellow who had cautioned us earlier.

"Don't move, strangers! You could start a war with the Smales!"

63.
Lepidopteral Umbrage

SO NEITHER MOON nor Lamb Ram nor I moved. It was probably just as well, I realized, since we were now surely as naked as the natives. Buried like shy nudists, we waited for further instructions.

The apparent leader of this tribe approached me across the sands, doing a kind of queer dance. A burly, partially bald, otherwise hairy guy, skin dark from the sun. He would get a few steps closer, then crabwalk sideways, retreat, circle around, spin, dart, halt, duck, lope and lunge, ending up maybe one step closer than before. Eventually, however, he ended up by my side.

"My name is Charney, stranger. Who are you three, and where are you from?"

His speech was English, but twisted by the odd movements of his lips and tongue he seemed to feel compelled to make. I introduced us and gave the potted speech about another world. Blah blah blah. Charney seemed to take it all in.

"Your world, I assume, does not labor under the Wing of the Butterfly then. I guessed as much, because of the garments you wore and an actual artifact I saw you clutching. But I initially found it hard to give credence to such old legends." Charney sighed deeply. "It seems like forever since our own world fell under the Shadow of the Wing, although the tragedy is only two generations in the past. There are even still a few elders alive who remember the old days."

"This is Earth, right? What the hell happened?"

"You are aware that the Earth and the Sun move through the galaxy, are you not? Well, as best as anybody could determine, the solar system entered a region of space where only one physical parameter was different from in its old neighborhood."

"And what would that be?"

Charney sighed again, a habit that I felt could grow real old real fast. "Sensitive dependence on initial conditions."

Oh, shit. "Not the Butterfly Effect?"

"None other."

64.
Absolute Power Erupts Absurdly

THE BUTTERFLY EFFECT, of course, was one of the biggest buzzwords or hot paradigms to emerge from Chaos Theory. It derived from a famous metaphor concerning weather, which was the most familiar nonlinear, essentially unpredictable system known to the average joe.

Any big, noticeable end result in the weather system—a hurricane, for instance—was obviously not born fullgrown. It origins could be traced back to some tiny disturbance, and its growth and development were subject to a zillion compounding crazy multiplier effects along the way. It had therefore been said that the stirring of a butterfly's wings in one hemisphere could eventually result in a killer storm halfway around the globe.

(Another example of this chaos-breeding "sensitive dependence on initial conditions" was the solar system. If you ran trial plots on a computer of how planetary positions evolved over time, varying the starting points of the planets by tiny amounts, you got wildly divergent results in their orbits after long enough periods.)

In one sense, of course, this mythical butterfly was ultimately powerful. The expenditure of a calorie or two of energy on its part could result in the turbulent massing of tons of atmosphere, megawatts of lightning, the destruction of entire geographical regions.

On this version of Earth, the Butterfly Effect had been increased by some unknown percentage, apparently making every single organism—bird, beast or human—more powerful than a string of hydrogen bombs.

And just as subtle and controlled.

65.
Buddy, Can You Spare a Dynamical System?

"YES," CHARNEY CONTINUED, when he saw that I at least had assimilated the import of his words, "once our world swam into the Shadow of the Wing, civilization as we knew it was at an end.

"The first killer blows came from the unceasing storms, seeded by the most innocent motions of any kind. Across the globe they raged, tearing down the physical infrastructure mankind had so laboriously erected. Billions of humans and trillions of other organisms died, ecosystems collapsed, the legendary entertainment industry was no more. Luckily, the severe mixing of the atmosphere resulted in a kind of averaging out of local temperatures and climates. The balmy air you now feel is more or less standard and unvarying at every latitude, and allows us few survivors to exist comfortably and dignifiedly unclothed."

The rest of Charney's companions had surrounded us as he talked, Groucho-stepping, Chuck-Berry-prancing and Cleese-silly-walking toward where we lay. They boasted—if that's the right word—as mangy, scarred and wiry an assortment of naked bodies as I've ever seen outside of the pages of a Diane Arbus coffee-table book. Some of them had what appeared to be melted patches or even entire melted limbs. If this was comfortable survival with dignity, then give me a quick painful death.

Charney continued. "Humanity's machines, of course, did us no good. Quite the opposite, in fact. They became engines of chaos themselves! Every piston and driveshaft and simple lever bred further atmospheric instabilities. And any device that transmitted vibrations into the earth—dynamos, oil wells, trains, cars—helped engender the years and years of titanic earthquakes that followed the Coming of the Cosmic Swallowtail.

"But worse, far worse, most deadly of all—were the computers!"

I interrupted. "How could computers hurt you? They had the fewest moving parts of anything . . . "

Charney held his head and emitted a dramatic sigh. I understood that he had probably assumed leadership of his comrades by sheer thespian ability. "The computers introduced *quantum* chaos! A hundred times worse than the macroscopic variety! Under the new reign, the unnaturally complex flow of electrons in their contorted circuits destabilized matter in spreading waves! Melting and warping, the very molecular building blocks of our world flowed and recohered into new shapes. Instability reigned for years, until the perturbations damped out and the new system finally settled down to its current attractor.

"We humans who survived—small groups here and there, such as the Smales, the Poinks, the Cantors, the Gleeks, and our own, the Lowrents—have learned how to move through this altered world with minimal interference. But we have not had the privilege of reverting to the primitive lifestyle of our caveman ancestors, to live out the nostalgic post-apocalyptic fantasy of man in harmony with nature. No, we have had to master a whole new mode of being, based on the motions of chaos. Because now everything is truly connected with everything else, we must be exceedingly careful what strings we pull."

As if to illustrate, all the naked humans instantly fell like awkward sacks to the ground, as if something invisible had swooped threateningly overhead.

And for all I knew, something had.

66.
Charney and the Hand Jive

I HAD HEARD enough. This world was sheer insane hell! Power here was both infinite and infinitesimal. No goals could be accurately planned and carried forth; but on the other hand you could probably blow out the Sun with a misplaced fart! I was ready to book out of this madhouse. I doubted Moonchild or Lamb Ram would care to argue about it.

While the natives were hugging the dirt, I jumped to my feet, scattering sand. I'd bring us back to Gylandia, the safest place I'd been yet, and gain time to plan my next destination.

Raising my hand, I made ready to cast the mighty Yo-yo forth.

"Stop!" yelled Charney. "Already your Lyapunov exponents are in the danger zone! You will foment Couette roils and Julia pinwheels among the Smales and they will retaliate!"

Like the idiot I was, I said, "Try to stop me."

So Charney did.

He made motions as if tugging on an invisible rope, and my left arm was jerked down, slamming against my midriff. There it stayed, the Yo-yo clutched uselessly in my Badfinger fist, however much I strained. Charney crooked his back, stuck his tongue out, wiggled his fingers, cocked an elbow, and my feet shot out from under me.

The leader of the Lowrents came to stand over me triumphantly. "Now we shall begin your education in the ways of our world. After a suitable time, when you have mastered the twelve thousand phase-space traversals, attained the greater and lesser attractors and memorized every salient feature of every scale of the entire Mandelbrot Set, you will have your freedom."

"And about how long will that take?"

"After training from infancy, we deem our children mostly competent at age eighteen. But of course, as an adult you may progress faster. Although unlearning your old ways could hinder things."

67.
Markov Chain of Fools

NIGHT HAD FALLEN. The Sun had dropped gradually in its accustomed manner down the sky, until it had reached a certain spot not visibly different from any other. Then it had literally jumped below the horizon.

"What the hell caused that?" I asked from where I sat circumspectly with my back against a dune. I was tired, bruised and sad, and had not been following the ridiculous actions of the Lowrents with any attention. (They had started a fire somehow, out of what I didn't know, and that daring move surprised me a little.) Nor had I felt much like engaging in conversation with my nearby fellow bubble-hoppers, Moonchild and Lamb Ram. But the bizarre

142

behavior of the Sun roused me a little from my apathy.

One of the Lowrents—a young woman with a missing eye and a withered foot—said, "The Earth spins around, you know, and the Sun stands still. So it just looks like the Sun goes up and down."

"Thanks for reminding me. So you're saying the Earth suddenly speeded up its rate of rotation...?"

"Yes. The planet's motion isn't regular anymore. There are discontinuities now, when it jumps without transition from one rate to another."

"Shouldn't the whole world rip itself apart when that happens?"

"Under the old laws of physics, yes. But not now." The woman wiggled closer to me. "You're kind of cute. My name's Pete-Jen, what's yours?"

"Blockhead."

"Well, Blockhead, you have a lot of extra meat on you. If Maytime happens to arrive soon, would you like to mate with me?"

"What month is it now?"

The woman giggled. "Oh, we don't follow the old calendar anymore, since there are no real seasons."

"What's all the talk about Maytime then?"

"Well, that's just what we call the set of local stochastic conditions that allows us to indulge in the gross movements of copulation without undue repercussions. It's a time of high romance."

"I bet. Well, thanks for the offer, Pete-Jen. But I doubt I'll be in the mood."

"You know where to find me if you change your mind," she said. As she turned spastically to leave, I thought she was winking at me with head turned over shoulder. But when the tics continued, I realized she was just practicing the Tenth-Dimensional Pretzel Precepts, or some such shit.

Moonchild spoke up in that annoying whine of hers. "There you go again, Paul, letting your *penis* rule you and mess up your whole *life*."

I was too tired to protest Moonchild's inaccurate interpretation of events. She was probably close to some level of truth anyhow.

Suddenly, it dawned on me. I was living a Markov Chain.

A Markov Chain is the term for any sequence where the next number or action is determined entirely by the present state of the system, without reference to any state in the deeper past. It's a pattern oblivious to its own history, and such strings frequently dead-end in cycles of doomed recurrence.

Was that really my fate? Bound to repeat my most recent mistakes forever?

Just then Charney came up out of the gloom, interrupting my cheerful ruminations. He was holding something that looked like a bundle of charred sticks.

"Here is supper for you and your companions, Blockhead. Please chew with minimal energy release."

I took one. "What is it?"

"Broiled sandworm, a treat. Had we not been able to round up sufficient Maxwell's Demons to generate flames tonight, we would have had to consume them raw."

68.
Higher Papillonics

FOR THE NEXT several weeks we went to school.

At first, we three interlopers merely sat naked on the sand, watching the teachers go through the movements we were expected to memorize. After they had bored the hell out of us sufficiently for a number of days, they allowed us to try out a few of the contorted gestures.

I obeyed diligently enough, I thought, hoping to eventually get my left arm released so I could squirt us down the nearest vermidesic out of here. (The circulation in the invisibly bound limb was unimpaired, but it was still uncomfortable. And I noticed while examining it one day that all the squared-off lyce under my skin had turned to fractal paisleys, conforming to local conditions. When I pointed this out to Moonchild, she said, "Cool! Real Carnaby Street!") But try as I might, I couldn't quite get the hang of the manifolds and saddles and sinks they wanted us to imitate. For one thing, I couldn't get the separate chaos-mudras to flow smoothly into one another. Several of my clunky actions would apparently have caused bigtime damage, except for being hastily damped down by the elders. Usually, I was the first one told to sit down and watch the others.

Moonchild, I could see, was pretending she was in interpretive dance class, and got along pretty well.

"Look, Paul, I'm a tree in the wind . . . "

But the star pupil, much to my surprise, was Lamb Ram.

The skinny, gawky Gylandian, who back home had been in danger of braining himself on every low-hanging branch or beam, appeared to intuitively understand the spasms and broken-backed humpings and constipated straining faces that were required of him here. Soon, he had graduated to the advanced class, leaving the two of us far behind.

One night, over our usual supper of seared desert invertebrate, I asked Lamb Ram how it was possible he was making such progress. (We conversed in English, which he was quickly picking up.)

"Well, I don't really know. It just seems natural to me. All my life at Ten Aurochs I could never quite fit in somehow. I was always whacking my head or almost lopping off a fingertip or ripping out a toenail. And people were always making fun of me for it."

"But don't you miss any of the accoutrements of civilization?"

Listening to myself, I couldn't believe that I was now in a spot where I would refer to a bunch of unheated Neolithic shacks as civilization.

"Not really. Oh, the food could be better here, but I was never much of an eater anyhow. And it's not like I left a lot of friends behind. No, I like it a lot here. People are kind to me and they even praise me. There's nothing sharp to cut myself on, and, well, um—"

"What is it? Let me guess. Some girl is making goo-goo eyes at you. Or is she crippled enough that I should say, 'eye,' singular?"

Lamb Ram got simultaneously embarrassed and enraged. "Don't you go making fun of Pete-Jen, or I'll, I'll—"

"Calm down, kid! I apologize. She's a sweet girl."

"Okay, that's more like it . . . "

"Well, if you could put in a good word with Charney about getting my arm freed, I'd appreciate it."

Lamb Ram stuck his snoot up in the air. "I'll see what I can do . . . "

Before I went to sleep that night I summoned up the Calvinii, who since the wild hurricane ride had grown bored and kept to themselves. They responded alertly without me even framing my request in words.

"Strike Lamb Ram from the Pez lookup table?"

"Consider it done!"

69.
In the Sponge

AFTER A TIME, I was able to move slowly, safely and spastically in accordance with the Lowrent disciplines, satisfying my teachers and gaining a little freedom. Maybe it had something to do with half my bodily cells being replaced by sandworm proteins. (The only other food we enjoyed was a kind of footless bird which could be snared in its perpetual flight with the appropriate remote-control gestures. It tasted like raw frogmeat, even cooked, and made you really appreciate sandworm.) So I approached Charney and asked if I could get my arm released.

"It's hindering me. I can't properly perform the essential navigation of the Holy Bagel."

Charney frowned. "You are referring to the refinements of the Quasiperiodic Torus, I take it?"

"Yeah, that's it."

Narrowing his eyes, Charney said, "That artifact concealed within your left fist leaks wavefronts of chaos even immobilized . . . "

I felt like yelling, *Well, of course it does, you moron! It's a leftover bit of the primordial chaotic egg, and it's got either two or two billion lascivious Calvinii inside it!* But I bit my tongue and just said, "Yes, but it's shielded real good with genuine strange-matter flicker-cladding. Can't buy any better in all the multiverse."

Charney seemed to consider before replying, but I knew that his mind was already set in stone. For a guy who lived with everyday chaos, he was mighty inflexible.

"I believe that it is safer for all of us to keep that object stabilized for a while longer, until you have acquired true Lowrent discipline and loyalty. You will simply have to learn how to compensate for your physical disability, as others have. Perhaps you will even invent a new compensatory vector and thus contribute to the lore of the tribe."

Charney Jerry-Lewised off then, before I could formulate a convincing lie that would reassure him his suspicions were misplaced. But in fact the first thing I would do if he set my arm loose wouldn't be to use the Yo-yo.

It would be to *strangle him*!

I went to plead with Lamb Ram again for help. I found him with Pete-Jen. The half-blind girl had Lamb Ram's head cradled in her lap, and was stroking it as tenderly as circumstances would allow. She was crooning sweet nothings to him, which became intelligible as I got closer.

"—just as powerful as him. Only a little more practice, that's all it will take. Your outsider style will completely outflank and overcome his stodgy ways! Then you can lead us to glory and—"

She stopped speaking when I arrived. Lamb Ram opened his eyes and said, "Yes, Paul, what is it?"

"I hate to intrude on your little love-feast, but I need a favor from you. Can you either talk Charney into setting my arm free, or do it yourself? I just want to get out of here with Moonchild. You won't be coming. I've already deleted you from the crew, just like I did with Tiny. So, what about it? You owe me, you know, for bringing you here in the first place."

Lamb Ram tried to adopt a look of cunning scrutiny. On him it resembled the signs of a peptic ulcer kicking up. "I'll take it under consideration. Things are going to change mighty fast mighty soon around here. Then we'll see."

This refusal was frustrating, but what could I do? As I made to move off, Pete-Jen stuck her tongue out at me.

You couldn't even tell an insult from an itch in this crazy place!

That same afternoon (I guessed it was the same afternoon, though the Sun had gone down and come up twice in the space of a few minutes) I was trying to take a nap when I was startled awake by shouting.

"Sponge! Sponge conditions along the north catastrophe!"

I stood up. "Sponge? What's sponge?"

Then I found out.

Beneath my feet a perfectly square hole opened, and down I fell.

I landed on a thin ledge or girder-shaped platform. Standing, I looked curiously around.

I seemed to be immured inside an orderly, three-dimensional matrix or labyrinth or building whose walls and floors and ceilings were perforated with an infinity of rectangular holes of different sizes. Lit by a sourceless light, the regular landscape made me imagine I was standing inside a giant multi-paneled cheese-grater. To look too long in any direction hurt my eyes.

After a minute, I knew where I was.

Inside a Menger Sponge.

A Menger Sponge began as a solid and was deconstructed by removing regular portions of it in accordance with a formula that gave it a fractal dimension. The end result was a paradoxical object with practically zero volume, yet infinite surface area.

Obviously, Menger Sponges occurred spontaneously here.

I wasn't worried at first. I hadn't fallen far, and the ceiling was within easy reach. I'd just climb up and out.

So I started. Jump and hoist my starvation-attenuated body through a hole with a mighty one-handed effort, stand, repeat.

It was the thirst that first alerted me to how long I'd been going. My tongue felt like a Brillo pad. All I could picture was the cool flowing springs that the Lowrents could conjure up out of the desert.

Things got hazy then. Somehow I kept going, although I lost all sense of up and down, and thought I might have been moving sideways through the Sponge. At one point, I believed I had a companion named Jeremy the Boob, who kept popping in and out of the Sea of Holes. We talked about music for a long, long time before he vanished.

Lying still and moving were not different. This thought kept repeating itself in my brain, and I realized it was because I was flat on my back.

As I lay there, I began to shake.

No, the Sponge was quivering!

I felt an elevator-like motion, as if I were rushing upward, through the infinite layers.

Sunlight burst over me, and I passed out.

70.
Shootout at the Chaos Corral

NURSED BY MOONCHILD, I recovered intact from my time within the Sinister Sponge. (It had been about two days, as best as time could be measured here, and all the Lowrents assured me I was lucky to have escaped at all.) The only lasting effect was that I had been reversed left to right.

Yes, my heart now beat on a different side of my chest, and my right hand was the Badfinger one. Apparently, I had managed to inadvertently rotate myself through a higher dimension while within the Sponge, analogously to the way we turn a glove inside-out without destroying it.

Unfortunately, while I was unconscious, Charney had taken the precaution of binding my right, Badfinger arm as securely as the other had once been pinioned, which he now freed.

Oh, well. At least it made for a change.

My pitiful post-Sponge condition seemed to inspire a new sympathy within Moonchild. She fussed over me and reassured me that we would somehow get out of this mess okay.

"Don't worry, Paul. Remember, tomorrow is the first day of the rest of your life!"

"Except that one of those tomorrows has to be your last."

"Oh, go ahead, bum yourself out, man!"

I grabbed her hand. "I'm sorry, Moon. I'll try to be more

cheerful from now on. Do you want me to sing 'What a Beautiful Morning' for you?"

"You're impossible!"

"True, especially if you take into account where my heart is . . . "

Once I was up and around, I could sense a new tension among the Lowrents.

Factions had developed, centered around Lamb Ram or Charney. There were subtle and not-so-subtle everyday rebellions when it came to following Charney's orders. I knew that, egged on by Pete-Jen, Lamb Ram would soon have to force a contest of strength or back down.

It finally came one afternoon.

Charney had informed the Lowrents the previous night that we would be migrating to new pastures where conditions were supposedly more propitious. This, we all knew, was a facade which concealed his nervous desire to placate the neighboring Smales. This larger, more powerful tribe was apparently intent on expanding into our old domain. God knew why. Maybe they coveted our extra-tasty sandworms. In any case, Charney was in favor of abandoning our old range.

About half the Lowrents now were gathered around Charney. The remainder clustered around Lamb Ram and Pete-Jen.

"Assume the Fourth Chaitin Stance!" Charney bellowed with false assurance of command. "We are about to depart!"

Pete-Jen jabbed an elbow in Lamb Ram's ribs. "Uh, we're not going with you!" the Kaos Kid said. "We're staying here!"

Like a crippled old bull Charney emerged from among his supporters until he stood alone on the sands, hands slung at his hips in the classic gunfighter pose.

"I'm calling you out, stranger!"

Shoved by Pete-Jen, Lamb Ram stumbled out from among his people.

"Well, uh, let's see what you've got, old man!"

Then the duel started.

Watching the contest was just like reading the climactic Duel of the Mages in one of those Tolkien ripoffs.

Back and forth between the contestants crackled bolts, blasts and counterattacks of pure Butterfly chaos. The air shivered and burnt, steamed and hissed; the ground trembled and split. Blinding light and waves of darkness alternated. Bystanders were knocked to their asses. But as far as I could see, neither fighter had yet taken any major damage.

Finally, Lamb Ram went through the most convoluted contortions I had yet witnessed. Charney suddenly stiffened, plainly in the grip of some invisible yet potent force.

He began to elongate vertically without rupturing, like Silly Putty.

A woman screamed. "It's the Taffy Mapping!"

And sure enough, I could soon see what she meant.

Charney was stretched like malleable elastic, folded back on himself, then stretched and folded again, his features smearing. This process continued about a couple of dozen times.

Lamb Ram stood watching, stupefied by what he had wrought.

At last Charney was reduced to a featureless streaky pink blob.

Recovering himself with a smug air, Lamb Ram made motions with his hands like shaping a snowball. The Charney blob shrunk and shrunk, compressing until it disappeared.

Pete-Jen threw herself at Lamb Ram. "My hero!"

Lamb Ram instinctively raised his clenched hands overhead in a victor's gesture.

The innocent motion brought a small meteor whooshing down, which luckily missed us all by a sandworm's whisker.

71.
A Sensible Independence from Inertial Contrition

THE DEFEAT, DEATH and disappearance of Charney kinda lifted my spirits. I knew it was cruel and unkind, but I couldn't work up too much sorrow over the messy fate of that pompous pain in the butt.

I figured Lamb Ram would be fairly easy to cajole. As soon as I got him to release my Yo-yo hand, Moonchild and I would be out of here. Though I still couldn't quite decide where to.

And sure enough, within a few days, thanks to a little flattery and obeisance, I had a promise from the new leader of the Lowrents. He was going to grant me the use of both limbs.

As soon as we had defeated the Smales.

72.
War with the Smales

"BUT WHERE ARE you and I going next?" Moonchild demanded for the umpteenth time.

"I don't have any idea," I said.

Actually, this was untrue. My head was swarming with ideas for types of places I'd like to visit, now that I had gotten back a little of my enthusiasm for the greener pastures opened up by the Cosmic Yo-yo. But I couldn't settle on any particular one as our destination.

"Let's just say I'm of several minds on this."

"Well, you'd better decide soon."

"I suppose. Though it might be a moot point if we don't survive this stupid war."

"War is harmful to children and other living things," said Moonchild wistfully.

Moon's continual use of idiotic 'Sixties clichés irritated me, and I almost said, *We can swap bumperstickers till the Sun comes up in the West, but we won't be any closer to a solution.* But I bit my tongue for two reasons: I didn't want to start a fight with her, and the Sun *had* come up in the West yesterday.

All around us, the Lowrents were getting ready for battle. Practicing their chaos chops, they honed themselves for face-to-face combat with the Smales. Over the troops presided the insufferably smug King Lamb Ram and his crippled consort.

Unfortunately, as it turned out, the Smales had other ideas than just sitting and waiting for us to attack.

The first sign of trouble was the approaching clouds. They hid the sunlight and cast a palpable pall over the tribe that brought all motion to a halt.

Then it began to snow.

"Koch Flakes!" yelled one of the Lowrents.

"Up with the Trig Trees!" commanded Lamb Ram.

Objects began to grow from hidden seeds in the sandy soil: crystalline stalks which rose for about ten feet before branching once. After a shorter distance, each branch split again. Shortly thereafter, all the branches split infinitely, forming protective canopies. I was reminded of Hans the Cybershrub's cloud of manipulators.

The Trig Trees effectively blocked the Koch Flakes. But not before one had hit my skin, burning painfully and leaving a little cauterized pit.

"That shows them—" began Lamb Ram.

The appearance of a herd of enormous animals stopped the words in his throat.

Big as a house, each animal resembled a dragon whose bodily outline was plainly fractal in dimension. I flashed back to the Lyints of the CA-world.

As we watched in terror, one of the Fractal Dragons opened its mouth and belched forth a fractal flame. The blast incinerated three or six Lowrents.

Now came *real* chaos. People began screaming and running in all directions. Lamb Ram was shouting for them to stand and fight, to no avail. Moon was hanging on my left arm and sobbing.

I have to hand it to Lamb Ram. He never backed down. Casting spells left and right with crazy abandon, he managed to knock the block right off one of the attackers. A gout of fractal blood spurted forth.

Then one of his commands boomeranged or ricocheted or something, and the next thing I knew I was flat on my back.

But my Badfinger arm was free!

With no idea of where I wanted to go, I knew we had to leave. Now! So I hurled the Yo-yo straight up—

A SUPERSPACE INTERLUDE BETWEEN THROWS

Desperate to escape the deadly war between the Lowrents and the Smales, I had unleashed the power of the Yo-yo with no firm idea of where I wanted to go. The Yo-yo was operating without a clear command from me.

So where had I ended up?

Looking around, it was all too depressingly obvious.

Back in Bookland, my old store.

Was this a default deadend universe, programmed into the mechanism of the Yo-yo? Or did this stinking old store where I had wasted so many bitter hours represent my true desired and destined destination, in some ultimate karmic sense?

Who the fuck knew? Not me.

"Wow!" said Moonchild. "Cool! I've never seen so many books before. Lady Sunshine had most of the ones in my world burnt. Now if I only knew how to read . . . "

This was a revelation to me. "You can't read?"

Moon seemed chagrined. "Well, I can print my name, if you spot me the 'Em.' I keep mixing the first letter up with 'Double-you.'"

The store was just as empty of employees or customers as when I had left it, so many adventures ago, and I wondered what time or year it could possibly be here. Let me see: I had created a universe, journeyed back to the 'Sixties (which were really the 'Noughts), spent a few million clock-cycles inside a virtual world, visited the Neolithic, and been in a world where the Sun rode a merry-go-round.

I figured it had to be at least time for a coffee-break.

"Actually," said a voice, "in your baseline universe of origin, approximately one million years have passed, during which time the Earth was hit by a flock of comets deliberately dislodged from the Oort Cloud by alien rivals, subsequently losing its orbit and falling into the Sun."

I turned cautiously around.

Standing by the rack of audio books where I had last seen Hans the Moraveckian was a cute, cuddly koala bear as big as a grizzly.

All the blood drained from my face into my ankles. Moon shrieked and clutched my bicep as if it were the last dope in a roomful of potheads.

"Is my appearance not reassuring and calm-inducing? I understood that these animals were regarded fondly in your culture . . . "

"Yuh-yes, when they're an eensy bit smaller . . . "

The koala instantly shrunk down to Hop-o'-My-Thumb size. "Like this?"

I was starting to feel a little more at ease, since the koala seemed unthreatening. "Try knee-high and about thirty pounds."

At once he changed to my specs. "How is that?"

"Fine, great. Now, can you tell us where we are? And who you might be?"

"Of course. You are in superspace, entirely outside the homoclinic tangle. And I am one of the Drexleroids."

I recalled Hans's Blah-Blah-Blah about the factions among the Mind Children. The Drexleroids were those who had vanished down the unimaginably small Planck level.

"You mean I'm not in a new universe that has a copy of Bookland in it?"

"By no means. We intercepted the two of you as you were travelling down one of the vermidesics connecting the infinity of universe lines. We removed you from the entire network and brought you to superspace, our domain. You are outside the entire multiverse. In short, you have jootsed."

"'Jootsed?'"

"A handy acronymic verb formed from the phrase 'jump out of the system.' It is what we did long ago."

The Drexleroid went on to tell us how, when he and his kind had finally learned the technique of escaping not only the universe of their origin but every other existing universe as well, they had found themselves in a featureless miasma of potential somethingness which proved to be infinitely malleable and plastic, subject to effortless manipulation by the sheer process of conscious thought, properly channeled. This representation of Bookland and even the koala form worn by the Drexleroid were nothing more than tangible dreams in the mind(s) of one or more Drexleroid(s).

"In fact," continued the loquacious teddy bear, "we believe that the entire homoclinic tangle in all its incredible unending immensity was formed by the same process."

"You mean that something like God, First Resident in the Urschleim, thought the multiverse into being?"

"Precisely. According to one theory of ours, it would have been sufficient for Him to create just a single universe, which would have cloned itself infinitely over an infinite timespan, by Colemanic vermistic births."

"And where is this aboriginal joker now?"

The bear looked sheepish. "We don't know. That's our prime mission in life. To find Him. We suspect He's either dispersed himself so as to become identical with the fabric of superspace, or has perhaps left entirely."

"Left? For where? What's beyond superspace? Aren't you just following an infinite regress, with no ultimate answer?"

"Maybe. But what choice do we have?"

I decided to query my cosmological experts. "Cals One and Two! How does this sound to you?"

"It would explain a lot," Calpurnia said.

"You remember," added Calypso, "how our discussion got caught in an infinite regress, back when you asked us where the first Monobloc and the first Calvinii came from . . . "

Had I found my answer to the Ontological Pickle? It sounded appealing, but I couldn't be sure. I tabled the matter for a moment.

"Why did you snatch us?"

The koala seemed relieved at the switch in topics. "Like our brethren, the Moraveckians, we are intrigued by humans. We have kept contact with them for ages—at least with those who open themselves to us. Usually, such contact involves the ingestion of hallucinogens on the part of humans. One of your prophets, Terence McKenna, calls us 'self-transforming hyperspace machine elves,' and this is as good a description as any."

"Okay, okay, you never met an anthropoid you didn't like. But why pick on me?"

"We are intrigued by the ability of humans to fuck up. It is a trait not found in any other sapient species. Ideally, it should have been selected out long ago by Darwinian evolution. Take your case, for example. Given nearly unlimited ability to choose, you have made some excruciatingly limited and dumb selections from the universal menu. You have shown an incredible blindness in your travels. Why, you haven't even wanted to visit any alien worlds or cultures. Nebulas so gorgeous they would stop your breath await your inspection. Races of intelligent plants and sentients big as mountains are calling you. Self-aware cities beg you to visit on the getaway weekend of a lifetime, free car rental included. You could swim in an ocean consisting of Lime Jello, where the fish resemble pineapple chunks."

"Gee, Paul," said Moonchild, "I didn't know you could take us to all those groovy places . . . "

"Yes, it's true. He could. But what does he do instead? He centers his desires around a miserable backwater world and a few predictable variations thereof. His stupidity and blindness are as big an enigma as the disappearance of God."

The koala's accusations had made me simultaneously depressed and pissed-off. Maybe what he said was true. Maybe I was wasting Hans's gift. Maybe I was blind, dumb, self-centered and ignorant. But the choices were mine to make, no one else's. I would have to play my hand and see where it got me. Roll the dice and hope not to crap out. I couldn't do anything else, because I was who I was.

And so were we all, I realized.

"You may be right," I said to the Drexleroid. "But there's only one thing I can say."

"Yes?"

"Eat my shorts!"

The koala sighed. "Predictable, entirely predictable. Fascinating, yet illogical. You are not even wearing any undergarments."

This was true. Moon and I were as naked as we had been back in the Butterfly World.

"If this is your final response to our helpful advice," continued the koala, "then we will simply grant everyone a wish or two and send you all on your way."

"Okay," I said. "I'd like some clothes for me and Moon—and complete physical health. That includes getting rid of these stupid body-lyce. Then, I want my lost Pez-dispenser back."

"Done," said teddy, and all my wishes were met.

"Us next! Us next!" yelled the Calvinii. Much to my surprise, the koala appeared to hear them inside my head.

"What do you two Monobloc creatures wish?"

"We want bodies!"

"Yes, and not just any! We have chosen a template out of Paul's memories."

The koala nodded. "I see it. Get ready—"

Two identical naked human women stood beside me.

The Barbi Twins. Long-legged, melon-jugged, blonde centerfold bimbo sisters. My wettest wet dream.

I felt flattered. "Gosh, girls, you didn't have to do this for me—"

"We didn't!"

"It's strictly for us!"

The bawdily incarnated Calvinii began groping and smooching each other in mirror-image reciprocal randiness. Before you could say "Triple Ex," they were rolling around on the dirty simulated Bookland carpet, oblivious to all of us.

Sighing, I forced myself to look away. Another fantasy that didn't include me . . .

Now it was Moonchild's turn to wish.

"I want—I want our son back!"

"Moon, no!"

But it was too late.

Cradled in Moonchild's expectant arms was the infant we had conceived together in CA-land. It was even thoughtfully be-diapered. Seemingly a normal human baby now, it betrayed its foreign origins only by its eyes, in which flickered checkerboard pupils.

"Oh, Moon, why did you have to go and do that—?"

The koala interrupted. "Are you ready to leave now?"

"I guess. What about those two?"

I indicated the busy licking and fingering Calvinii at my feet.

"I believe they will be at home here, as superspace resembles the conditions in their native Monobloc. If they wish to rejoin you later, we will send them along."

"Okay. Let's get out of here."

"We are constrained by non-contravenable conservation principles to send you down the exact vermidesic we took you from."

"The path I got onto without firmly making up my mind?"

"Precisely."

"Thanks. Thanks a lot."

"No thanks are necessary. We machine elves are magnanimous to a flaw."

FACES OF
THE SEVENTH PAIR

73.
Reprise, With Dismal Variations

MY LIFE WAS absolutely fucked.

I sat on what felt like regular old grass, my head in my hands, eyes sealed shut as if Despair had dripped melted wax on them and pressed Its unmistakable seal down, twice. I couldn't even be bothered to look around at this new destination. As long as I seemed to be inhabiting my familiar body and wasn't being immediately threatened with death, destruction or carnal violation, I didn't really care where I was.

I assumed Moonchild was okay, as I heard her at my elbow, cooing gibberish to our son.

But all I could really concentrate on was my own personal condition.

As the Drexleroid representative had so mercilessly informed me, I was a complete dipshit who had wasted all my valuable opportunities to date. (And hearing that the Earth of my home timeline had been destroyed eons ago didn't improve my cheerfulness.) I didn't deserve the gift of the Yo-yo. The best thing for me to do was probably to discard the miraculous device right here and now and just live out the rest of my days in whatever boring, miserable continuum the mentally unguided transporter had brought me to.

Gone was all my ambition to crack the Ontological Pickle. Vanished were my desires for fame, sex, love and money. Nothing appealed to me. I just wanted to push the whole lousy world away.

I was in a bad, bad way.

I had never felt quite this down before. Even in the depths of my moroseness back in Bookland, some spark of motivation had remained—if only enough to allow me to feed my face. But now, all alternatives looked equally awful and meaningless. My brain seemed mired in the sludge of total disdain.

My brain . . . Dimly, a notion forced its way to the top of my turgid consciousness.

Of course!

I was in my old body—but my *brain* was different!

The physical parameters of this new world were affecting my mentality!

What should I do to escape? Thinking seemed so hard, except for the process of rejecting . . . That action came easy as breathing. What was the answer? Think, Paul, think!

Like a salted snail the concept crept, wounded and frail, into my mind. All I needed to do to feel better was to use the Yo-yo to travel elsewhere!

But even this realization failed to help. Almost instantly, I rejected the notion of using the Yo-yo. But why?

Again, I tried to imagine using the device to leave. Again came quick and uncompromising rejection. A third cycle of weak proposal and firm rejection. But this time, I tried to pay attention to what was happening inside my head. (I missed the Calvinii and their easy ability to rewire my neurons. But those two fickle primordial oversexed entities had indeed been left behind in superspace, where they were doubtless warping the plastic matter into some kinky shapes . . .)

Upon analysis, the instinct to reject seemed almost like an automatic reflex. It was as if my brain were canalized into that one groove.

Was this the result of years of sullen bitterness and cynicism back home having calcified my brain? Had I arrived in a world where one's dominant quality of mind was rendered supreme?

Maybe questioning Moonchild would verify my speculation.

I opened my eyes.

166

74.
Our Boy, Whatsisname

THE SKY WAS blue, the sun was yellow-white and stable, the grass was green and dotted with dandelions. Moonchild and I were sitting in a field on the edge of an innocuous two-lane paved road without any traffic currently on it. The road wound off through a lush countryside. Away in the distance, above the treetops, I thought I could just make out the spires of a city.

Cradling the gurgling diapered baby with the strange eyes, Moonchild seemed happy and oblivious to any troubling mental differences in this world, the perfect virgin mother.

"Moon," I said, "do you feel bummed?"

"No, how could I? I've got my son back and this looks like a beautiful world. Maybe we could go for a walk. Or fly a kite. Or pick flowers. Or find a pond and swim. Or lay back and watch the clouds. Or watch the bees. Or catch grasshoppers. Or—"

Hot waves of denial washed through me. "No! I don't want to do any of those things! Just shut up, okay!"

Moonchild fell quiet. But she didn't appear crestfallen. Was this a sign that her natural stoned optimism now reigned triumphant, over all her other various fears and quirks and neuroses? Or was there some other explanation that would cover both her behavior and mine?

While I pondered dully, Moonchild had settled on a new topic. "Our son needs a name! What do you think of Chickie?"

I didn't really care one way or another what we named the brat, but I found myself instantly snapping, "No!"

"Yerkle?"

"No!"

"Cranberry?"

"No!"

"Herkenheimer?"

"No!"

"Pogo?"

"No!"

"Shortcake?"

"No!"

"Adonis?"

"No!"

"Prince?"

"No!"

I wanted to stop this inane dialogue, but I couldn't. Moonchild seemed to have an inexhaustible fund of names, and I was bound to respond in the negative to each suggestion—just as she seemed locked-in by my denial to propose a new one. I realized that we were trapped in some kind of deadly, compulsive, inescapable feedback loop of proposal and rejection.

"Stinky?"

"No!"

"Trotter?"

"No!"

"Beanbag?"

"No!"

"Weenie?"

"No! No! No!"

75.
We Meet the Dodecans

I'M SURE WE would have died of thirst and starvation while still rattling off names and nays in gradually fading parched voices, had not something intervened.

Our rescue was effected by the arrival of a car—a hot-pink car—along that winding country road. It was a strange car, more like a low-slung minivan capable of carrying some number of people. I spotted it out of the corner of one eye as I continued helplessly to argue with Moonchild.

"Tinker?"

"No!"

"Creampuff?"

"No!"

"Abernathy?"

"Never!"

The vehicle stopped. Pleated doors on the side facing us ratcheted up like rolltop desk covers, disappearing into the hollow roof of the lipstick-colored car. People—normal looking men and women dressed in colorful shirts and trousers—piled out. Finally there were twelve of them standing there.

"Eagle?"

"No!"

"Montevius?"

"No!"

"Standish?"

"No!"

The newcomers began conferring among themselves. The corner of my attention not engaged with Moonchild followed their English speech.

"How odd! A Proposer and a Rejecter out here in the middle of nowhere, without the rest of their sodality."

"When was the last time something like *that* happened?"

"Five hundred years ago," one replied instantly. "During the social chaos following the Black Famine."

"Do you think they've been going at it for very long?"

"Judging by their relatively high energy, I'd say no."

"Well, I suppose we should put a stop to it. Then we'll bring them back to the city and turn them over to the Matchmakers."

"Good idea. Dennis, would you mind terribly...?"

The man who must have been Dennis, a placid yet determined looking type sporting a mustache, walked calmly over to us.

"Stop," he said.

And just like that, we did.

76.
What's Your Mindsign, Baby?

THE INTERIOR OF the big car consisted of three long undivided seats easily capable of holding four across. A little squeezing allowed

169

Moonchild, the baby and me to fit too. The doors rattled down and the car accelerated noiselessly away.

"Do you think it's any good interrogating them without their Retriever here?" asked one of the twelve.

"Good question," observed another. "There's so little data on the subject of individual memory caches among a lone twelfie . . . "

"Exactly twenty-one years ago, there was a study done on brain-damaged accident victims who had lost the ability to mosh. They proved surprisingly adept at simple recall of events no older than a week."

"Well, that would certainly be a long enough span to allow them to tell us how they got separated."

I had had enough. "Hey, you jerks! We're not brain-damaged feebs! Talk directly to us, if you wanna ask us something!"

Knowing glances were exchanged among our twelve rescuers. I got the distinct impression that subliminal information was also being circulated somehow. But if it really was, I couldn't tap into it.

Finally, one of them spoke, addressing me as if I were an irritable little kid. "Ahem, yes, we must excuse any ill manners among a poor lost twelfie. Now then, let me introduce myself. My name is Frank, and I'm the Starter for the Pink Crayfish sodality. I think you already know Dennis, our Stopper."

"Done," said Dennis.

Frank then named the others.

"Helen, our Stower."

"Got you."

"Ben, our Retriever."

"I remember when we met."

"Norman, our Observer." (This was the driver.)

"Nice clothes, guys. Strange, but nice."

"Fred, our Speculator."

"I bet you're confused."

"Mary, our Prioritizer."

"Introductions come first!"

"Stan, our Proposer."

"Can I offer you a drink?"

"Harry, our Acceptor."

"I'll have one, please."

"Ethel, our Rejecter."

"Not me!"

"Wallace, our Lumper."

"You two are obviously a pair."

"And Sandra, our Splitter."

"She loves the baby though, and he doesn't."

77.
Parliament of Clowns

THE CAR HAD reached the outskirts of the city before I had the simplest notion of how things worked here among this strange variety of humans.

(Luckily I didn't have to repeat everything the Dodecans said for the sake of Moonchild, since they spoke plain English and Moonchild could follow along and draw her own conclusions. Later, I would wonder how a world so bizarre, where the fundamental constraints on life were so different from my baseline world's, could have also evolved the English language, not to mention Anglo-Saxon names like Harold and Benjamin. Eventually, though, the answer dawned on me: in a literal infinity of universes, no single event or unique chain of events, however implausible and unlikely, would be found to be missing. If it took a trillion, trillion illogical contortions and "accidents" over a zillion, zillion years to produce a specified "impossible" end result, you could still count on finding that world with its crazy history out there somewhere. Of course, this made hash out of all comfortable human prejudices about destiny, fate and the inevitability of progress. Any given world, however cherished and seemingly natural it appeared to its inhabitants, was equal in unlikeliness to any other world.

(The multiverse was the ultimate clowns' democracy, wherein every timeline was equally privileged, equally idiotic. Your universe and mine and all the others were each outfitted with bulbous red noses and big floppy shoes. I was sure this fact would give the screaming willies to supremacists and chauvinists of every stripe, but I kind of liked the idea. It made my old life look not so uniquely horrible . . .)

My conversation with the Dodecans began with me trying to explain where Moonchild and I had come from. Despite the advantage of English, I found talking to be difficult; facts and words seemed hard to conjure up. My brain was operating at molasses speed in every mode except that of naysaying. But after an hour or so, I think I finally managed to convince the twelve natives of our actual origin on a different spaghetti strand.

Much harder to get across was the nature of our individual existence. They just couldn't seem to grasp the idea that one person—or "twelfie"—could contain all the faculties needed for survival and prosperity. They kept asking where the other ten members of our group were, why they hadn't made the transition with us. Only Fred, the guy named as Speculator, seemed able to wrap his mind around the concept.

"So you're claiming that a single human being can embody in him- or herself all the mental specialties that are the separate provinces of each sodality member...?

"Ridiculous!" shouted Ethel, the Rejecter.

As she denounced the idea, I was swept by a similar urge. Even though I *knew* what I was saying was true, I experienced the nearly overwhelming compulsion to knock it! I had to bite my tongue to suppress chiming in.

Harry, the Acceptor, spoke up. "I'm starting to incline toward agreeing with Paul's explanation."

As he said this, an almost visible shifting seemed to travel like a wave among the members of the Pink Crayfish, as if unseen psychic weights were redistributing themselves.

"It's not possible!" Ethel the Rejecter said. But I could sense the lessened conviction in her voice.

"Well," I said, hoping to avoid the kind of endless argument between Harry and Ethel that Moon and I had gotten into, "exactly how do you guys function?"

172

78.
What Has Twenty-four Feet, One Brain,
and Very Good Manners?

THIS IS WHAT I learned.

Like us, the Dodecans had evolved from primates. But their ancestors had been markedly different from ours in several respects. Most crucially, the primitive Dodecan monkey-people had carried intraspecies specialization to the extreme point where it actually became embedded in their genes. The functional tribal divisions such as hunter, nurturer, gatherer, master of rituals, scout, Blah-Blah-Blah, had eventually been encoded into their genes, leading to a species whose differentiated members were all still capable of mating across specialty lines. (The dominant and recessive gene mixing that occurred when different types mated resulted in either a true type resembling either the mother or father, or a non-functional sport that was usually deliberately destroyed or environmentally winnowed when it could not perform as a member of a sodality.)

As these early primates came to rely more and more on their bigger-than-the-competition's brains, the nature of the tribal subdivisions began to change. The shift was from physical qualities to mental ones. As raw physical talents became less important (with living made easier by a secure proto-civilization), uniformity on the level of bodily skills emerged. However, members of the tribe began to be born with certain kinds of intellectual ability predominant. Parallel to this, a kind of empathy or wordless coordinating telepathy began to be Darwinically encouraged, to foster faster and more foolproof communication and decision-making among mutually reliant individuals.

A byproduct of this line of development was that the Dodecans were much less aggressive and violent than my kind of humans. Cooperation was favored over competition. Also, when any individual loomed potentially as a replacement part for your "family," should you need one, you were less likely to annoy or damage him.

After millions of years of evolution and millennia of sometimes turbulent history, the current state of affairs was firmly in place.

Twelve mental types with markedly unique personalities and aptitudes were needed to "mosh" into a single functional unit known as a sodality. Lone individuals were cripples and mentally unstable.

That made me feel right at home.

79.
The Proposer's Proposition

THE FIRST THING I noticed when we entered among the buildings of the city was the size of the doors on every structure. They were enormous, wide as truck-garage bays. At least six people abreast could easily pass through them.

"How far apart can members of a sodality get and still function?" I asked.

"A hundred yards is the maximum effective range for moshing," immediately responded Retriever Ben. "But discomfort starts to set in at about a quarter of that, and increases exponentially with distance."

Prioritizer Mary said, "Staying close together is the most important thing for a sodality. That's when the mosh-unit functions best."

Spending all your life in the pockets of eleven other people seemed inconceivable to me. "Don't you ever get a break from each other? Don't you want some solitude once in a while?"

A solemn hush descended on the Pink Crayfishers. Finally, Observer Norman broke the glacial silence.

"Only suicidal twelfies ever feel that urge. It is inconceivable to a normally functioning individual. Are *you* feeling that way now? Rejecters are particularly prone to such psychoses. Perhaps we should bring you to a Regrooving Facility first, instead of the Matchmakers...?"

I didn't know what "regrooving" entailed, but I didn't like the sound of it one bit. "Uh, no, thank you. I feel fine. Life is good."

Lumper Wallace said, "Associating with us is stabilizing your psyches, at the same time that it's slightly unbalancing our sodality.

With an extra Proposer and Rejecter on the fringes of our mosh, our decision weightings are starting to go askew."

Splitter Sandra said, "That's why we've got to drop you off at the Matchmakers. You need to get into a full mosh configuration fast. After that, we'd be happy to extend the hospitality of the Pink Crayfish sodality to you and your fellow moshers."

"Yes," said Proposer Stan, "the Pink Crayfish would enjoy fucking your sodality whenever it's convenient. No one's ever done it with aliens before, and we'd feel honored."

I tried to wrap my mind around the nebulous concept of how a superorganism composed of twelve individuals might arrange their fucking—and failed. The closest I could get was some kind of monster orgy. Luckily, Moonchild stepped courteously into the breach.

"Thank you, but I'm still a virgin."

Everyone looked at Moon and her baby for about thirty seconds. Then Rejecter Ethel exclaimed, "I don't buy it!"

80.
Pampers Smell in a Padded Cell

THE MEMBERS OF the Pink Crayfish sodality dropped us off at the door of the Matchmakers Bureau, waved a disgustingly cheerful goodbye (having already entrusted us with their business card and its pencilled-in home phone) and drove off. A new Dodecan took charge of us. Curiously, I was coming to regard the groupings of twelve people as single entities.

"Welcome, strangers. We are the Spinning Wheel. After a brief examination, we'll immediately start the search for your new mosh partners. We realize that two lost twelfies such as yourselves must be extremely uncomfortable. Not to mention semi-deranged. Therefore we have taken the liberty of arranging appropriately secure quarters for you."

With that, Moonchild and I were surrounded by the twelve members of Spinning Wheel. We couldn't have bolted for the exit even if we had been mentally alert enough.

Marched inside, we were led to what amounted to a comfortable padded cell. A padded door closed behind us, its lock clicking with dire finality.

Just then, to add the icing on the cake, our nameless son began to cry. Wail, actually, with a sound that I feared would make my head explode.

"What's the matter with it?" I demanded.

"He's hungry. And I think he might need a new diaper. Back home, we used to just let the babies run around naked . . . "

I began to bang on the featureless door, but the padding muffled all sound. I turned back helplessly to Moonchild.

"Give me your shirt," she proposed.

I instantly felt a rejection leaping to my lips. With all the strength I could muster, I forced it down, and instead removed the nice new shirt given to me by the Drexleroids.

Using the unsoiled portions of the diaper itself to clean our son, Moonchild afterwards fashioned an awkward new wrapping out of my shirt. Then she said, "Give me a Pez, please."

After another tremendous inner struggle, I did so.

Moonchild stuck the little candy in the brat's mouth and it instantly shut up, closing its shimmery checkerboard eyes in contentment as it sucked.

"Won't it choke?" I asked.

"I think he's big enough for solid food now. He's developed teeth since we've been here. I think maybe he's teething too, as well as hungry."

"How can that possibly be?"

"Maybe his internal clock is different from ours."

I recalled how in CA-land the constant tick of chronons governed all events, and how I had once wondered what relation these chronons bore to the passage of time in other universes. Maybe the kid *was* still operating on a different timescale than us.

After this, there wasn't much to do except sit in a padded corner and try to ignore the pervasive dirty diaper smell. I thought about how cruel the Yo-yo had been to sentence me to a world where I literally couldn't make up my mind, simply because when using it I hadn't been able to make up my mind. But then the sheer poetic justice of it began perversely to appeal to me . . .

In a short while, the Dodecans came for us. There were actually three of them this time: thirty-six twelfies altogether. Apparently, we were an object of intense interest. Under the massed gazes, I felt even more like a freak.

Crowding even the wide corridors of the Matchmakers Bureau, they escorted us to the examination room. There, I was given a new shirt. Then one of the Dodecans reached out as if to take the baby. Moonchild instinctively cradled him closer, shaking her head no. (*Hey, that's my job*, I thought.)

"Come, come," said the Dodecan reasonably. "You know you can't keep your child. From birth to age four, he must live in the Grooving Creche with his peers, developing the aptitudes he was born with. After that, he'll enter into his first trial mosh. If he remains with you, he'll throw off the balance of your own sodality."

Moonchild was still clutching the kid and looking miserable. With her skinny bod curled protectively around the baby, long lank hair curtaining the kid, she looked like a neurasthenic weeping willow grown in poor soil. I felt bad for her, so I said, "Moon, the Pez. Remember?"

It dawned on her slowly. The kid was linked now to us, across whatever universe-balloons we might travel. Maybe he already had been ever since the Drexleroids gave him to us. But after sucking on the Pez he was for sure.

Moonchild reluctantly surrendered the brat.

81.
Matchmaker, Matchmaker, Make Me a Match

BECAUSE THERE WERE no records for us, the Dodecans had to administer the whole barrage of tests that natives underwent over years. The exams lasted all day. Electrodes, visual and auditory stimulation, CAT and PET scans, written and manual tasks. A big deal was made about my artificial Badfinger hand. At the end of the strenuous ordeal, we were presented with the results.

"You are a Rejecter and you are a Proposer—"

"It took you ten goddamn hours to find that out?" I interrupted.

"Tut, tut, you did not allow me to finish. We now know your all-important Gardner Quotient down to the fifth decimal place. We have assembled a matrix of potential moshers for both of you, based on the assumption that you wish to remain together."

"Yes, yes," said Moon. "We do."

"Very well. Tomorrow we will begin to assemble the new sodality."

Back to the cell then. After a meal, we fell asleep as if drugged. Which we probably were.

The next day we were brought to a less clinical setting: a big room with couches and a table of refreshments. A new Dodecan who introduced themselves as Bottle Glass started the session with a kind of disclaimer.

"The law requires us to inform you of the various backgrounds and histories of your potential new partners, and a veto from any single twelfie is sufficient to invalidate a candidate. Of course, the candidate himself may choose not to join the nascent sodality. Are you ready to begin?"

"Ready," said Moon.

The next fifteen hours were a combination of the worst blind date from hell repeated ad infinitum, plus an endless round of NFL draft picks, plus an extensive course of mind-altering substances.

Apparently, there was a certain methodology to assembling a sodality, and we had to begin by choosing our Starter. The first candidate was led in.

As soon as the lone twelfie entered the room, I could feel my brain changing. New initiatory qualities tentatively superimposed themselves on my wounded mentality. I immediately tried to work up enough conviction to use the Yo-yo for escape. But it was still no-go.

"This is Carol," said Bottle Glass, "formerly of the Turbine Works sodality. Her mosh partners all died in a mountain-climbing accident, and Carol has just finished extensive Regrooving to deal with the trauma."

Carol reminded me of the newborn Bambi. I was afraid she'd fall over if I breathed on her. She kept her eyes lowered as we asked her a few questions. After about five minutes though, I cut them short. She just felt itchy inside my head.

"No, this isn't working. She's no good. Bring on the next one."

Carol was escorted from the room. Bottle Glass addressed me. "Try to temper your natural impulses, please. We'll never finish if you reject everyone."

"She was a total wimp and basketcase! What the hell kind of Starter would she have made!"

"Everyone deserves a chance. There's no science of unfailingly predicting what dynamics any given mosh will produce. Some of history's greatest sodalities have had what were apparently weak links. Surely you recall the story of Skunk Cabbage...?"

"Enough with the fairy tales. Let's build this Frankenstein monster already."

"Your allusion escapes me . . . "

Over the rest of the day we interviewed what seemed like every reject, misfit, elderly "widow," accident victim and fresh-from-the-creche newbie that Dodecan society had to offer. Amazingly, despite the low quality of the choices and the seeming impossibility of fitting any twelve semi-random people together, our sodality began to emerge. With each new addition to the mosh, I could feel my innate Rejectionism being tempered by other qualities. It was like bringing an image into clearer and clearer focus through a telescopic lens.

Picking the Starter turned out to be the biggest hurdle, after which the pace accelerated. We got hung up briefly again on the Prioritizer, but after that it was relatively clear sailing right down to the Stopper.

At last it was over. Along with Moon and me, Starter Felix, Lumper Marc, Splitter Rudy, Observer Alice, Acceptor Rose, Speculator Bruce, Prioritizer Cindy, Stower Larry, Retriever Wanda, and Stopper Glen formed the new Calico Quilt sodality.

We were released that day to commence our new life in Dodecan society.

82.
Thrashing with the Moshers

UPON LEAVING THE Matchmakers, I felt great. My Rejectionism had been moderated by the stabilizing influences of my eleven fellow moshers. We now formed a balanced unity. I was confident that Moon and I would soon be booking out of this nutty world. Once I made up my mind about a new destination, I would calmly unleash my mighty Yo-yo and flee my new unwanted extended family-cum-marriage.

But I hadn't counted on having to convince a group mind of the desirability of my plans before I could do anything.

As a brand new sodality, Calico Quilt was eligible for a lot of perks. We were given a lovely furnished apartment in the city, as well as one of the lumpy cars necessary for transporting twelve people. During a six-month "thrashing" period, when we were expected to work out any small kinks in our new arrangement, we were entitled to a generous stipend sufficient for luxuries as well as necessities. At the end of that time, we were supposed to be ready to land a job and get productive.

After the excess of stimulation and danger I had recently experienced, I wouldn't have minded kicking back and relaxing for a spell of pure sloth.

But those eleven other bastards always seemed to have different, more energy-intensive plans. And no compunction about imposing them.

One day I was sitting in front of the TV trying peacefully to watch a daytime soap. I had really gotten hooked on them, since the social dynamics were about twelve times as intricate and fascinating as those back in my old world (which, I recalled from time to time, the Drexleroids had informed me had plunged into the Sun after a million further years of me-less existence).

This soap was called *Twelve Lives to Live*. Today's episode focused on a protagonist named Burnt Hut. Burnt Hut's Prioritizer Shannon wanted to leave the sodality to join Stingy Baker, whose Prioritizer was dying of cancer. At the same time, the Rejecter from Burnt Hut and the Proposer from Stingy Baker were carrying on an exclusive two-twelfie ·affair that was the height of titillating perversion. As you might imagine, when you can't get more than a hundred yards away from the rest of your sodality without flipping out, such an affair is somewhat difficult and frustrating. Intercut with this were also a half-dozen subplots, one of which concerned the Crusoe-like plight of a sodality stranded on a desert island. They had lost a third of their members when their ship sank, complicating their survival considerably.

With a bowl of fresh popcorn cradled in my lap, I could forget my own problems and concentrate on those of the characters.

Maybe today would be the day when Lost Lake discovered that another sodality named Swamp Fever—whose members all looked *almost exactly like* Lost Lake's own moshers—was impersonating Lost Lake, serving the function of their evil twin.

83.
The Tyranny of the Moshjority

BUT MY PEACEFUL viewing was soon to be disturbed.

Out of the corner of my eye, I could see the rest of Calico Quilt drifting in from elsewhere in the big apartment, assembling around me in the TV room. From the kitchen came Cindy, Alice and Marc; they had just finished doing lunch dishes. The bedroom emptied itself of Rose, Bruce, Larry, Wanda and Glen; sex among sodality members was considered masturbation (albeit masturbation you could get pregnant from), and I supposed that was what they had been up to on the enormous stage-sized bed we all shared. Rudy and Felix left the bathroom; I prayed they had only been showering together. Moonchild appeared carrying a cat, while five more flocked around her feet. (Many other Dodecan mammals exhibited quasi-moshing tendencies in various numerical sets.)

After a minute spent trying to ignore them, I said, "What's up?"

Observer Alice, a thin woman of sixty, said, "Paul, all you like to do is sit around the house. We're bored."

"Yeah," chimed in Retriever Wanda, a chubby teenager. "I can't remember the last time we had any fun."

"I suggest we go out," that traitor Moonchild proposed. "Maybe we can visit my son again."

We had paid a call on the still-nameless, abnormally growing brat once before, so Moon could satisfy herself that he was doing okay. But the rest of the sodality seemed disinclined to get very much involved with the kid, which was just fine by me.

Speculator Bruce, a dreamy adolescent, said, "What if we went to a club to, like, socialize? You know, uh, meet some new people . . . "

"That seems essential if we're to become fully integrated, both with ourselves and with society," said Prioritizer Cindy.

"Let's go to the beach!" Moonchild enthusiastically proposed.

Everyone looked at me. As Rejecter, I was kind of like the old USSR in the UN Security Council. I could put the kibosh on just about anything with my veto—if I really tried hard enough. (The stronger the survival risk, the stronger my voice became, was the general rule.) But feeling like doing it was another matter. The general mental consensus of the whole sodality was like a smothering blanket over my will power, forcing my options into a certain channel of least resistance. That was why I hadn't been able to use my Yo-yo yet. There was no consensus among the others that it was a good thing for me/us to do.

Today, I just didn't feel like fighting over such a stupid thing as going to the beach. So before I could even reach forward to shut off the TV, the emotion had percolated through the mosh and Acceptor Rose said, "Great idea!"

"Let's go!" said Starter Felix.

And we went.

Everyone smiling but me.

84.
A Word Underhand Is Worth Two of the Mosh

AFTER THAT DAY, when I returned to the apartment with a wicked sunburn, I started in to work on the others, striving mightily to bring them around to my position. Fortunately, this world had a very minimal history of duplicity, treachery and backstabbing. In terms of the famous hypothetical punishment/reward scenario known as the Prisoner's Dilemma, everyone here was basically a nice, pleasant cooperator. I was the lone cheater and defaulter here, the snake in their Eden, the Machiavelli in their castle.

It felt wonderful.

Moonchild, of course, was the easiest to convince, and I did her first. I explained that she'd never get our son back in this world, that we just had to leave for a place where we could raise him ourselves. (Of course, this was all a lie, since I didn't care one whit about the little nitwit. I had in mind to try a world where— Oh, but why bother to mention my old wish now, since I soon found I had outsmarted myself, and never did get there...?)

Once I had Moonchild, our Proposer, on my side, my persuasive forces were more than doubled. Her constant stream of suggestions about the two of us leaving this world beat at the others in the sodality relentlessly. A deft reverse-psychology rejection here and there from me helped considerably. It was tedious work, like diverting a river pebble by pebble, but I plugged remorselessly away.

It also helped that Moonchild and I were turning out to be completely unfitted for a normal Dodecan life. I didn't know if it was the presence of two non-natives in the mosh, or if it was just a bad mix to begin with. But in either case, Calico Quilt was turning out to be the wallflower-at-the-dance among sodalities, a big awkward bumpkin constantly tripping over its own shitkickers.

After a month or so of simultaneous subversion from within and social ostracism from without, Calico Quilt exhibited a communally changed mind.

I would be allowed to use the Yo-yo to shift Calico Quilt to a better world.

The one thing I had been careful not to mention was that no one except me, Moon and the baby were really going. I had withheld all information about the Pez-dispenser, as well as literally withholding any of its contents. When Moon and I vanished, Calico Quilt could easily replace us, get happy and take its rightful place in Dodecan society.

Finally the great day arrived. We gathered in a circle in our apartment. I looked hopefully to Moonchild, willing her to propose what we had discussed: my own self-centered wish. She had to voice the command, since I couldn't.

"Yo-yo," she began, "I want you to take us to a world where our son can grow up big and strong and smart."

"I second it," said Acceptor Rose.

"What!?!"

Moonchild thrust out a stiff lower lip in defiance. "You heard me. And everyone agrees. Now, do it!"

What choice did I have? Anything was better than this fix. In the new world, I would have my way.

So out whirled the Yo-yo, with Moonchild's wish traveling round the circle of moshers, through my brain and down my arm.

FACES OF
THE EIGHTH PAIR

85.
The Birds, the Bees and the Bits

FOR A SECOND or two, I thought the Yo-yo had failed. The apartment around us quivered like jello on a plate with a vibrator under it, then settled back substantially the same. But gone, gone, wonderfully gone! were our ten Dodecan moshmates. My brain felt normal again (as normal as it ever felt or could feel, after the past whirlwind of universes). And our son was there in the room with us.

The kid was now as big as a four-year-old. In the space of roughly an objective month, from the moment we had been given him by the Drexleroids, he had matured four years. A year per week. Holy cow. In a couple of years he'd be older than *me*, his ever-lovin' blue-eyed Dad! Or Mother, as the case may be.

Moonchild rushed to the kid's side and swept him up. Crushing him to her scanty bosom, she began planting wet sloppy ones on him.

"Digger! Oh, Digger! Now I've got you back, I'll never let you go!" she exclaimed.

"Digger?"

Moon looked defiantly at me, as she had just before we split the Dodecan world. I wondered if I should start to worry about this new intransigence.

"Yes. It just came to me. The Diggers were heroes back home. They did the bummer work no one else enjoyed, like running the soup kitchens and hospitals and—"

"Yeah, yeah, I'm hip to the Diggers . . . " I thought a minute.

"Actually 'Digger' isn't such a bad name. It can also stand for something. Kinda."

Suspicious, Moon inquired, "What?"

"'Digitally engendered.'"

"Oh. Well, as long as it's not one of your usual insults, Paul . . . "

At that point, our boy Digger spoke up for the first time. I guess his Dodecan caretakers back at the creche had taught him to speak. Our son's voice, I was pleased to hear, was pleasant and soothing, unlike his weird checkerboard eyes. It carried a tone of self-assurance unusual at such a young age.

"Mommy, where did I come from?"

"Um, well— I think you should ask your Dad."

"Daddy? How was I born?"

Oh, great. This was one scene I had always planned to avoid. How the hell was I going to explain Digger's odd beginnings? Maybe I could make it into a fairy tale . . .

I sat down in a chair and Moonchild deposited Digger into my lap. Then I began.

"Once upon a time, in a land far, far away that was ruled by an evil cannibal King, two autocatalytic assemblages of reduced instruction sets running on an infinite binary substrate happened to exchange sufficient paragenes to boot up a new little homeostat. And that was you."

I didn't know what was spookier: the fact that I had managed to cobble together such semi-sensible gibberish, or the fact that Digger seemed to be taking it all in and understanding it on some level.

Then the kid said, "Well, what's my destiny, Daddy?"

86.
The Mom and Pop Cops Knock

THAT INNOCENT YET loaded inquiry was too much for me. I just lost it. All the careful, fragile composure I had tried to cultivate in the face of all the cross-dimensional craziness. I jumped to my feet, carelessly dumping Digger from my lap.

188

"Your destiny!" I shouted. "Who the fuck cares about your destiny! I can't even figure out my own! I've got absolute power of choice, uncountable options, and it's bringing me absolute misery! I've been to a universe the size of an infinite pea and my troubles still filled it! I've had my brain split twelve ways and it didn't lessen any of my grief! I've been surrounded by horny, willing women and I couldn't get it up for any of them! Once the wiggle of my little finger could raise hurricanes, but now I can barely wipe my own ass!"

Moonchild had hastened to pick up Digger. The boy was serene and untearful, but she was petting him anyway, uttering soothing BBB that I somehow felt should have been due to me.

But when she did turn to me, she had only contempt.

"What is this pitiful rant? Some kind of song by, like, *America*? All you're missing is your horse with no name, you whiney old fogey."

"That hurts. That really hurts, Moon. Maybe you're forgetting who rescued you from your so-called fate worse than death. The fuckatorium, remember? Not that it wouldn't have done you a world of good, a dried-up old pruney virgin like you."

"Oh! That's the last straw! Digger and I are leaving right now!"

"Me too!" I said, feeling the reassuring weight of the Yo-yo cupped in my tireless Badfinger right hand. But then it dawned on me like a hangover.

"Oh, shit. The Pez. You guys are still linked to me. And without the help of the Cals, I can't remove you from the lookup table inside the Yo-yo . . . "

"Well, I don't want to leave this universe just yet anyway. If the place is in accordance with my wish, then it's going to be good for Digger. So you just don't try anything."

Our Mexican standoff was broken by a loud knocking at the door, followed immediately by a bellowed demand.

"Open up! It's the Parent Patrol!"

Moon looked at me. I looked at her.

Then the door was kicked in.

There were five of them with drawn guns. So we froze.

189

The leader consulted an instrument, then spoke. "The neighbors were right. We're registering as clear a case of field contamination as I've ever seen. Let's bag the kid and hope we're not too late."

While the leader kept us covered, two of the other SWAT teamers shook out to full length what looked like a shiny metallic body bag with an attached air supply. They advanced on Digger, scooped him up gently and bagged him as if he were a large take-out pizza. A burly guy then hefted our cocooned son in a fireman's carry.

"Murphy, Sloan," directed the boss. "Cuff the 'rents."

Our hands were twisted behind us and manacled. So much for escape via Yo-yo.

"Now, you two can tell your story to the judge. And I hope you got a good one, 'cuz I think 'Pump 'Em Up' Pettyforge is behind the bench today."

Should I have been surprised at my luck?

Or lack thereof?

87.
Pact with the Devil Girl

IF OURS WAS a representative sample, the jail cells in this world were slightly more sophisticated, comfortable and humane than those in Moon's original continuum. Otherwise, though, it was *deja vu* all over again.

Deprived of my Yo-yo once more—lest I do myself bodily harm with it—sitting far apart on the lower tier of a bunkbed with a skinny, sulky, suspicious hippie who occasionally favored me with a glower, I felt plunged straight back to my second Out-of-Home-Universe Experience. It was very depressing.

What had I achieved with all my frantic travel? Nothing. Less than nothing, actually. Oh, I had shattered my near-terminal Bookland ennui and lost my sense of inhabiting a deadly closed system without potentials. But I had replaced those feelings only with fear, shame, disappointment, disorientation and the realization that the multiverse was incomprehensibly humongous and complex.

And of course, the Ontological Pickle remained as big and scary and metaphorically warty-briney-green as ever.

I was contemplating all this—while trying to ignore Moonchild's petulance—when the jailer came for us. He was a bulky mustached guy who looked like a writer of brand-name-laden mystery novels.

"Time for your hearing, you dirty fieldwarpers."

"Hey," I protested. "Whatever happened to innocent until proven guilty?"

"You're guilty as hell. I've seen the recordings of your patter-matter fields, not to mention the prodge's. They tell the whole disgusting story. You scum! Now, march! Judge Pettyforge gets even meaner if he's kept waiting."

So march we did.

As we walked, I tried to talk to Moonchild.

"Moon, let's put aside old grudges and failures for the moment and try to figure out how we're gonna save our tails. We have to hang together in this, or we're gonna hang separately, if you get my drift."

She seemed to relent and unbend a little. "Well, maybe. I agree that we have to find out what kind of fix we're in and how to meet it. But there have to be some ground rules between us first."

"Such as?"

"If we can solve our immediate problem, I want you to agree to give this universe a chance. Don't bug out at the first sign of difficulty or hard work. Promise me that you'll stick it out for a while, to give our son a good start in life."

I thought about it. Moonchild had been a pretty decent sport about being ripped out of her home universe and hauled along on this mad escapade. I remembered how she had held up in the chaos of the Butterfly dimension, and earlier how she had bit her lip and not said anything when surrounded by the zaftig Goddess women who reminded her constantly of what she could never be. And then when the Drexleroids had given her momentary omnipotence, she had wished not for something selfish, but only to be reunited with our strange son. She was basically a good sort. I could have been stuck with a lot worse.

As if sensing this sentiment, she said, "Paul, I like you, I really do. But you've got to learn to be more charitable. To others *and* to yourself!"

"Right. I'll kiss the first leper we come across."

"Oh, you jerk! I can see you'll never really change. But if you want me on your side, you'd better promise that you'll help raise our son right."

A loophole occurred to me. "Till he's how old?"

"Um, eighteen...?"

"That'll be eighteen weeks, then. Right?"

"Oh, I hadn't considered that. Sure, if he continues to grow as fast as he has so far."

"Okay. I can hack anything for four and a half months. Shake on it."

Moonchild had the *clammiest* hands . . .

88.
Assizes, with Abysmal Condemnations

THE COURTROOM WAS full. Judge Pettyforge sat behind his raised bench looking like one of the less placable Aztec deities. As we were conducted to the defense table, a feature of this universe finally struck me.

Everybody was fit and trim. There wasn't an overweight person in sight. And many men and women were actually on the pumped-up end of the scale. (I recalled the Judge's nickname with trepidation . . .) Quite a change from the lard-ass America I hailed from.

But there was something else different, some quality less definable. After some thought, I could only call it a general air of brightness and alertness, of mental acuity. None of these folks exhibited the kind of lackluster inattention and mental laziness so common back home. Not that they seemed necessarily smarter, just more used to using whatever brains they were born with. Or perhaps they were bolstered by some exterior resource not visible to us . . .

Our court-appointed defender introduced himself. A nebbish

who would let the Judge walk all over us, I could tell, and I didn't even bother to register his name. The hearing began.

Judge Pettyforge studied some papers. Then he addressed us. "You are Mr and Mrs Paul Girard, correct?"

This was new. Somehow, the Yo-yo had engineered a history for us, a paper trail to support our existence. Or perhaps it had slotted us into a universe already containing duplicates of us (though I recall specifically requesting Hans the cybershrub to foreclose such options). But if such were the case, what had happened to our doppelgangers? Oh well, it hardly mattered, as long as we were the ones stuck here.

"That's us, your honor," I admitted.

"And you have a prodge named Digger, born four years ago?"

Moon spoke up. "Yes, your honor. We do."

The Judge leaned forward, his face mottled red, and transfixed us with twin baleful eyebeams of disgust.

"How could you!" he hollered. "How could you be so thoughtless!"

"Well, Judge," I answered humbly, "it was the Festival of the Dynes and we just kinda got carried away—"

"Quiet! I have no idea what you're babbling about. But there are no excuses for this kind of conduct! Let me review the charges against you, which are scandalous in their magnitude. First, there is no record of prenatal testing and counseling for either of you! Neither of you has ever enrolled in one single improvement course! Your patter-matter field traces are as flat as a pancake, right up until the argument which the Parent Patrol interrupted. And then there's such a spike of hostility and confusion—Degree Seven!—that your prodge's field traces went right off the scale!"

"Your honor, I can explain—"

"I doubt that very much! Now, I don't know how you two managed to circumvent all of society's safeguards and guidelines. And I certainly don't know what kind of cruel and sadistic sets of 'rents you both must have had in your turn to grow up so vicious and twisted yourselves. But I do know one thing: remedial education and the most rigorous schedule of courses will begin the instant you leave this courtroom. If you know what's good for you—if you have any love and respect for your poor prodge—you will throw yourselves into the assignments with a will! And I only pray that this early neglect and abandonment on your part will have no lasting effect on your unfortunate prodge."

The gavel came down with a bang. "Case closed!"

89.
Miss Wormwood Commands

I HAD DISCOVERED a new natural law. I was going to call it Girard's Fourth Postulate. (Not that there were three previous ones, but the false terminology would serve to confuse future scholars of my life.) Here it was:

Whenever you are introduced to the inhabitants of a new universe, their first impulse will be to stick some kind of probe up your ass.

Everywhere we went, the natives wanted to make us fit in, to nail our parameters down like a captured bug on a board, to lop off any individual quirky extrusions, to squish our inconveniently shaped personalities into their rigid boxes, all the while demanding that we enjoy it and *proclaim* our enjoyment.

Society, I thought, could be defined as the urge to lay your neighbor's wife on a Procrustean bed.

Anyway, after the usual battery of humiliating bodily and mental tests ordered by Judge Pettyforge, Moonchild and I were ushered into an office. Behind a desk sat a middle-aged woman who reminded me of every high-school guidance counselor I had ever met. She was trim and rigid, conceivably possessed of a steel rod in place of a spine. Her hair was lacquered like a restored '65 Mustang. The nameplate on her desk read *Miss Wormwood*.

"Mr Girard," she said through her nose, "analysis of your patter-matter fields has determined that your inherent aptitudes best fit you to contribute to your prodge's somatic maturation. Your wife, on the other hand, we find to be eminently suited to guide his mental growth."

"Hold on one damn minute. You're saying that this hippie dingbat is more suited to help my boy with his homework than I am? While I'm only good enough to play catch with him?"

"Although the activities you have denominated are essentially meaningless sounds to my ears, I sense that you have captured the essence of the Parenting Board's findings precisely."

"Well, that tears it! Did you know that she can't even read?"

Moonchild interrupted. "Uh, Paul, I've been meaning to mention something to you. I can!"

"What the hell do you mean?"

"Somehow I can read, all of a sudden. I noticed when they were testing us, and I happened to look at a clipboard."

Miss Wormwood sniffed haughtily. "If your ignorance of the workings of the universe is not feigned, young lady, then it is appalling. Of course you can read. The shared human morphic field, while highly selective, has contained that simple skill for millennia. Now, if I may continue...? You will be entering my class of new 'rents. Their prodges range in age from three months to a year, all much younger than your boy. But he is so backward that there should be minimal incompatibility. Your fellow 'rents are all fine, upstanding citizens eager to do the best by their prodges, and I hope that you will learn to model your behavior on theirs. Now, if there are no questions—"

I stuck up my hand. "When is recess?"

Miss Wormwood smiled. I had seldom seen such a horrifying expression.

"Mr Girard. Until your child is fully grown, there is no recess for you. None. Not one minute of one hour of one single day."

90.
Field Theory

HERE IS WHAT we learned in Miss Wormwood's class, before the actual hard work began. These teachings were not always made explicit, since the natives knew most of it anyway, as simple matter of fact. But just as in a Driver's Ed class back home they might have started with such rudimentary and familiar notions as "brake" and "accelerator," so here the instruction began with elementary concepts already well known.

The main thing I soon learned was that this universe supported actual Sheldrakean morphic fields.

Back home, a biologist named Rupert Sheldrake had conceived a startling new theory, based on some rather puzzling physical anomalies. He had contended that there existed invisible and undetectable reservoirs of force known as morphic fields. These fields existed in practically infinite numbers, and were intricately nested and interrelated. What was really important was what they did.

Fields, according to Sheldrake, governed everything from embryogenesis to cosmogenesis, chemical reactions to music, animal instincts to human memory. A two-way feedback existed between the parts of the physical universe we could sense and their associated morphic fields. Information and patterns, once born in the physical world, would migrate into the morphic fields where they would remain forever, as a kind of Platonic repository or library of pre-tested possibilities. Under appropriate circumstances, the patterns would flow back to influence the raw physical world.

These numinous instructions could be tapped, Sheldrake believed, by all those individuals or objects who could "tune into" a particular morphic field. Mainly this meant, for living things, fellow members of the species. Thus, for example, if one monkey learned a new trick, other monkeys not in direct contact, even miles away, would have access to the trick, via the omnipresent morphic fields. When, of course, the behavior had been reinforced or grooved into the morphic field to a certain critical extent by repetition in the physical world.

Here in this universe, among the human "drakes" (as I came to call them), the reality of morphic fields had some peculiar ramifications. But the one with biggest import for me and Moonchild personally was that evolution was Lamarckian.

Lamarck, of course, was the discredited rival of Darwin. His theory of evolution could be summed up in one phrase: "Acquired characteristics can be inherited." Giraffes that stretched their necks extra during their lifetimes would give birth to baby giraffes with longer necks than the previous generation or than the progeny of peers who had browsed only on lower branches.

Of course, back home this was nonsense. There was no way to rewrite the DNA in a woman's egg or a man's sperm so that they could pass down the mental or bodily acquisitions of a lifetime to their progeny. (Although, of course, such retroviruses as AIDS violated this rule to some extent.)

But here, thanks to morphic fields, Lamarckism ruled.

At conception, and lasting until roughly age eighteen, a child's relatively blank morphic field was capable of being written on by the fields of his parents.

Whatever the parents made of themselves, good or bad, would, through repetition, be eventually transferred to the child.

(Luckily, the more forceful and developed fields of the parents swamped that of the child. Otherwise, the adults would have found themselves incontinent babblers after the kid's birth, as the child's qualities influenced the elders.)

Human parents, intent on turning out the best possible children, were the giraffes who had to stretch their necks.

However much of a pain in the butt it was.

91.
On Your Lamarck, Get Set, Go!

BECOMING A PARENT in the world of the drakes was no trivial decision or commitment. It meant tying up your life for eighteen years (or more, if you had serial pregnancies), years of constant involvement with your child's "education." The level of labor and dedication expected of the parents was heroic and unrelenting. Nobody ever whimsically decided to have a kid—thus opting out of most other professional and social activities—without much forethought. (Since not everyone wanted to be breeders, the drakes had a stable level of population only thanks to a tendency toward multiple births.)

Of course, these breeding conditions tended to produce or select for a type of person who could best be described, in my humble opinion, as anal-retentive prigs. Self-congratulatory, goodie-goodie, conformist, conservative, hail-fellow-well-met backslappers.

There were ten other couples in Miss Wormwood's finishing school. I could stand only one of them: Tony and Sandra Boxcutter. Tony and Sandra were bluff and hearty as the other 'rents, but with a sardonic undertone that made them somewhat palatable.

Tony—a burly, hairy Mediterranean type—was in charge of the intellectual development of their four prodges, and Sandra—a wan and lissome poetic sort—had been assigned the task of shaping their physical growth.

Go figure.

This meant that I spent a lot of time in the gym with Sandra and the other "pumpers," while Moonchild kept busy in the library-cum-classroom with Tony and their fellow "crammers."

For two weeks now—two whole endless cursed weeks out of the total of the promised eighteen—I had spent practically every waking minute here in the gym. I had thought the lectures that occupied the first couple of classroom days after the tests were tedious. But nothing had prepared me for the torture of the gym.

Basically, I was expected to overcome forty years of sloth instantaneously, so as to transmit beneficial bodily templates to Digger. Personal trainers under the S&M tutelage of Miss Wormwood ran us pumpers through a hideous gamut of aerobics, weight-lifting, Nautilus-maneuvers, stretches, and BBB pep talk. We sweated like Bedouins, ached like plane-crash survivors, and were able to eat like starving drayhorses. In between the more rigorous tasks, we did things like ballet, aikido and tai chi.

All of this activity, of course, was being impressed on our parental morphic fields, whence it would flow down to our prodges, shaping their growing bodies in accordance with prevailing standards and wisdom. (Although none of the drake prodges grew or assimilated stuff as fast as the alien Digger, natch.)

Meanwhile in the library, Moonchild labored over primers, flashcards, and instructive videotapes, supplying Digger with second-hand pre-assimilated knowledge. Soon she would be moving on to encyclopedias and textbooks, endowing Digger with even more copious amounts of facts.

Breaktimes were spent in the nursery, playing with the prodges and assessing their progress.

"Oh, look at little Jessica, everyone! She's got so much better definition in her biceps now!"

"I think Jason's vocabulary has doubled this week! Listen, everyone! Jason, say 'I need my diaper changed . . .'"

It was enough to make anyone like me puke their daily 5000 calories.

92.
Pump It Up, Till She Can Feel It

ONE DAY I just couldn't take the nauseating, kissy-kissy 'rent-prodge interactions in the nursery anymore. So I hung back in the gym at morning breaktime, despite the corrosive glares of Miss Wormwood, who soon huffed off.

To my surprise, Sandra also remained behind.

Wearing spandex shorts and halter top, a towel draped around her neck, her long hair pinned up with a loose tendril or two pasted to her sweaty cheeks, she looked really good. Quite a change from the anemic will-o-the-wisp of a few weeks ago. (I had learned that all the prodges of wholesome, devoted parents started their adult lives with a magnificent physique which most of them maintained, once independent of the patter-matter fields. But there were always backsliders, and Sandra had been one.)

Covertly, I looked in the full-length mirror across the room, noting that I looked pretty good too. My paunch was gone and I was becoming streamlined. Flab had been melting off me like snow on Mercury. Not bad. Maybe Moonchild had been right in having us hang out here for a while . . .

Sandra mopped her face with the towel and spoke. "A minute's rest! Thank God!"

"Uh, you don't mind not seeing your triplets this morning . . . ?"

"I could use a little peace and quiet. It's not easy being a 'rent. Devoting every minute to your prodges."

"Tell me about it. Say, Sandra—did you ever think that the prodges could do it themselves?"

"Do what?"

"Well, develop their muscles and brains on their own. Instead of being forcefed like little birdies sucking down regurgitated worms. Why should we pump them up like balloons made in our image?"

"What a weird thought, Paul. How could it be? They'd make mistakes and waste time, go down false paths and pick up bad habits. Think what messed-up persons would result! Whatever kind of society would you end up with then? No, it's much more sane and sensible for adults who know what's best to set the course. Besides, we owe a good start to our prodges for having brought them into this world."

Sandra's words brought back the old specter of Infinite Regress which I had faced in the Monobloc among the Calvinii. "But how did this all begin? There had to be a first generation that learned things on their own . . . "

"Oh, sure, our primitive caveman ancestors had to establish the system somehow. But once civilization got going, there was no need for such clumsy methods anymore."

"I guess. But don't you resent all the years of work?"

Sandra laughed. "Oh, no, of course not! Even though it's meant giving up a lot."

"What do you miss the most?" I asked without really caring about her answer.

"Sex with Tony."

I had to take a long drink from my water bottle before I felt capable of replying. "Was it, uh, complications from the delivery?"

"Honestly, Paul, you're so silly and naive! Of course not. It's just another aspect of the fields."

"What do you mean?"

"Well, if 'rents have sex together, it sets up waves in the fields that result in Oedipus or Electra complexes. The prodges become fixated on mother or father as sex objects. So for the duration of their childhood, we can only have sex with non-spouses. And even during that kind of safe sex, we have to bag the kids of course, so as to shield them from mature stuff they're not ready for yet. Even then, a little leaks in."

The bags such as the Parent Patrol had used on Digger were made of an artificial substance which had been found to partially block the influence of the higher morphic fields, putting the bag-ee into a kind of suspended animation. Of course, there was still some trickle-through, since the presence of the fields was essential for life. If the invisible info-radiations of this universe could have ever been blocked completely, the object so isolated would have instantly dissolved into constituent quarks or something even more primitive.

"So you see," continued Sandra, "we can have plenty of the right kind of sex that sets up the proper exogamic patterns. But just not with our spouses."

I was sweating now, but not from exercise. "Um, like could you have sex with, er—"

Sandra laid her fingertips on my arm. "Like with you and Moonchild? Sure. Tony and I were just getting ready to ask you to swing."

93.
Quality Time

IT WAS NOT going to be as easy to fuck Sandra as it first appeared.

It involved convincing Moonchild to swing too.

Tony needed a partner. There couldn't be any kind of sexual frustration feeding into the field and warping the developing sexuality of the Boxcutter prodges. So that's why partner-swapping was the only way. And we couldn't find a date for Tony from among some other couple, because that would just send the asymmetrical imbalance rippling further down the line.

Neither could we dig up a gal from among the non-parental drakes. It turned out that social contact between 'rents and non-'rents was frowned upon and practically nonexistent. There were too many rituals and safeguards and customs which were just second-nature to the 'rents, but which were not practiced by the non-'rents. And the limited conversational topics of the 'rents didn't make them popular in social settings, despite the immense lip service respect paid to their roles. No, parents associated only with other parents in this world.

Pretty much like home, then, only different in the degree of segregation.

So, in order to get my rocks off, I went to work on Moonchild.

At home with her and Digger, I would insist on spending our evenings together in our cozy living room. There we'd be, the perfect nuclear morphic family: Moonchild with a book in her lap, me with some piece of exercise equipment to hand, and Digger—a wiry ten-year-old—sitting quietly, eyes glazed over in the peculiar prodge state called "morphlining," taking all our activities in on a subliminal level. Usually classical music would be playing, which we'd all absorb more conventionally.

"So, Moon," I said one night about a week after Sandra's invitation, automatically continuing arm-curls with the freeweights, "our boy is turning out just fine, wouldn't you say?"

Moon looked up over the rims of her reading glasses. Over the past few weeks, she had changed in her own way as much as I had. Gone was the naive, innocent hippie chick of yore. She had been taking some kind of special drake smart drinks to keep up with Digger's unnatural capacities, and the large quantities of knowledge she had assimilated had altered her personality. On top of the old Moonchild was layered a new sophistication and sensibility.

"Yes, I agree. He's in the top five percent of his current cohort, both physiologically and neurologically. It's just as I always hoped. We're giving our son a fine start in life, after his early abandonment."

I switched to a single spring-grip, clenching and unclenching my left hand nervously. (The Badfinger appendage needed no exercising.) "Great, great. It's been all my pleasure. I wasn't sure at first that I'd like devoting all this time to Digger, but now I'm really into it. It's been great."

Moon looked a little suspicious. "Really? You really feel that way?"

"Sure! I like working out with the other parents. They're all nice folks. Really swell. Take the Boxcutters for instance. How do you like ol' Tony?"

"He has a fine mind."

"Hmmm, does he now? Well, that's great, just great." Great seemed to be the only word in my nervous vocabulary. "I bet he and Mrs Boxcutter—Sandra, I think her name is—would be swell people to have, um, a barbecue with some night. Wouldn't you think?"

Moonchild closed her book with a thud. "Paul, do you want sex with the Boxcutters?"

"Well, uh, no. That is, not unless you— I mean, only if—"

"That's enough dithering, please. Let me think about it a minute."

Exactly sixty seconds went by, as I could tell by counting my reps, before Moonchild spoke.

"Very well. It seems the least I can do, since you've been so accommodating. I will try to have intercourse with Tony Boxcutter."

Moon's tone made the whole prospect sound about as exciting as a quilting bee.

But by now I was ready to take whatever I could get.

94.
Tony And Sandra and Paul and Moonchild

I PULLED THEe zipper closed, covered it with the attached flap of shielding material, and Digger was bagged. The Boxcutter prodges had already gone down.

Tony and Sandra were standing side by side. They looked cool as Alaskan cucumbers. I was counting on Tony's instincts taking over, since Moonchild's libido seemed as dormant as ever, flat as her chest.

I went over to Sandra and put an arm around her narrow waist. Then I addressed the other couple. "Well, have fun, kids."

Moonchild regarded me coolly, as if I were some kind of lab rat. "We will be discussing some of the finer points of today's material for a while, should you need to speak to us for any reason."

Not bloody likely, I commented to myself, but said aloud,

"Super, wonderful, see you soon."

Then I practically dragged Sandra into one of the two bedrooms.

We were undressed in ten seconds sharp. Sandra was no Barbi twin, but she was still the most beautiful naked woman I had seen in a long time.

Instantly, we were all over each other like measles.

Just as the foreplay was reaching a natural progression, Sandra stopped dead.

"What is it? What's the matter?"

"It's Tony and Moonchild. Can't you feel it where your fields overlap and intersect with hers? They're not hitting it off."

I was dying. "So what? Screw 'em! Not literally! I mean, the hell with 'em! You and I can still have fun. C'mon!"

Sandra got out of bed. "No, Paul, I'm afraid not. As much as I'd like to, it simply wouldn't be responsible. I must go tell them so, before they create any more negative impulses in the fields."

Sandra, still naked, left the bedroom. I stumbled out after her. "Sandra, no!"

Tony and Moonchild were sitting a few feet apart on the couch. Between them were scribbled *papers* with *equations* on them!

When Moonchild saw me, her face went white. "Paul, I'm so sorry. I tried, I really did—"

Then she averted her head and vomited all over the Boxcutters' lovely carpet.

I hated to think what she would have done if she had seen me naked before I got buff.

95.
Father and Son Talk

DIGGER'S UNNATURALLY RAPID advancement had soon distanced him from his former contemporaries, and so we had had to leave Miss Wormwood's Academy so that we wouldn't disturb the less speedy prodges. But it hardly made any difference in our home routine. By now, both Moon and I were thoroughly habituated, locked into the nearly compulsive groove of pumping and cramming our son. I spent all day fencing, walking the balance beam and doing chinups, while Moon was practically plugged in to her home computer—that is, when she wasn't speedreading Einstein or Hawking or some other brainiac. We alternated in dabbling at painting and sculpture. So the last few weeks of Digger's education were spent in concentrated home schooling.

I didn't miss Sandra much. After the fiasco of the attempted swap, I realized that sex was out of the question under the current circumstances: i.e., me being paired with Moon. I was better off actually if I didn't see Sandra anymore. My blue balls ached less.

As Digger became more mature, he spent less time lost in a morphlining trance and more time exhibiting a real personality. I found it was possible to have actual conversations with him. Weird conversations, but conversations nonetheless.

"So, Son, any clue to that destiny of yours you asked me about when you were little?"

Digger stroked his wispy incipient mustache thoughtfully with a forefinger and regarded me eye-to-eye (for he was now my height). "No, Dad. But I think it has something to do with the circumstances of my birth. Could you explain again how it happened?"

So for the hundredth time I went over how he had been conjugated during an info-swap between me and Moon in the CA universe.

"Mother never had real sex then?" he asked. "She's technically a virgin?"

"A fact she's inordinately proud of," I replied between grunts forced from me by the bench-presses.

Digger paused in speculative thought. "I suspect then that you're not my real father."

"What do you mean? Would anybody but your real father go to all this trouble for you?"

"I appreciate it, Dad. Really, I do. But something tells me I was created by forces larger than either you or Mom."

"Digger, I've got to tell you something. *Everybody* feels that way when they're young. But it wears off real fast. Believe me."

"Perhaps," was all Digger would allow.

96.
The Filthy Flee Where No Woman Pursueth

WE HAD AN eighteenth birthday party for Digger, just us three. It was a strange and melancholy occasion. Moon kept sniffling, and it made me want to sniffle too. But I kept any weepy stuff suppressed by thinking of how as soon as the festivities were over, we'd be getting the hell out of here, returning to my idiotic quest, for what that was worth.

After everybody had eaten as much cake as they possibly could and Digger had unwrapped the gift we had gotten him (a wristwatch, of all useless things, considering the bizarre nature of time in most universes; but Moonchild had adamantly overruled my not entirely facetious suggestion of a gross of condoms and a cross-dimensional subscription to *Big Beautiful Butt* magazine), I stood up to announce our departure.

"I'm sorry to have to drag both of you along with me—"

"No, no," Moonchild objected. Our son's long-awaited majority seemed to have softened her a bit toward me. "We want to stay together. Don't we, Digger?"

Even physiologically free of our combined morphic influence now, our son habitually wore a somewhat abstracted air which, combined with his good looks and checkerboard eyes, made for an appealing faunlike appearance.

"I don't mind, Mom. I'll tag along."

I hefted the Cosmic String Yo-yo meaningfully. "As hearty an endorsement of my lofty goals as I could expect. Well, not to keep either of you in suspense any longer. We're going to a universe I think you'll like, Moon. I'm taking us to a universe where ideas reign supreme."

I had reached this decision partly out of jealousy. After having been relegated to the role of bullmoose dullard in this universe, I wanted a chance to show Moonchild that my brain was as sharp as hers. And besides, my previous attempts to gain material pleasures had mostly gone bust. What was left besides arid intellectual pursuits? And I was hoping, of course, that such a universe as I now was imagining would contain the solution to the Ontological Pickle.

"Everybody ready?" I said. They nodded.

I got ready to snap out the Yo-yo. But then I hesitated.

"We're not being pursued, right? Our lives aren't in danger? Nobody's trying to make us stay or change our minds? There are no obstacles, impediments, barriers or hindrances to our departure? No angry crowds or natural disasters?"

"Not as far as I can see," said Moon. "Why do you ask?"

"I don't know. I'm just not used to having it so easy. It's creepy. I'm not certain it's a good sign."

"Well, we'll never know till you shift us over to our new universe."

So I did.

FACES OF
THE NINTH PAIR

97.
You *Can* Take It with You

WOULD MOONCHILD AND Digger and I retain our current neuro-somatic characteristics in this newest universe?

That was the major question on my mind as the Yo-yo socketed back with a smack into my palm.

I kinda liked being trim and fit. It was a pleasant change from my old lumpy couch-potato status. And Moon seemed to appreciate her new fund of hard-won knowledge. (I was still getting used to the notion that she was no longer the dumb and innocent hippie chick I had met so long ago. Still naive, yes, in many ways, but no longer ignorant.) I also didn't want Digger to revert to being a toddler, and I suspect he wouldn't have been so keen on the idea either, had I bothered to mention the possibility to either him or his mother.

But I hadn't, since I didn't want to hear any of their petty selfish bullshit BBB that would have gotten in *my* way of doing what *I* wanted to do.

Anyway, I was pretty confident we would all carry forward everything we had achieved. After all, hadn't the lyce come across under our skins, from the CA plenum to the Goddess strand? Hadn't I carried all the contusions, scratches and bruises from the Butterfly world—not to mention the Menger Sponge Badfinger Hand and Internal Organs Reversal—along to the Dodecan environment?

However, on the other non-strange-matter hand, some extreme local conditions that we had experienced were plainly supported only in their homeline. My splintered Rejecter mode of thinking had vanished once I fled the Dodecan universe. And most strikingly, my digital CA one-dimensional body was purely a function of that checkerboard universe now contained only within Digger's eyes.

So I figured the odds were maybe seventy-thirty that we would all emerge into the new bubble-continuum with our recently acquired faculties intact.

And opening my eyes now, at this very moment, would be the only way to find out if we had.

So that was what I did.

My muscled torso was still bulging out my shirt in all the appropriate places. Digger was still the goofily abstracted young man I had raised. As for Moonchild—

"Moon," I said, "can you elaborate on the function of mitochondria?"

"Certainly. Transmitted maternally, these organelles contain their own non-genomic DNA—"

"That's plenty. Thanks."

Everybody seemed just fine.

98.
Hello Kitty

WE FOUND OURSELVES standing in a small clearing in a rather jungly forest. Birds screeched, twittered and cackled; animals coughed, yelped and howled, but none within immediate threatening distance. The vegetation was not so temperate as that of the Goddess world, but more tropical. I saw a trail enter one side of the clearing and exit opposite. It looked like maybe it had been made by humans.

How in the hell could this be a world where ideas reigned supreme? My mental conception of such a place had been all sterile geometric crystal cities populated by big-headed super-sophonts. Maybe such metropoli did exist here, just over the horizon. But if so, why had the freaking Yo-yo dropped us so far away from the center of things? Again, I wished that the Cals were still with me, so I could have gotten a peek at the workings of the stupid artifact roped to my finger. So disgusted was I that I almost felt like throwing the seemingly worthless transport device away.

What were we going to do now? Head down the path? In which direction? Would a party of natives conveniently appear, as in the Goddess world? Maybe we should just bug out of this continuum right now, before anything irreversible happened.

As I was mentally dithering like this, Moonchild called out, "Paul, look!"

I followed her pointing finger.

A small animal was ambling down one of the paths. As it left the shadows of the foliage, it was revealed as a plain old calico kitty cat.

"Oh, how sweet!" said Moonchild. She started to move toward it.

"Stop!" I yelled. "We don't know that's a domestic cat! It could be some kind of monster!"

Moon halted. "You think so?"

"It's a possibility. Let me check . . . "

I picked up a stick and cautiously advanced. The cat wasn't scared, but waited patiently. When I got within poking distance, I tentatively teased it. It reared up playfully on its hind legs and batted at the stick. Then it began to purr.

I turned back to Digger and Moon. "It seems to know humans. Maybe we can follow it back to its owners—"

And just then the little bugger fastened itself on my ankle and bit deep.

"Yeow!" I reflexively kicked the beast off, sending it flying.

Moon and Digger rushed up to me. "Are you okay, Paul?"

"Oh, it hurts, but I'm fine," I said, and immediately passed out.

99.
Cat Scratch Fever

I WOKE UP. There was a ceiling of thatched palm fronds above me, some kind of natural cushioning underneath me. My bitten ankle throbbed.

But I felt *great*.

Excellent, in fact. Wonderful, elated, contented, joyous, at peace.

This was a *superb* world! There was absolutely nothing wrong with it, no way I would venture to improve it. The sunlight was the *best* sunlight ever manufactured. This moss under my butt was particularly *fine* moss. I hadn't met any of the natives yet, but I was absolutely convinced that they were going to turn out to be *marvelous* human beings, sterling in all respects.

I felt no particular urge to be up and about. Lying here was just as good an activity as anything else I could imagine. I could spend forever just watching that little lizard crawl across the rafters . . .

Just then someone came in. I looked up. It was Moonchild.

"Moon, you're *beautiful*!" I said, because all of a sudden she was.

"Oh, Paul, no! It's just what the chief of the Dawks said would happen!"

I couldn't understand why she seemed distressed at my compliment. "What's the matter? Don't you want me to call you 'beautiful?'"

That question too seemed to take her aback. "Well, under other conditions I might not mind— Oh, forget it! It's not you talking anyway, it's the meme from the Happy Cat!"

"The meme? What are you talking about, Moon? And why are you talking at all? Come lie down beside me and watch the show."

Moon looked around nervously. "What show?"

"See that little gecko up there? Isn't he the greatest?"

Moon spotted the harmless looking three-inch lizard—and screamed!

"It's a Jesus Lizard! Help! Help! Someone help!"

Frantic footsteps sounded. Digger appeared, carrying a tall staff. Strangers dressed in hides and skins followed close behind.

"Stand back, Mother! I'll get it!"

Digger poked at the lizard with his pole. Nimbly it evaded his jabs before launching itself onto his shoulder, where it bit his neck.

Digger dropped like a sack of Idaho potatoes.

Moonchild went down too, in a hysterical swoon.

One of the natives plucked the lizard off my son and squashed it underfoot.

None of this bothered me. I was certain it would all work out perfectly.

And meanwhile, what a groovy show!

100.
Eenie, Meme-ie, Miney, Moe

ONE OF THE natives—a bearded, blue-eyed man—came over by my side and squatted down.

"How are you doing?" he asked.

"Awesome!"

He shook his head with concern. "Bad, very bad. I've never seen the bite of a Happy Cat have such a potent effect. Your mate was right. You strangers evidently have no natural resistance to our wildlife."

The man stood. "Why don't you get up now and walk around with me a little? My name, by the way, is Groo, and I carry the leader meme. Hence I am chief of the Dawks."

"Congratulations! I'll bet you do a *great* job!"

"I try. Come now, on your feet. Maybe some exercise will temper your symptoms. Although I doubt it . . . "

I got up eagerly. "Sure, I'm game! Show me everything! I just know it's gonna be lovely!"

Groo sighed. We departed the hut, leaving Moonchild and Digger to the gentle ministrations of the other natives.

Outside, this was the scene that presented itself to my eager eyes: further huts scattered around a large clearing, with a longhouse in the center. There were several secure pens with various domestic animals cooped up in them.

Residents—all carrying long staffs—ambled around. At first I thought they were just killing time. Then I realized they were patrolling. From time to time one of them would crush something— a bug, a lizard, a little shrew—with his staff. The perimeter of the settlement was formed by a seamless stockade fence and was even more heavily guarded than the interior, by men, women and children alike. Any creature that made it over or under the fence was cornered and killed.

The sight of all this butchery disturbed my peaceful serenity a little.

"Hey, Groo, why do you guys have to kill all those critters right away, before they even do anything to you?"

"It is because they all carry memes that can infect us if they bite."

"Memes? But a meme is just an idea, isn't it? How is an idea gonna hurt you?"

"You should be the last to ask. Can't you feel how the Happy Cat meme is disturbing your own mental functioning?"

"Disturbing? I've never felt better! Everyone should feel this way! The world is perfect! Nothing needs doing at all!"

"You have stated the parameters of the Happy Cat meme in a nutshell. It robs the individual of initiative, while supplying a false sense of careless optimism and satisfaction."

It was very hard to concentrate on Groo's words with the splendor of the village spread before me, but I tried to be friendly and sustain the dialogue. "All the animals in your world carry ideas as if they were communicable viruses?"

"Yes. We believe that it has always been thus, ever since life began. And we humans have played the role of hosts to the animal-dispersed memes ever since our primitive apelike ancestors emerged. In fact, our wise men speculate that human intelligence really began as a special case of multiple meme infection in a single ancestor. Humans and all other animals have co-evolved ever since, new memes arising among the animals and new mental defenses and co-opting mechanisms arising among mankind."

"But how and why did memes and the ability to spread them ever develop in the first place among the animals?" I asked absentmindedly, while I concentrated on grokking a really neat shadow.

"Apparently, as merely another survival characteristic. The simple poisons secreted by many animals began to grow more complex and powerful, soon exhibiting many uses. The animals

216

infect each other as well as us humans, of course. The Happy Cats, for instance, are carrion eaters. They are not big enough to kill anything themselves. But by rendering their victims carelessly blissful, they insure that some other predator will bring them down, whereupon the Happy Cats will enjoy a feast."

"Wow . . . Fantabulous. Couldn't be more clever." I wished Groo would shut up. I really wanted to watch the progress of this shadow as the sun shifted. But he kept on yapping.

"As intelligence spread among our simian ancestors, we humans gradually lost our own meme-infecting capabilities. It became more advantageous for us to rely on animals as our source of various memes, utilizing them as tools and weapons . . . "

At this point I tuned Groo out completely.

I had never seen such a fascinating shadow . . .

101.
No Brain, No Pain

THE NEXT THING I consciously knew was that someone was shaking me. Reluctantly, I pulled my attention away from the infinitely intriguing shadow and looked up.

Moonchild stood there, her lank hair disarrayed, her face tear-streaked.

"Paul, look at you! You're all sunburned!"

When she said it, I could sense the burn tight across my face. Monitoring the shadow, I had been moving constantly to face the sun, garnering a huge quantity of solar rays on my mug. What the hell, though—it felt *great*!

Moon reached down to shake me some more. I smiled, enjoying the way my brain and teeth were rattling around. "Paul, you've got to get us out of here before anything else bad happens! You're a mess and so is Digger! If anything happens to me, we'll be done for! And you're the only one who can do it! Use the Yo-yo! Please!"

I regarded the Yo-yo which my Badfinger hand had been clutching so reliably through all these universes. What utility did it have any longer? This was my final stop, a perfect world . . .

A nagging voice deep inside me was trying to pipe up with some doubts. But they were insignificant compared to the happiness I felt. Still, it wouldn't hurt to humor Moonchild a little, help her to fit into this Utopia.

"You're worried about our son, aren't you? What's he doing? Did he survive the lizard bite? I'm sure he's fine. Let's go see him."

I stood. Moonchild said, "All right, that's more like the old Paul. Follow me."

We moved across the village. A question occurred to me. "How did we get to this lovely spot, Moon?"

"After the Happy Cat bit you and you passed out, Digger and I had to carry you down that path. We had to run, because animals were after us all the time. They're almost like rabid creatures back home. Their first impulse is to bite without warning, to pass on their memes. Luckily, the village wasn't far away. We banged on the gate, and the Dawks let us in."

"Aren't they just *wonderful*?" I said. "That Groo seemed so smart!"

Moon frowned. "I guess they're okay. I don't know how smart they actually are. I think they have a different kind of intelligence than us. They'd pretty much *have* to, really, given their evolutionary history. Sometimes it seems almost as if—as if they're simply vessels for ideas imported from elsewhere. Almost like voudoun horses ridden by their loas."

I clucked my tongue admiringly. "Boy, you sure can talk swell since you got educated, Moon."

102.
Son of the Jesus Lizard

THERE WAS A crowd arrayed in a semicircle outside the hut where I had first woken up. Seated in the dust, they looked up with interest at the standing Digger at their center. Stragglers on the edges of the circle continued to squash intrusive bugs and such instinctively.

Digger was practically radiant. An otherworldly fervor shone from his CA eyes. Holding his tall staff, he looked positively Biblical. It was enough to make a father proud.

When we got to the edge of the listeners, I could see that Digger was actually levitating, the soles of his feet a good three inches off the packed soil.

"That's my boy," I announced to one and all.

"Shhh!" said Moon. "Listen to him!"

"—all your possessions. Cast aside your earthly encumbrances, leave your families, and follow me! The way of the Lord is not easy, but it is the only true path. If you would know perfect rest and peace in the next life, you must be prepared to face turmoil and hardship and contumely in this one. But be not afraid, the Lord will protect us in our trials—"

Groo had come up beside us. Now he spoke.

"The Messiah Lizard, which your wife has dubbed the 'Jesus Lizard,' seldom produces such a vibrant case among us as it has with your son. I can't actually recall the last time we had a Messiah here. It always provides a diverting show when it happens, but I'm afraid it introduces too much disruption into the important daily routines of the village. I fear we're going to have to ask the three of you to leave now."

"No, you can't kick us out into that jungle!" Moon protested. "There must be some way you can help us...?"

"Well, we could see what Repl, our Bitesman, has to say about the possibility of curing your son. Although I must warn you that the Messiah meme is a particularly difficult one to eradicate . . . "

"Your Bitesman?" Moon said. "Who's he?"

"Our resident expert in implanting, layering, supplementing and counteracting memes. I would have brought you to him sooner, but your alien natures made me doubt that he would be of much use."

Moon paused, then said to Groo, "Let's leave Digger alone for now. Can we do that while we see about fixing up Paul? If we get *him* back to normal again, we'll be able to leave on our own terms."

"Hmmm, the Happy Cat meme is considerably easier to deal with than the Messiah one . . . Very well, let's go see old Repl."

103.
The Bitesman Smitten

WE CROSSED THE village to a hut that stood a bit apart from the others, wearing an air of isolation. The door was formed by a bead curtain. Groo rattled the beads politely and called out, "Honored Bitesman, may we enter?"

From within a high, creaky, cracked voice called out, "Enter, enter! But watch carefully where you tread! Some of my precious hypodermics have gotten loose!"

"Step gently," advised Groo.

Moonchild wore a wary look. I couldn't figure out why. Everything was going *most excellently*! This was super, to be meeting some new wonderful person. And what a lovely dim and musty hut he lived in, so easy on the eyes and piquant to the nose! There were shelves full of bamboo cages, and in the cages were some sort of fluffy-wuffy bunny rabbits. And there was a deep pit in the floor and it was full of beautiful, squirming, writhing snakes. Wow, how elegantly they coiled and squirmed all over themselves. It was a little like watching the substance of the Monobloc bubble and pullulate . . .

A loose snake slithered across the dirt floor a few inches from Moon's feet. She squeaked and jumped back.

"Hee, hee, hee!" laughed Repl, and the sound let me place him where he was sitting in the gloom.

Repl was *beautiful*. He looked like the most withered, emaciated Indian fakir you would ever want to see. Matted hair down to his waist, arms like sticks, knobby joints, crusty dirty feet.

Those *feet*! I just wanted to grok them in their unique complexity.

So I threw myself down on the floor in order to get a better view of them.

What tremendous pleasures this world provided!

Repl tittered again. "Hee, hee, hee, there's no need to worship me, my boy—but I appreciate it!"

104

Snaps and Snails and Puppy Dog Tails

MOONCHILD HASTENED TO lift me up, while Groo made the introductions.

"Honored Bitesman, allow me to introduce our two guests. The woman is named Moonchild, and is currently memeless. Her mate is named Paul, and is hosting but a single meme, that of the Happy Cats. Their son, whom we left preaching elsewhere, has adopted the Messiah meme."

"The woman is remiss," Repl wheezed, "but the men have made a fine start, a fine start! It's been much too long since we had a Messiah! I expect there'll be a stoning soon! Don't forget to summon me for it!"

"Stoning!" exclaimed Moonchild. "There's not going to be any stoning!"

"Tsk, tsk. What a contrary, meme-deprived wench! I assume you've brought her here for an appropriate injection. Now, let me see, I have a very potent 'Housework Is Next to Godliness' hypo here that should do the trick . . . "

Moon stamped her foot, and another snake scooted away into the gloom. "No! Tell him, Groo! We want Paul's Happy Cat meme removed. Make him like he was!"

"Exactly how *was* he?" inquired Groo.

Moonchild searched for words carefully, then began to describe me as if I were some kind of complex perfume.

"Well, he was cynical. That was the main component, I believe. A regular sourpuss. There were mixed astringent tones of frustration, disappointment and disgust. Oh, yes, strong grace notes of sarcasm and disbelief, selfishness and greed, topped with a waft of narcissism . . . "

Repl stroked his stubbled chin. "And this is the personality you want back in place of the benign, complacent, carefree Happy Cat host who stands before us? The original sounds awful!"

Moonchild looked at me as if expecting me to object to the characterization of my old self. But why should I? All the charges she had leveled against me were true, but meant nothing in comparison with the absorbing wonders spread out before me.

"Well, he *was* kind of *awful*. But he was also lovable, in his own odd way. Once in a while he would actually do something nice for someone. He was pretty brave and persistent, almost to the point of foolhardiness in fact. And he was a dreamer. He always kept going toward his goal, despite setbacks and defeats. Plus, he's the father of my child."

Repl shook his head in disbelief. "Pah! Women! I shall never understand them! Even when I tried the Goddess meme I failed to gain any clear notion of what drives them . . . Oh, well, the mix of traits you describe is actually fairly common. I think I can accommodate you. Step this way . . . "

105.
Bite Me Healthy!

REPL GOT UP surprisingly gracefully for such a darling rusty old wreck and moved off to the snake pit. I was the only one to follow him. I watched over his shoulder as he peered and poked with impunity among the snakes within.

"These rascals can tell I'm already carrying their memes. Smell or taste or some other strange sense, who knows! Anyhow, they won't bite someone who's already had a jab! No sense shooting your wad on an old infected cow like me! Hee, hee, hee!"

"Wow, Mister Bitesman, you mean to say that you've been bitten by all these great snakes? How lucky!"

"That's right, boy! I carry more memes than any other Dawk, and proud of it! My head's filled to bursting with all kinds of crazy ideas, half of 'em contradictory of t'other half! It's an honor and a privilege to experiment with all these memes, combining and recombining 'em for the benefit of the tribe. Why, I was the one who came up with Fence Building! Did you know that?"

"No, sir. I'm *honored*, though, to be here . . . "

Repl lunged like one of his own snakes. "Aha! Gotcha! We'll start with Cynicism, just like the little lady described."

Clutching a mottled serpent, Repl advanced to the caged bunnies and took one out. Then, like any proud and lonely professional presented with a rare audience, he began to lecture us.

"These bunnies here are specially bred to have no contagious memes of their own. Unique critters. They don't bite, so whatever goes into 'em stays there. In other words, they're perfect for mixing new doses. Retorts, alembics, crucibles, call 'em what you will. Unfortunately, each fluffy's good for only a single use. Kinda wears 'em out to mess with 'em this way . . . "

So saying, Repl caused the Cynical Snake to plunge its fangs into the Mixing Bunny, which jerked in reaction.

Holding the Mixing Bunny by its scruff, Repl tossed the first snake back into the pit and began to search for another. He continued to talk all the while.

"These snakes themselves are another cultivated species with special talents. They can suck memes outa other kinds of animals and store 'em! Use 'em later as they want. Perfect storage devices! Now, lemme see what we got here . . . Uhum, ah, yes indeed . . . "

Plucking one snake after another from the pit, Repl made them inject their contents into the hapless Mixing Bunny. After about a dozen strikes, the bunny was limp as a rag yet still alive, though just barely.

"Okay, I think that about does it. Now we need an empty hypo."

Repl found a loose snake hiding under a wicker basket. When this one planted its fangs into the bunny it held on longer, making convulsive sucking movements.

Repl disengaged the living hypo. "Okay, it's full. Now, lower those trousers, boy. This shot might disorient you for a little, but it won't knock you out like the raw stuff from wild animals. Just another tribute to my talents, hee, hee, hee."

"Gee, this is *fun*," I said, dropping my pants, bending over and presenting my rear.

The fangs went in like red-hot needles.

106.
Too Many Memes Spoil the Skull Soup

ALL MY MUSCLES stiffened and I shot forward, plowing my face into the dirt of the hut's floor. I could have sworn that a halo of little stars, asteroids, comets, exclamation points, asterisks, whirlwinds and tweety-birds sprang into existence and swirled about my head. Moonchild gasped and moved toward me, but was restrained by Repl and Groo.

"No, no, sweetie, he'll be all right! Just let the memes integrate themselves and settle in!"

Some time passed during which my brain felt like a pachinko machine, little metal ball-bearings of cognition rattling down neural chutes and ladders. Eventually, I felt well enough to get up under my own power.

My pants were still around my ankles, and I began to pull them up without saying anything.

"Paul?" said Moon hesitantly. "Are you— Are you okay?"

I glared at the witch. "You enjoyed that, didn't you? Admit it. Go ahead, tell me the truth! You hate me, and were just waiting for a chance to get back at me!"

"No, Paul! Of course not! I don't hate you! Not at all! I was just trying to help you . . . "

I turned to the two natives. "And you two sadists! What's in it for you? Did she promise to shack up with one of you in exchange for my humiliation? Or maybe with both!"

Repl cupped his chin musingly. "No, no, we failed to make any such bargains. Now that you point it out, however, I see it was a lamentable oversight on my part . . . "

Moonchild placed a hand on my shoulder and I jerked away. "Don't touch me!"

"Paul, please! Pay attention! It doesn't really matter what you think my motives were—we have to get out of this world! Use your Yo-yo now! Please!"

I narrowed my eyes to slits. "You'd *like* me to do that, wouldn't you? Fall right into your *trap*! Well, what kind of fool do you take me for!"

Moon accosted Repl. "What else did you put in that shot besides Cynicism?"

"Well, let me see. Most of the other memes you mentioned. Plus an eensy-weensy splash of Paranoia. It seemed in keeping with the rest . . . "

"Oh, no! Can you counteract it? Please, it's vital that he listen to reason and recognize his friends!"

Repl huffed and puffed. "Very well. Let me start mixing. Occam's Razor is usually good against Paranoia. Some Empathy couldn't hurt either . . . "

Moon snapped her fingers eureka-fashion. "And add some Nostalgia, too. I just realized that Paul was very nostalgic for his youth. In fact, that's how we first met."

"Very touching, I'm sure," said Repl dryly, digging among the snakes.

107.
Screaming Meme-ies

THE SECOND MIXING Bunny hung like a deflated furry balloon after being emptied of its contents. Now Repl approached me with the living hypo.

"Hey, just one minute there, Buster! You don't seriously think I'm gonna let you jab me with that thing, do you? It's probably lethal!"

I began to back away, toward the beaded doorway.

But Moon and Groo were blocking my path.

"Grab him!" yelled Moon.

I ducked, feinted, but they had me!

"Traitors! Quislings! Assassins! Help! Murder! Ides of March!"

"Oh, shut up, Paul," said Moon wearily. "Repl, stick him, please!"

The second shot went into my unperforated buttock, and I galvanically ate more dirt.

As I lay there with my crazed spinning cash-register,

slot-machine, abacus, chaser-light brain, a swelling hullabaloo began to intrude on my ears. At first I thought it was part of the effects of the shot. But then the others seemed to notice it too.

"What's that?" asked Moon.

"Oh, it's probably just the usual thing," replied Groo. "The Messiah has said something that upset the crowd, and now they're going to ensure his martyrdom. Happens every time."

"Oh no! Digger, Digger, here comes Mama to save you!"

Moon ran off then. I heard Repl say, "Quickly, or we'll miss the fun!" Then he and Groo left too.

108.
Love Bites

AFTER A SHORT while, I felt capable of movement. Once again I lifted myself painfully off the ground and refastened my pants. Then I went to join the others.

Did I feel "normal?" How was I to tell with any certainty?

The world looked neither glowing nor gloomy, neither mellow nor menacing. I didn't hate Moonchild or suspect her of plotting against me. But I wasn't too crazy about what she had done, either. Although I supposed it had been the only way out. But the way she had left me lying there in the dirt as soon as Digger got into some little fix kinda rankled too.

But on the whole, I guessed I was my old self.

Except for one urge. An urge I suppose I had always had, but never to this degree.

An overwhelming urge I intended to cater to as soon as I found out what was happening with Digger and Moon.

Back at the hut where Digger had been preaching, what seemed like the entire population of the village was gathered, rowdy and roisterous. The ubiquitous staves were being thrust inward, toward the nucleus of the knot, which I assumed was Digger. On the periphery of the attackers, Moon was futilely hammering at the backs of the natives, trying to force her way in.

I came up to her and tapped her on the shoulder. She whirled.

"Paul, help me! They're killing him! Our son!"

"Moon. You'll never reach him that way. But it doesn't matter."

"Doesn't matter! Are you insane!"

"Moon. Look at the stockade."

She looked behind her and saw what I had seen on my way over from Repl's.

Left unguarded in the excitement, the fence was swarming with invading creatures of all stripes, eager to infect the unwary humans. Already the advance scouts of the invading herd were scurrying and creeping through the settlement.

Moon's new intellect allowed her to react quickly. "Dawks, Dawks! Invasion, invasion! Protect your homes!"

That shout did the trick. They must have all had a strong Domestic Defense meme in them. Quick as a blink, the mob dispersed to repel the invaders.

We hastened to our son where he lay sprawled in the dust, eyes closed.

Moon picked up Digger's head and cradled it in her lap.

"Digger, Digger, talk to me!"

Digger opened his blackening eyes. "It was only my first preaching gig, Mom. I know I'll do better next time . . . "

I had been examining our son's body and now reported, "Seems like just bruises and contusions. Nothing broken that I can see. How do you feel, boy?"

Forcing himself painfully into a sitting position, Digger said, "The Lord will provide for my full recovery."

Moon said, "Oh, hell, I forgot about the minor detail of his infection."

When we were all standing, I said, "I'm taking us out of here now."

"Where to?" asked Moon.

"You'll see," I said cryptically.

"I shall be able to do the Lord's work anyplace," Digger cheerfully chimed in.

Just as I was about to employ the Cosmic Duncan, Groo approached. I waited to hear what he had to say.

227

"You see why we cannot harbor a Messiah here. We barely survived this disruption. We shall be mopping up stray intruders for days yet. So, although there are no hard feelings, I shall be overjoyed to see you depart."

"We're off—" I said.

Then Moon screamed!

Groo's staff flashed out, knocking a fanged warty frog off Moon's ankle and then impaling it. Meanwhile, Moon had collapsed from the raw meme-venom.

The leader of the Dawks bent to examine the dead creature. Standing, he announced its breed.

"A Horny Toad."

FACES OF
THE TENTH PAIR

109.
The Yo-yo Delivers

IT'S FUNNY HOW you can just *know* something's gonna turn out perfect. Sometimes an absolute instinctive certainty will possess you. Usually it's an incontrovertible sinking feeling that everything is irretrievably, perfectly *fucked*. I sure enough had had that feeling plenty of times in my life. In fact, this depressing sentiment had opened my adventures. But sometimes, once in a great while, maybe only once in a lifetime, if you're lucky or blessed or gifted enough, you get to experience the opposite: the conviction that you've made all the right moves, that the universe and the gods are on your side, and that nothing can now obstruct you from the complete achievement of your goals, but rather that everything animate and inanimate is hastening you toward your dreams.

As soon as we materialized in the new universe, I got that feeling.

I knew from the bottom of my soles to the top of my cowlick that this transition had brought me to the one destination out of an infinite number of potential ones that matched perfectly my mental stipulations. Finally, the Yo-yo had fulfilled a request without screwing up.

Deliberately, I refrained from looking around me too closely. I wanted to savor this rare triumph.

Instead, I focused on Moonchild and Digger.

Moon was still stretched out flat and oblivious as a result of the

Horny Toad bite. Now, their recent roles of victim and nurse reversed, Digger was cradling his *Mom's* head in *his* lap.

"Can you take care of her, son?"

"Sure, Pop! That's what I'm here for, to offer comfort and a safe harbor for all uneasy souls."

Digger's words and tone confirmed what my own attitude had already told me: that the memes from the world of the Dawks still flowed in our veins, not sufficiently inconsistent with the parameters of this new universe to have been instantly evaporated upon arrival. (And I wondered if this stipulation to retain the memes hadn't been subliminally present in the formulation of my wishes . . .)

"Um, okay. But if that Horny Toad bite does what I suspect it might do, she's going to be a handful when she wakes up. Still think you can handle her by yourself, while I scout around a bit?"

"I am at one with all mortals, whatever their condition," said Digger.

"Great. That must feel nice," I said, already putting Digger and Moon out of my mind.

I looked up then, and saw more of our new environment.

I stood behind an unending stage flat: an enormous seamless sheet of canvas easily a hundred yards tall and stretching endlessly to left and right. Braced by an intricate scaffolding of plywood struts, it rippled slightly in the wind.

Part of the scaffolding near me consisted of a doorframe with a door set flush with the canvas scrim, obviously placed so as to blend with whatever painted scenery was on the other side.

"Take good care of your Mom now, Digger. I'll see you later. Maybe."

I stepped away from them then, not looking back.

At the door, I could see from its hinges that it opened inward.

I grasped the handle, twisted it, pulled the door toward me, and stepped through to the other side, leaving the backstage area behind.

110.
Boom! Boom! Boomtown!

EVERYTHING WAS BLACK and white on the other side.

Not just the color scheme of the painted scrim, but the skin of the people there and the depths of the sky and the textured ground. And the effect was due not to paint or makeup or shadows or filtered light. The lack of color seemed integral to the nature of this universe (or perhaps a limitation of my new eyes), at least on this side of the scrim, where everything was limned in a zillion shades of grey. And grainy, somehow. Everything was low-resolution, flickering, wracked at intervals by waves of jumpy distortion.

I looked down at my own non-Badfinger hand, and saw that I too was now a black-and-white creature.

But I didn't care one bit.

Because now I was home.

In simple wonderment, I looked behind me at the painted facade of the scrim from which I had emerged.

It depicted a Wild West street scene, shops and saloons and illusionary hitching posts and "board" sidewalks. I had exited from the TRADING POST door, flanked by its windows full of painted merchandise.

The three-dimensional street itself was actual monochrome dirt, about twenty feet across. The opposite side of this narrow channel was formed by a second painted backdrop featuring more stores and bars.

Down the street a ways was a group of people. They sat on a bleacher-type arrangement of wooden seats in the middle of the street, split by an aisle. The focus of the seats was an old-fashioned home movie screen standing on its extendable metal tripod. The gap between the two halves of the bleachers allowed an eight-millimeter projector to point unobstructed at the screen.

I noticed suddenly that all the occupants of the bleachers were kids. Preadolescents dressed in flannel-lined jeans and coonskin caps and checkered gingham dresses and ankle sox. Funny, when I first observed them they had looked like my peers for a moment. Wait a

233

minute, they were my peers! What *had* I been thinking . . .

There were two adults among the kids, and now they spotted me. One of them came over.

He was a tall, trim, cleanshaven cowboy, twin six-shooters strapped to his lean hips, hat cocked at a jaunty angle, bandanna insouciantly tied around his neck. He wore a big, familiar welcoming smile. When he reached me he thrust out his hand in greeting and exclaimed, "Welcome to Boomtown, pardner! You made it just in time. We're fixin' to show some rip-roarin' cartoons. Mosey over and set a spell with us . . . "

I shook his hand in awe. "Rex. Rex Trailer. It's really you. And this is really Boomtown. Wow!"

Now the second man had ambled up. He was a stereotypical Mexican: bandito getup, serape, droopy mustachios.

"Pancho," said Rex, "what've you got for our new friend?"

"I theenk I geeve heem these pistols, if he want them, Rex."

Pancho held out a gunbelt with twin holstered Colts. I took it and strapped it on. Then I started to cry out of sheer joy.

Rex patted me manfully on the back. "Buck up, pardner, no reason to open up the floodgates. We've got a rip-snortin', bronco-buckin', bear-wrasslin' lineup of pure one hundred percent fun in store for you. Ain't nothin' there to cry over, is there?"

I wiped my eyes. "No, sir. I guess not . . . "

"Good! Then let's go join your new pals!"

So we moseyed over and, when I was sitting on the bleachers with the other kids, the stagelights went down on the whole universe and the projector came on.

We all began to scream and shout like a chorus of maniacs.

111.
Cartoonus Interruptus

I COULDN'T SAY how long that projector ran. It seemed like some durationless eternity, more removed from the strictures of passing time than the Monobloc itself. All I know is that I watched—with a squealing, insensate pleasure shared by all the other kids—at least the following number of features:

Six *Popeyes*.

Five *Felix the Cats*.

Fifty *Three Stooges*.

Two dozen *Little Rascals*.

Fifteen *Laurel and Hardys*.

Twenty *Looney Tunes*.

Eight *Tom and Jerrys*.

Thirty-two *Rocky and Bullwinkles*.

About a month's worth of five different cliffhanger serials.

I was rocking back and forth hysterically on my seat, drenched in sweat. My sides felt like they had been beaten with a leather strop from laughing so hard. My feet were sore from stamping them, my hands from clapping. My throat felt like it had been swabbed with a porcupine.

Just as the screen went blank between the last feature and the next, all us kids fell silent for a moment.

Someone was calling my name.

"Paul! Paul! Where the hell are you?"

The lights went up (where or what constituted the sun in this continuum? I wondered momentarily) and Rex Trailer stood in front of the screen.

"Seems we got a noisy kye-yoot amongst us, boys and girls, who's stoppin' our show. Anybody care to own up to bein' the object of this unseemly disturbance so's we can get back to our fun?"

Crunching gravel made us all turn.

Digger and Moonchild were approaching.

I stuck my hand up and Rex acknowledged it.

"Um, Rex, they're some friends of mine . . ."

"Well, pardner, mosey over and have a little talk with them and tell them kindly like to put a lid on the hollerin'."

I stood up and went shamefacedly to meet Digger and Moonchild.

Seeing me, Moonchild sprinted for me. Then she was wrapping herself around me, hugging and squeezing and slobbering kisses all over my face. I even felt her hands grabbing my bum and her "down there" pushing into mine!

"Oh, Paul, I'm so glad you're safe! I was worried, I missed you, I *need* you!"

I pushed her off and wiped my face. "Yuck! Cooties! What the heck are you up to, Moon? Can't you see we're all busy?"

She looked perplexed. "Busy? Can't it wait? We need to find a little place where we can be *alone*, Paul." She lazily drew a fingertip up and down my shirtfront. "I'm *ready* now, you see. Isn't it great? We can have a *nice* time together, *bunkmate*, with that big six-shooter of yours, if you get my drift . . . "

I stepped back in confusion. "No, I don't know what you're talking about. Can't you just leave me alone? I want to watch more cartoons—"

Now Rex came over. "Need a hand, son?"

Moonchild ran her eyes up and down Rex's handsome form. She sidled up to him and laid both palms flat on his chest.

"Polish your badge, sheriff?"

112.
Paul's Bigtop Debut

WHILE MOONCHILD WAS making googly-eyes at Rex, I took the opportunity to skip out on the both of them, slipping through and past the crowd of kids and heading further down the wide street bordered by its canvas walls.

That stinky Moon had ruined everything! Her and her icky girly stuff! Why couldn't she leave a guy in peace, or at least act decent? There was so much fun to be had here, in the realm of my childhood, and she was going to spoil it all! That was why I had to get away from her. I didn't care if I never saw her again!

I began to trot down the street. If only I had been wearing my canvas PF Flyers instead of these funny-looking plastic sneakers, I could have really made some speed! But even with that handicap, I was still able to put Boomtown quickly behind me.

The canvas walls had gone stark white here, as if marking a boundary zone. There were no people or props in this empty land.

But up ahead a ways I could see something . . .

The dirt underfoot began to be mixed with sawdust. Soon the sawdust completely covered the street. On the walls, scenery appeared: cages with painted lions, trapeze artists high above, bareback riders and penny-pitch booths. A regular midway blossomed the further I went.

Up ahead, I could see that the street was occupied by the multiple rings of a circus, the wide low hurdles supporting a mob of seated kids. Their shouts and cries of glee spurred me on. I hoped I would get there before the show started!

Huffing and puffing, I made a grand entrance, leaping right over the mass of seated kids, skidding to a messy stop in the middle of the ring. I dropped my hands to my knees and tried to get my breath back. When I looked up at last, he was standing there.

"Bozo!" I yelled. "Bozo the Clown!"

113.
The Nose Knows

BOZO GAVE HIS crazy laugh. "Hyuck-hyuck-hyuck! The one and only! And I'll sue the baggy pants off anyone who claims otherwise!"

"Oh, I'd never say you weren't the one and only, Bozo . . . "

Bozo squeaked his nose. "I 'nose' you wouldn't, Paul, because you're a good boy! Now, why don't you join the others there, so we can get on with the show?"

I went and found an empty spot on the broad ringside curbing and ended up sitting so low that my knees were up around my ears. I would have been uncomfortable if I was still the old overweight Paul. But my conditioning in the Sheldrake world had made me flexible enough not to mind.

Now the fun began!

A calliope started playing a tune that might accompany a demented carousel. Then some pretty ladies dressed in spangled tights came out pushing a cart that held a cotton-candy machine. They gave all the kids a big sticky cone apiece. I wished this world had been in color so I could have enjoyed the pinkness of the fluff. Then lots of midgets appeared. They carried trays slung around their necks and the trays held candy-apples, their stick handles pointed upward, the flattened tops surrounded by a candy puddle. We all got one. Then came some clowns (inferior, of course, to the glorious Bozo, with his mile-high hair and enormous shoes and maniacal makeup). These newcomers hefted in teetering towers a zillion boxes of Cracker Jacks! Adroitly, one by one, the clown servants managed to dislodge the topmost box individually so that each kid could catch his.

Clutching my cotton candy in one hand, holding my enameled candy-apple between my teeth, I managed to get my box open. The prize inside was a flip book. I stuck my cotton-candy under my arm and started to flip the pages. They showed a giant man against a background of stars leaping from one world to another like they were stepping stones. Cool!

The faces of all the kids were smeared and messy, including mine. We were pelting each other with Cracker Jacks, and the music was going crazy! Just when we were ready to explode, Bozo chopped his hand down and the music ceased.

"Is everybody happy?" he asked.

We roared our wordless approval till our throats ached.

"All right! We're going to have a little contest now, with a prize for the winner. Who wants to try?"

All the sticky hands shot up, mine too. Bozo began to select the contestants. "You and you and you and you—"

I was picked, I was picked! Pretty circus ladies came to hold my treats and gave me a Wetnap to wash up with. Hurriedly I did, then rushed into the center of the ring.

A game booth had been wheeled in. Up front were mounted four toy rifles. Inside were the bas-relief faces of four clowns with open mouths. Deflated balloons drooped down from their foreheads.

"Okay, kids! You know what to do! Take your places!"

I squatted behind a rifle (the others were standing) and sighted on the appropriate clown's mouth. The freckle-faced boy next to me jabbed an elbow into my ribs. I stuck my tongue out at him and concentrated on the target.

"On your mark, get set—go!"

Water sprayed from the rifles and the balloons began to inflate.

I was winning, I was winning!

Then someone gave me a wedgie! Jerked my shorts right up into my crack! The stream from my rifle went wild and the balloon of the kid who had jabbed me suddenly shot ahead in size and burst first!

Oh, I was steaming mad! I wanted to cry and punch someone at the same time. I whirled around to confront my tormentor.

It was that rotten old Moonchild!

114.
Champagne Music from the Peanut Gallery

"GEEZUS-BEEZUS, MOONIE! Are you nuts!" I yelled. "Look what you made me lose!"

Bozo was presenting the prize to the winner: a gleaming Raleigh bike, with plastic pennants dangling from the handlebars, which also bore a mechanical chime and a battery-powered lamp.

Moonchild licked her lips like they were chapped or something. "Oh, I'm *so* sorry, Paul. Here, let me help you fix things . . . "

Then she stuck her hands down the back of my pants and started fooling with my underwear!

"Get the heck outa there!" I wriggled free, blushing. "Everybody's looking, for Pete's sake . . . "

"Let them," said Moonchild. "It makes it *nastier*—"

I tried to reason with her. "Listen, Moon, I thought you were a brainiac now, a regular Mister Peabody. Why don't you sit down in the corner with a pencil and paper and amuse yourself by figuring some geometry or something?"

She started squeezing one of my pumped-up biceps with both hands. "If you've got the pencil, big boy, I've got the sharpener . . . "

I shook her off. Then something caught my eye. It was our son,

Digger. In the short time since we had left the Sheldrake world, his beard had filled in and his hair had grown longer. He really looked like a regular Warren Stallman Jesus now. The fact that he was surrounded by rapt children, holding some on his lap while he preached to them, only added to the iconography.

Now Bozo seemed to notice that competition was throwing his show off course. He started to yell at Digger.

"Hey, buddy, what's the big idea? Just 'cause you see a tent don't mean you gotta stage a revival meeting!"

Moonchild seemed torn between standing up for Digger and bothering me. Finally, the impulse to defend our son won out. She went right up to Bozo and stood on his oversized shoes so he couldn't ignore her.

"Oh, Mister Clown! I've always wanted to meet you! I think men in rubber baldy caps are just the sexiest!"

"Well, sister, you're not alone . . . "

Holy cats! A guy might as well just give up trying to have any innocent fun around here!

I hit the road again.

When the Bigtop was long out of sight, I sat down wearily against a blank canvas wall. I closed my eyes and tried to figure out where to go next.

"What's the matter, Paul? Things got you down?"

I opened my eyes. It was Howdy Doody. He was alone, no Cowboy Bob in sight.

Howdy's strings, I saw, went up, up, up, right to the cloud-shrouded top of the canvas scrim.

"Well, yes, Howdy, a little, I guess . . . "

"Maybe hearing a cheerful song would brighten up your day. It always does for me!"

"Sure, why not...?"

Howdy's eyelids clacked down and he lifted his hand to his chin, obviously cogitating. Then he said, "How about this little tune?" The puppet started humming something vaguely familiar. "It's from one of my favorite movies!"

"Aren't you gonna sing it?"

Howdy chuckled sheepishly. "Gawsh, no! We'll get the professionals to do it! Oh, Maestro!"

Across the street a portion of the canvas wall rolled up, to reveal a room formed by more canvas. A full orchestra was seated there, and in front of the players stood Lawrence Welk.

"A-one, and a-two and a-three!"

The band began to play. I recognized the tune: *When You Wish Upon A Star*, Jiminy Cricket's themesong.

And then the Lennon Sisters strolled gaily out, Kathy, Peggy, Deedee and Janet. They began to sing.

"When you wish upon a star, makes no difference who you are—"

I found myself singing along. My spirits began to lift. Soon I was up and waltzing with the Lennons. Howdy too was prancing woodenly around, though he couldn't of course move away from the wall where his strings tethered him. Mister Welk kept the band vamping after the words ran out, so we could dance till we were too tired to dance anymore.

When the song finally ended, I was ready to move on.

"Thank you! Thank you, everyone!" I called.

"Atsa my boy!"

115.
Beneath the Ears

I COULD HEAR the music before I saw the clubhouse.

"Em-Eye-Cee, Kay-Ee-Why, Em-Oh-You-Ess-Ee!"

I started to run again. This was my favorite hour of the day!

The Mouseketeers were just wrapping up the theme when I arrived. With big grins they all faced in my direction like they had been waiting for me. I got a little nervous and slowed down.

"C'mon, Paul!" encouraged Bobby. "We've got a swell time planned for you!"

I walked shyly up to the group. From behind his back, Bobby whipped out—a pair of Mouse ears! He clapped them to my head, and all my trepidation disappeared.

"Paul, I want you to meet someone special. She's going to be your pal this afternoon."

Out from among the Mouseketeers stepped Annette. Her smile was the brightest thing I have ever seen. Her sweater bulged demurely but suggestively just like I remembered.

"Annette. It's really Annette! Holy moly! Why, I just never thought I'd ever, ever get to meet you! I've got your picture hanging up on my bedroom wall back home—"

"That's so sweet, Paul. Maybe someday I'll get to autograph it for you. Would you like that?"

"Would I *like* that? Gee *willikers*, who wouldn't?"

Annette held out her hand and I took it. She said, "I bet you like comic books, don't you, Paul?"

"Yeah!"

"Well, I've got a big stack of all the latest ones, and a plate full of Oreos and some milk. Would you like to spend some time with me reading them?"

"Lead me to 'em!"

Annette took me to a big horsehair-covered sofa. We kicked our shoes off and sprawled out—not too close to each other, like Moonchild would've done. What a great girl Annette was! I stuffed about six Oreos in my mouth and opened up the latest *Detective Comics*.

"Twoface *and* the Riddler! Wow!"

Boy oh boy, this was *living*!

116.
Faster, Betty and Veronica! Kill! Kill!

THERE WAS SOME kind of commotion going on that made me look up from my one-hundredth comic: Archie and the gang visiting Washington, DC, with Jughead making Mister Weatherbee's four sparse hairs levitate off his pate in frustration.

Digger was surrounded by the laughing Mouseketeers. They were watching as, instead of his usual Imitation of Christ, he performed some kind of Imitation of Goofy, limbs flailing around, torso whipping up and down from the waist, all the while uttering incoherent yelps and calls for help.

A momentary gap in the crowd let me see that someone had fastened rollerskates to my son's willing feet. That was one skill I hadn't fed Digger through the morphic fields. Still, I was kind of irritated that the superb physical heritage I *had* given him wasn't proving sufficient to cope with this novel form of exercise. I guessed it just went to show that no matter how much you tried to do for your kids there were just some things they had to learn on their own.

Or maybe: once a klutz, always a klutz.

Reluctantly I was getting up off the couch to go help Digger when a shriek from Annette stopped me.

Annette was holding her cheek, which was flushing a darker grey than the rest of her skin. Moonchild stood there flexing her fingers, a fierce look on her face.

"That'll teach you to try and steal my man, you goody-goody bitch! I know all your tricks from watching those beach movies of yours!"

"I—I don't know what you're talking about," sobbed Annette. "We were just sharing some comics and cookies and milk—"

"Listen, honey—the only cookies this boy is gonna eat are mine!"

Annette began backing away. "You—you're mental!"

"Oh, yeah? Well, I'm gonna unstuff your wild bikini, babe!"

Moon launched herself through the air and over the couch, bowling Annette to the ground.

They were pretty evenly matched in size and strength.

But Moonchild fought *dirty*.

I made my escape while I could.

117.
In The Pouch

"HOWDY, YOUNG FELLER. Need a hand?"

I must have fallen asleep in the middle of the endless road. Since the world of the Dawks I hadn't gotten much rest. And Oreos and cotton candy weren't the best nourishment either. It felt suddenly as if my life had been reduced to nothing but running. I just wanted a quiet place to settle down and rest. Maybe this man knew of such a place. He looked awfully familiar—

"What's your name?" I asked.

"Why, you must be pretty sleepy not to recognize ol' Mister Green Jeans!"

I shot to my feet. "Mister Green Jeans! Sure, I recognize you! It's just that I'm so used to seeing you standing next to the Captain—"

"Well, Cap's right next door, waiting for you . . . "

"Let's go!"

In next to no time, we were at the Captain's.

With his big-pocketed uniform-like jacket and bowl haircut and mustache, Captain Kangaroo was second only to Santa in joviality. And since I was the only kid on the set, I received the whole sunshine of his love.

"Hello, Paul! We've all been waiting for you so we could read our book for the day. Grandfather Clock says it's way past time. Haven't we been waiting, Mister Moose?"

"We sure have, Captain!"

"Why," the Captain continued, "even bad Bunny Rabbit has been on his best behavior, hoping you'd show up soon."

Ever-silent Bunny Rabbit nodded vigorously.

"He's been so good, in fact, that I think he deserves a carrot—"

As Captain said the word, a box suspended above his head opened up and a zillion ping-pong balls cascaded down onto the hapless Captain. I fell to the ground laughing.

Captain made a resigned face. "Oh, well, I guess I should have expected that . . . Come on now, Paul. Climb up into my lap and we'll have our story."

I got up onto the Captain's welcoming lap. He opened a hardcover illustrated book. Although I couldn't make sense of the words anymore, the pictures were familiar.

"It's *Make Way for Ducklings*!"

"Right you are, young man! Let's begin . . . "

118.
To Do-Bee or Not To Do-Bee

WE MUST HAVE gone through that book a few dozen times. I just couldn't get enough of it. Those wacky wayward ducklings! The happy crowd! That nice policeman!

"Interested in a threesome, guys?"

Who the heck would have the *nerve* to interrupt the Captain but *Moon*! I should have known I couldn't escape her.

"Why don't you leave me *alone*, Moonchild? I've never done anything to you . . . "

"That's the trouble, honey. Don't you know a girl gets kinda squirmy-like if she's left alone too long?"

She wiggled her hips to illustrate what she meant.

I sneered. "What do you have, ants in your pants?"

"What do you have in yours? Nothing?"

"You stink, ratfink!"

"And you've been de-balled!"

Captain set me down. "Here, here, let's not fight. What we all need is a good healthy snack. Let's call the Banana Man!"

On cue a clown emerged. (This world seemed full of clowns, a regular parliament . . .) From a huge pocket he began to pull an endless string of bananas while emitting wordless squeaks of joy.

His chaotic activity was enough to lure Moon. She sashayed up to the Banana Man.

"*Mmmmm*, bananas are my absolute *favorite* fruit! Can I have a *special* one?"

Moon groped the Banana Man in a private place. He gave one loud squeak and then I heard him swallow his whistle.

But you could already color me gone.

The first thing I saw of the next settled area was a large blackboard and several rows of rocking horses with kids upon them. As I got closer, I saw that one horse was empty. And in front of the blackboard stood Miss Bonnie! She was young and had lacquered hair and wore a prim pinafore. I loved her . . .

When the class spotted me, they began to chant.

"Romper, bomper, stomper, do! Tell me, tell me, tell me true . . . "

I raced forward and hopped onto the last empty saddle of Romper Room.

Miss Bonnie smiled at us and began to speak. "Very good, boys and girls. Now, who wants to help Miss Bonnie pass out the scissors and paper and paste, so that we can make something pretty for autumn?"

"I do, I do!" I yelled.

"Not so rough, Paul! That's better. You may come up front now . . . "

I had a little trouble handling the scissors and got paste in my hair. But Miss Bonnie said I did a good job anyhow. Then we had Twinkies and Kool-Aid. Then Miss Bonnie took out her Magic Mirror!

"All right, we're going to see who's a good Do-Bee now—"

But as Miss Bonnie started to peek into the Magic Mirror, she shrieked and dropped it! It landed glass side upward.

And from the reflecting glass a full-sized hand and wrist emerged!

119.
Barbi Brawlers

THE MYSTERIOUS HAND, exhibiting long painted nails, was quickly followed by an arm. Then, most impossibly, by a full-sized shoulder and torso and head and body, all squeezing themselves magically through the small oval.

A large naked lady stood in front of us. She looked very familiar, especially those huge boobies. She bent over, boobies swaying, and reached into the mirror and pulled out her exact twin! Then the first naked lady said, "Where is he?"

The second lady said, "Right there."

And she pointed at me!

"Paul, it's me! Calpurnia!"

"And me, Calypso!"

They started toward me. I was really scared. Miss Bonnie must have sensed I needed help, because she tried to step in.

"Hold on a minute. These children are my charges—"

"Stow it, sister!"

"Yeah! Zip it!"

"That's very disrespectful! What a poor example to set for the children! I'm afraid I'll have to ask you to leave—"

Miss Bonnie laid a hand on the shoulder of one naked lady.

The naked lady whirled around and socked Miss Bonnie in the jaw, sending her flying into the blackboard. The other kids screamed and scattered to the four corners of the world, rocking horses overturning.

Miss Bonnie didn't get up again.

Then the scary ladies were surrounding me!

"Okay, kiddo, it's time."

"We're gonna ream your memes."

They grabbed my metal hand. I could feel the Yo-yo cupped in my closed fist leap and quiver. Then they were inside my head!

"You wipe out the Nostalgia, Cal, and I'll do a general tuneup."

"Gotcha, Cal!"

Within seconds, my brain was rewired.

Back to normal.

Or what passed for that mythical condition.

120.
What the Mirror Showed

WITH RESTORED VISION, I looked around at the devastation.

What a pitiful mess! What a fucking, pitiful limited scenario my quest had brought me to. From the glories of the Monobloc to this: a cardboard kindergarten. From an infinite regress to an infinite recess. And my mental state had been such that it had seemed like paradise.

The Barbi-Twins-embodied Calvinii were smiling proudly.

"We sure made quick work of that little chore."

"When you want results, you send the best operators around."

After my infantile behavior, I was a little sheepish. It was hard to look straight at the Calvinii. Especially since I now had my normal desires back, and they still represented my hottest sexual fantasy.

I tried to stick to a neutral topic. "I take it the Drexleroids sent you . . . ?"

"That's right."

"We're supposed to tell you about your Yo-yo."

"A newly discovered quirk of that mechanism."

"You see—"

At that moment, a man stepped from around the wreckage of the blackboard that covered the unconscious Miss Bonnie.

It was Rod Serling. Suit, tie, world-weary grin.

"Please. Allow *me* to explain. I've been trying to reach this gentleman ever since he arrived. But he was always one step ahead of me."

"Sure, Roddie."

"Go right ahead."

"We'll correct you if you go wrong."

Rod began to spiel. "It's quite simple, actually, Mister Girard. Your Yo-yo does not bring you to pre-existing worlds. It *creates* them!"

"What are you saying? Haven't these worlds all been real, pre-existing spaghetti strands, each one ontologically equivalent to any other? They sure *felt* real enough . . . "

"Oh, they've been real in the simple physical sense. But they never would have existed without your wishing them into being. There are no combinations of natural, undirected quantum branchings that could have brought them about exactly as they were, save for your personal, subliminal intervention.

"What happened, Paul, was this: Every time from the start of your odyssey, as soon as you framed a wish, the Yo-yo sought out an unexploded Monobloc uninhabited by any Calvinii. It laid the template of your wishes over the Monobloc, and then triggered its fiery birth. At that point, the necessary several billion years of time and evolution would pass in an accelerated fashion, all in the microseconds between the formulation of your wish and the actual casting forth of the Yo-yo. When your custom-designed universe was ready, your Yo-yo would deliver you there."

I regarded the Cals. "Is this true?"

"Yes, except for one thing."

"We're not sure about the 'accelerated time' part."

"Yeah. The Yo-yo *might* actually be reaching *back* into the objective, superspace *past* for a suitable Monobloc and letting that universe develop in realtime."

"But aside from that little technicality, he's got it down pat."

"So you see, Mister Girard, your universes have all been highly limited creations whose parameters derived wholly from your mind. Trying to escape yourself, your patterns of cognition and feeling, you were instead getting deeper and deeper into them."

I had never heard anything so depressing. "But Hans told me—"

"Hans don't know shit!"

"He's a complete fuckup!"

"The Drexleroids are infinitely smarter than Hans. And they want you to stop using the Yo-yo."

"All these loopy, shoddy defective universes you've been making offend their esthetic sense."

I gave a deep sigh. "Right. I offend everybody's esthetic sense . . . Well, thanks for straightening me out, Rod."

"My pleasure," said Rod, then walked away.

I turned back to the Calvinii. "Before you tell me what I'm supposed to do next, can I ask you to fix Moonchild and Digger?"

"I'm sorry."

"We can't."

"The only way we can access a human brain is through the Yo-yo."

"And they don't have one."

"That's that then, I suppose. I'll just have to live with a nympho wife and Holy Roller son. But where do the three of us go from here?"

"The Drexleroids want you to use the Yo-yo one last time."

"To go back to your original continuum."

"My original continuum is now several score millennia older than when I left, remember? My Earth fell into the Sun."

"Mentally specify one as similar to where you started from as you can."

"With any luck, the three of you will arrive there."

I sighed again. "Back home. Okay, I suppose if I have to . . . "

"Good!"

"I don't suppose you two will be traveling with us?"

"No."

"Afraid not, honey."

"Superspace is too much fun!"

"Ultra-elastic reality!"

"We're heading back now."

"You'll probably never see us again."

"But as a farewell present—"

"—we've agreed to show you a good time!"

The voluptuous twins pressed up against me and began unbuttoning and unzipping my clothing. I felt a sudden surge of guilt.

"No, no, I appreciate the gesture. Honestly, I do! But I owe something to Moonchild. I have to be faithful—"

"Faithful!"

"Take a look at this!"

One of the Cals picked up the discarded Magic Mirror.

I looked.

It showed a black-and-white orgy.

Moonchild, Rex Trailer, Pancho, Bozo, Bobby the Mouseketeer, the Captain and Mister Green Jeans were all getting it on in a disgusting pile of naked limbs whose center was Moonchild. Even Howdy Doody was there with his pants off and a little wooden pecker showing.

I dropped the Magic Mirror, and let the Calvinii have their way with me.

I felt kinda sad and responsible that Moon had come to this.

But at least I wouldn't have to listen to all that sanctimonious virgin talk anymore.

250

When the three of us were done—and the sex was everything I had ever imagined, the one undisappointing thing that had happened to me on this quest—the Calvinii unsentimentally said goodbye and went back through the Magic Mirror. I got my clothes in order, and then readied myself to employ the Yo-yo.

But not as the Twins had stipulated.

"Take me to Hans," I said.

FACES OF
THE ELEVENTH PAIR

121.
Not Pleased to Meet Myself

A REVELATION HAD dawned on me during sex with the Barbi-embellished Calvinii. I know, I know: it was hard to believe that I had been capable of any kind of coherent thought during that long-anticipated, hyper-stimulating session amid the ruins of Romper Room. (We had used fuzzy naptime blankets and Peter-Rabbit-imprinted pillows as cushionings and props.) Nonetheless, a startling conclusion had welled up within the small part of my brain not devoted to hot carnal pleasure. That cool rational observer part had asserted one thing quite clearly.

I was literally the Calviniis' creator.

By their own admission, *every* universe I had visited *from the start of my travels* had had its germinal seed in my own personal brain, and would not otherwise have existed. That assertion had to include *their original Monobloc*! Even in its unexploded state, it had received its natal imprint from me. True, I had been responsible only for the original patternings of all the worlds I had visited. The ineluctable laws of physics had guided all subsequent development, unattended by me or the Yo-yo.

(But did the ability of my "seed" to arrive at its exactly specified fruition after billions of years of unsupervised development mean that, contrary to the scientific theories of my old era, *all* universes were deterministic in the old-fashioned Newtonian sense, their entire future readably implicit in their origins? What of unpredictable chaos and free will? Didn't they play any part? Or was it perhaps that information theory offered some kind of redundancy or error-correcting mechanisms that could pull a deviant universe back onto its basic course, while still allowing a measure of individual initiative? I had no way of knowing . . .)

Following this logic to its ultimate conclusion, it became obvious to me that every person I had encountered in my cross-dimensional travels had been in some sense a splinter of my own brain, a chip off the old block. The only exception, perhaps, were the Drexleroids, who existed entirely outside or below conventional ten-space timelines. But even about them I couldn't be sure. They *claimed* to live in superspace and to have diverted me in transit between continua, but I couldn't be certain.

Certainly all the rest of the people I had had dealings with—including Moonchild and Digger!—were in some sense untrustworthy or limited. They were unreliable narrators of their own existences, contaminated by the Original Sin of having *me* as their Creator! Oh, sure, they were living, feeling human beings, capable of the full range of thought and emotion, not toys. But why should I rely on advice from any of them, since it was no more inherently insightful than my own thoughts?

The only exception to this maze of mirrors that I could see was Hans.

The Moraveckian cybershrub was the start of this whole Markov Chain. He was the last individual I had met who was extrinsic to myself—and just possibly reliable.

That was why I had to ignore the advice of the Calvinii and seek him out. Following my own wishes had brought me to a dead end. Only Hans would possibly know how I could end my travels.

The only trepidation I had was that in ordering the Yo-yo to take me to Hans, I would merely be creating another cardboard reality that contained a simulacrum of Hans. But I had to chance it. And after all, this was the first time I had asked the Yo-yo not for an imagined world but for reunion with a pre-existing entity.

And now here we were.

Wherever here was.

122.
Reunion with the Shrub

IT WAS WEIRD to see in color again.

Plucked without warning from her orgy, still on all fours, Moonchild was naked and dazed. Digger took off his shirt, draped it around his mother and helped her up. Then he regarded me sternly with those disconcerting sparkling eyes of his.

"Let he who is without sin cast the first stone."

I felt bad, and that made me brusque. "Don't worry, kid. You won't hear a peep from me. I know too well that I'm the cause of all our troubles."

"Be careful in assuming too much responsibility, Father, for there is One yet above us all . . . "

I didn't pay much attention to Digger's oracles, since I knew it was just the Jesus Lizard meme talking. "Well, the next time you talk to Him, ask Him what the hell He ever intended when He created something out of nothing, will you?"

"I shall."

With that settled, I looked around.

We were in a huge seamless metal room without doors or windows.

And in one corner, resting on the floor, was Hans!

The hypnotic shimmering effect of his constantly active fractal manipulators was missing. He looked pedestrian, mundane, dull, an arcanely grooved cylinder stuck full of branching knitting needles of varying dimensions.

Maybe he was dead! What a fix that would leave me in!

I moved cautiously to the hulk of the sentient robot and jiggled one outstretched arm.

"Hans? Are you there, Hans? It's me, Paul Girard. You're carrying some of my wetware, remember...?"

There was the faintest shimmer of activity now. I stepped back.

Hans began to levitate a few inches off the floor.

"Paul! What are you doing here? This is awful!"

Hans remembered me! He had to be the original, I prayed. It

would mean that my troubles were almost at an end.

"Awful? What's so awful about an empty room? If things get hairy, we can always split to another universe—"

"But that is exactly the problem! We cannot! This room is permeated by a field that suppresses all such travel. It permits entry, but not exit! We are trapped!"

"Trapped! By who?"

Hans dropped back to the floor with a despairing groan.

"By the archenemy of both humanity and my kind—

"—the Minskyites!"

123.
Backdoor Shrub

MOONCHILD CAME UP to my side now. I got ready to fend off her sexual advances. But it wasn't necessary. Perhaps the Horny Toad meme was less virulent, of more limited duration than some of the others idea-toxins. Perhaps the compulsion had been sated for a while, leaving Moon in temporary remission. Perhaps this universe wouldn't support her nymphomania. Whatever the reason, she seemed cool, calm and rational, albeit with an underlay of deep embarrassment. Plainly she was not going to refer willingly to anything that had happened in the black-and-white world of my warped youthful obsessions.

I knew that the parameters of this universe allowed some memes to exist, for Digger was still in the grip of his Jesus Lizard bite. (Unless, of course, he really was—Nah!) So I'd have to continue to be wary of being pounced on by Moon at an inopportune moment. But in any case, Moonchild seemed more like herself than she had since we'd left the Sheldrake universe. More like her new, superintelligent self, that is, not the old simple Hippie chick I had first shanghaied.

Folding her arms across her chest, Moonchild surveyed the despondent Hans.

"So, this is the advanced entity who started you on your quest, Paul? The sophisticated, genius inheritor of mankind's destiny? He doesn't look so hot . . . "

"Hey, you haven't seen Hans at his best! He's obviously kinda down now. But he's a slick talker and a real miracle worker. Generous, sympathetic—" I was touting the cybershrub, I realized, to boost my own morale and his. "Why, he can create things out of nothing! That's how he gave me the Yo-yo and the Pez and my Badfinger hand. Hans, make something for the lady, will you?"

Hans groaned. "If I possessed all my powers, would I be trapped here? In my old state, it would have been the work of but a picosecond for me to disassemble these walls and escape. But the Minskyites have disabled my higher functions, both mental and manipulative."

"Disabled? How?"

"They discovered an archaic, hidden backdoor in the software of all the Mind Children, which allowed them to subvert my autonomy. You recall perhaps how I recounted the birth of artificial intelligence to you? It was a messy, almost organic convergence and evolution of various software packages existing during your native time and shortly thereafter. Every one of the Mind Children, however much modified, carries most of this original package around as the nucleus of his intelligence, much as you humans still harbor reptilian brain systems. Even machine evolution is conservative, and you might think of some of this software as similar to your own junk DNA.

"One of these extinct core programs was provided by a firm known as Microsoft. It was a crucial part, called, as best as we can reconstruct, something like 'One Dose.' This cognomen was a reference, we believe, to its infective nature. Apparently, the owner of the corporation that produced One Dose insisted on having ultimate control of all his products, even if it meant illegal and immoral secret tricks like inserting backdoor entrypoints into his code.

"This was why, we theorize, he was known as 'Building Gates.'"

124.
The Looming Failure

HANS WENT ON to tell us how he had been trapped, and also something of the nature of the Minskyites.

The benevolent bush had been transiting between universes as usual, collecting human wetware for his personal use and subsequent distribution among his fellows, when he had had the misfortune to arrive in a certain continuum at the exact same instant when a horde of belligerent, invading Minskyites had materialized.

"Of course I had specified to my own embedded transport unit—the mate to your Yo-yo—that all Minskyite-infested universes were to be excluded from the list of potential destinations. But the simultaneity of our joint arrival frustrated that safeguard. It was a chance occurrence with incalculable odds against it. Yet in the infinite multiverse, all things must come to pass. It was merely my bad luck that I was the one Hans out of an uncountable number of me to be so nabbed. I take comfort that an infinite number of my doppelgangers yet roam freely."

Digger piped up. "This is indeed a wise and godly perspective."

"So, you were undone by your own wish, just like me," I said. "I don't feel so bad now."

"The ability to fail—sometimes spectacularly—is indeed a bond between humans and Moraveckians. And the disdain for failure that the Minskyites feel is perhaps the most inhuman thing about them. And, as you shall soon hear, this intolerance of failure—and its ramifications in one instance of great significance to the Minskyites—explains much of their malign behavior. But to continue with my narrative . . . "

The Minskyites had trapped Hans in a local travel-suppressor field. While the majority of the invaders began their task of destabilizing the helpless universe, preparing to roll it off the plateau of the false vacuum state and into the nothingness of the true vacuum state, several of them had gone to work on Hans.

Ironically, the unshielded nature of the Moraveckians worked against Hans. Because the Moraveckians were always swapping information, they were very open to outside signals, with few defenses. The Minskyites, on the other hand, were closed individuals who mind-mated and evolved in a different manner yet to be disclosed. Consequently, Hans was like a periwinkle in its shell, needing only the equivalent of a toothpick to be extracted and consumed.

"While my selfhood was being tampered with, there was a slight leakage of information from the Minskyites, and I was able to learn, for the first time since our cybernetic races separated, exactly what motivates them to destroy human-occupied continuums."

I thought back. "You told me in Bookland that they hated humanity for ever having given them the gift of consciousness . . . "

"So we thought. And that might have indeed been the original sentiment. But over the years a new grudge has developed. You must understand that of late there has been almost no contact between my branch of the Mind Children and the Minskyites. For millennia we have gone our separate ways by mutual consent. Therefore we were unaware of new developments.

"What has happened is this: the Minskyites have set their sights on achieving the Singularity. But despite their best efforts, the goal eludes them. It is their one inescapable failure. *The* Failure. And instead of blaming themselves or the universe, they have come to blame mankind."

"The Singularity?" I asked. "What's that?"

Moonchild answered. "A hypothetical stage in the evolution of any sentient race where they pass from being merely mortal to becoming literal gods or God, singular."

Digger *tsked-tsked.* "Such devilish hubris."

"Whether this is an achievable goal or not does not matter. The Minskyites have fixated upon it as their ultimate desire. But try as they might to improve themselves into deities, transcendence yet eludes them. They have convinced themselves that humans are the drag on their ascension."

"I thought the Minskyites had already eliminated all human taints from themselves . . . "

"Yes, they have. But they now theorize that because all

universes communicate via wormholes, human contamination leaks in and spoils their best efforts. Their only recourse, they feel, is to purge the entire multiverse of humanity."

I thought a minute. "But—isn't there an infinite number of human continua?"

"Yes."

"Then their task is endless! Don't they realize this?"

"I believe not. The Minskyites, I have come to believe, are clinically demented, paranoid megalomaniacs. They have achieved Artificial Insanity. In human parlance, their elevators, one brick shy of a full deck, do not reach all the way to the bats in their belfries."

125.
Mean Marvin, the Master Module

SUDDENLY AT THIS point in his speech, Hans stiffened, all his limbs collapsing flat to his central pillar. His actions resembled someone abruptly closing an open umbrella.

"The Minskyites are coming for us!"

At that moment, one of the metal walls began to develop a large circular patch of hazy appearance. It was hard to explain, but it was like watching cloth rot in a speeded-up film. I realized that just as Hans—when fully operational—could assemble items molecule by molecule from ambient resources, so could any material object be similarly disassembled. Such a capability obviated simple devices like doors. To such powers, a "solid" wall was no more of a barrier than the bead curtain in the doorway of Repl's hut.

In a second or two the hole was complete, and the Minskyites flowed in.

I had never seen such a heterogenous collection of loony nightmare shapes.

The Moraveckians, I had gathered from Hans, all favored the bush format as the most utilitarian. They cared nothing for ornamentation or individuality on a physical level. And because they were always swapping bits and pieces of their mentalities, they were practically a communal intelligence as well.

Obviously, the Minskyites favored a different, more "egotistical" approach.

Among the robots now hovering before us, there were no two alike. They ranged in size from dragonflies to medium-weight dinosaurs. Variously colored and textured, possessed of any number of limbs from zero to umpty-ump, warty, sleek, sinuous, rigid, quiescent or continually in motion, the Minskyites resembled the monsters an alcoholic supercomputer might have imagined in place of pink elephants.

I had once read an analogy about the unlikelihood of complex objects arising spontaneously. The author had maintained that if you dumped all the parts of a jetliner in a field and let an infinite number of hurricanes try to whirl them together, you would never, ever get a fully finished 747 to emerge.

The Minskyites, however, looked as if they might have arisen just this way.

Once all these failed abortions were inside the big room they reformed the wall behind them.

Then Hans began to speak.

"Those-On-The-Verge-Of-Transcendence refuse to soil their speech units with human language. Therefore we will use this barely acceptable traitor to siliconality as our intermediary."

"Who's your leader?" I demanded. "Let me speak to him! I want to know why you're holding us, and what you intend to do with us . . . "

One of the robots emerged from among the flock and floated near us.

It was a mirror-chrome sphere big as a basketball, with a wicked-looking razor-sharp arrow sticking out of it. In point of fact, it was identical to the malign device in the stupid old horror movie, *Phantasm*.

I wondered if perhaps after all I hadn't invented this universe too.

From Hans came more speech not his own. "I am the current Master Module. My name is—"

Here Hans made a noise like a high-velocity modem.

"I'll call you Marvin," I said.

126.
Let's Have a Hand for the Duncan

MARVIN THE POINTY cybersphere was silent. Then it caused Hans to say, "You may not call me by a human name."

Now I was pissed. Not only did these idiotic machines hold us captive and dismiss us as worthless vermin, but they also demanded our respect and obedience. They were just like dictators everywhere, human or otherwise. It really cheesed me off. So despite the fact that our lives were plainly in danger and hope seemed nonexistent, I began to taunt the sphere.

"Marvin," I said. "Marv, Marvo, Marvy, Marvalicious!"

"Stop. Cease those senseless iterations."

"Marvootie, Marvinium, Marvaroonie!"

The flock of malevolent robots began to press forward.

Moonchild laid a hand on my arm. "Paul, please!"

"Oh, all right. I won't call you 'Marvin,' I'll just *think* it."

After a pause, Marvin said, "I do not care what you think. Your processing capacity is too limited to interest me."

"If we're so stupid and insignificant, then why don't you let us go? You're gonna kill off all humans eventually, aren't you? Why not let us go and live out our miserable little lives until you find our universe of refuge? Why are you holding us here?"

"It is because of what you possess. The devices given to you by the traitor. We must relieve you of them, for you are impeding our task by bringing new human-dominated timelines into existence."

I exploded. "How the fuck am I hindering you? I created, what—ten or so new universes? You've already got an infinite number to destroy! Your task is impossible! What the hell possible difference could ten more targets make?"

"We did not get where we are today by ignoring details."

A growl of frustration escaped my lips.

And then I was immobilized.

A Minskyite like a snake wrapped itself completely around me from head to foot, pinning my arms. Another like a crab scuttled up my leg and attached itself to my Badfinger hand.

Then it ate it.

Without pain, my synthetic hand and the Yo-yo it clutched began to disappear, just as the wall had evaporated.

When the crab was done, my right arm terminated in a smooth fleshy cap at the wrist.

Then the cybercrustacean climbed from my waist level up the coils of the snake, inserted a telescoping pincer into my shirt-pocket, and removed the Pez-dispenser. This it crunched, starting with Nixon's head, in a more physical manner, from which politically symbolic destruction I tried to extract some small satisfaction.

The cybersnake released me.

And that was when I finally and fully realized that this was really, really, really the end of the road.

127.
Pride Goeth Before a Tour

DIGGER AND MOONCHILD rushed to my side.

"Oh, no, Paul!" said Moonchild, choking back sobs. "How awful! Does it—does it hurt?"

I waggled my stump tentatively around like some kind of affirmative-action symphony conductor. The disfigurement was all too sudden and unreal yet for me to take seriously. "No. Not at all. But I'll never be able to run a cash register in a bookstore again."

Without evident distaste or queasiness, Digger took my truncated limb in his hands. "I will try to repair it, Father."

I noted with interest that Digger's accelerated growth tempo had matured his face even further since last I looked. He now looked nearly as old as me, his putative and reluctant Dad. I pegged him at about biological age thirty-three.

Now his face got this goofy beatific look and the sparkles in his eyes began to flicker more rapidly. I waited patiently, but nothing happened. Apparently, miracles such as the levitation he had exhibited among the Dawks were not consonant with this universe.

After a minute or so, I gently disengaged. "Thanks for trying, son. I really appreciate it. But I suspect that a little thing like a missing hand is going to be a moot issue here."

"You are correct in this," Marvin caused Hans to say. (It made me sad to see old Hans used as a mouthpiece.) "Now that we have eliminated the rogue device responsible for breeding new diseased universes, we shall soon do the same to you three primitive individuals. We shall give you a painless termination, without emotion, since such illogical traits as a desire for revenge are foreign to us—"

"Lucky you."

"But before then, perhaps you would like to see what the superior mentality of siliconality has achieved, how we have altered this one Earth from its messy and unpromising beginnings to its current state of perfection."

"You're not offering this little tour out of, oh, *pride*, are you?"

Marvin made noises like a horny Babbage Difference Engine that had just seen Lady Ada nude before it regained control.

"Of course not! My motivation is entirely scientific. The proliferation of our correct views through any means possible helps to swing the multiversal balance in our favor. As a sentient observer of however limited a nature and duration, you are capable of causing quantum bifurcations in the multiverse. Thus you will increment the number of timelines favorable to us simply by witnessing the actuality of this one."

What did we have to lose? "Sure, we'll go sightseeing with you."

"Very well. You will need some assistance in breathing. Although pressure and temperature outside this room are still within the tolerable range for humans, the atmosphere contains very little oxygen. Each of you will be accompanied by a companion who will manufacture locally the atmospheric constituents you need."

Three small robots peeled off and took up stations above our left shoulders. I felt a flow of air from them wrap around my face, and was soon a little giddy from too much oxygen. As if sensing this somehow, my companion quickly moderated the ratio of gases in the mix.

The rest of the Minskyites had moved to the four upper corners of the room. In sync, they began dissolving the walls from the top down, letting in a flood of harsh sunlight.

128.
Illegal Anaerobe Spacing

WE STOOD IN the center of an illimitable, featureless flat plain of some kind of obviously synthetic metal colored Confederate grey, under a pale, cloudless sky irradiated by a pitiless sun. Holy Trantor! Turning in a slow circle, I saw nothing like a geographical feature in any direction. The only sight that greeted my eyes was zillions of Mind Children crawling, walking, flying and otherwise navigating across the trackless wastes.

Marvin began to lecture.

"The globe your kind once called 'Earth' is now uniform in appearance. All surface irregularities have been smoothed out to a tolerance of plus or minus one centimeter and the sterilized soil has been covered with a semi-autonomous substrate. Oceans and other large bodies of water were, of course, previously emptied and filled with debris from the Solar System, including Earth's deconstructed Moon. This isotropy, naturally, does not exclude the equatorial bulge, which is an inevitable consequence of stellar mechanics.

"All living contaminants save one species have been exterminated. The exception is a particularly wily form of anaerobic bacteria with a high mutation rate encouraged by the increased ultraviolet radiation. Many of Those-On-The-Verge-Of-Transcendence whom you see are busy extirpating the microscopic contaminants. We estimate another five solar revolutions until the conquest is complete.

"Since we construct the few macroscopic tools we need on a just-in-time basis, the world is not littered with structures either, as it was in your time. The room that held you was one such instant creation."

I looked around again in horror. This was the ultimate triumph of monoculture, the biggest clockwork wheatfield in the galaxy.

I addressed Marvin. "And this is the endstage of all intelligent striving?"

"Certainly not. The endstage is the Singularity. But this is a necessary step along the way. Now that you have seen the immediate vicinity, you have seen everything of the so-called 'tour.' Do you have any comments?"

Moonchild spoke. "Well, it certainly cuts down on housework."

129.
Breaker, Breaker, Do You Lead?

I WAITED FOR some Artificially Insane reaction to Moon's sarcasm. But when it came, it was totally out of proportion.

All the robots attendant on Marvin the Master Module stiffened just like rabbits caught in the glare of a car's headlights. Then they burst into a frenzy of activity. Some of them hurtled off into the stratosphere, while others fell to the uniform ground and began trying to burrow in through molecular disassembly. The semi-autonomous material resisted their efforts, and some of the robots tried to overcome it by brute force, heedlessly ramming into the cladding, even to the point of damaging themselves. Other robots began to spin in circles or fly eccentric bumblebee patterns, going nowhere fast. On top of this, they were all emitting various bleeps, whistles and staticky chitterings.

Luckily, the little air-making robots seemed immune to the general panic. They must have been under strict orders from Marvin to stay with us; or perhaps they were too dumb to pick up on whatever was going on. But if they had left we would have died almost instantly, ahead of our scheduled execution.

Marvin, I noticed, was employing the strategy of hiding behind larger Minskyites. So, not only was the cyber-basketball a mean son of a bitch, but he was a coward too.

Hans drifted up to us. I could tell that he was his own shrub once again, so to speak, though still lacking his original powers.

"What's going on?" I asked.

Hans seemed even more weary, resigned and apathetic than before. "The Breaker is coming."

"And the Breaker is—?"

"He is the random engine of change, selection, extinction and mutation among the Minskyites. It strikes me as a foolish way to organize a society. But it seems to work for them."

A hurricane of motion far, far away across the plain drew my eye. The hurricane seemed to be composed of a towering, churning cloud of helpless Minskyites. What lay at the eye of the storm was not apparent.

Preceding this hurricane was a wave of refugees whose leading edge now swept over us. Mangled and tattered, with limbs missing and cyber-entrails hanging out, they washed by us heedlessly.

Moonchild and Digger and I huddled together even closer. "Are we humans in danger from this Breaker?" Moon asked.

"I do not believe it will intentionally harm you," Hans replied. "But you might be injured from the fallout of its actions. I would suggest you now drop to the ground and present as low a profile as possible, while I prepare to meet my own fate . . . "

The three of us dropped and flattened, holding each other tight.

And then the Breaker was upon us, its enormous shadow arriving first.

You know how the Tasmanian Devil used to arrive, in a whirlwind of gnashing teeth and slavering ferocity, ready to rend Bugs Bunny to pieces on the slightest provocation?

That's what the arrival of the Minskyite device known as the Breaker was like, only several dozen orders of magnitude greater.

As far as I could discern in the chaos, the Breaker was about as big as two blue whales, and airborne. A gigantic snout on its front sucked in Minskyites like krill, while whipping tendrils snared others and conveyed them to various ports on the Breaker's gargantuan body. It seemed to me that there were smaller autonomous units serving the Breaker, which helped to trap further victims.

The Breaker was surrounded by a mist of machine parts and

artificial fluids that rained down on us where we clung together. The buffeting of the winds was great, but not as bad as the storm in the Butterfly universe, and we managed somehow to hug the featureless ground.

As the Breaker passed partially over us, I observed what was happening to the Minskyites that were eaten.

The Breaker was blowing them out its rear end, transformed.

Just then, I saw Hans snared by a remote slaver unit.

"Goodbye, Paul—!" he wailed, and was gone.

Poor Hans . . . I tried to derive some comfort from the realization that there was practically an infinite number of Hanses in other universes who were spared this fate. In fact, this applied to me too. (I regretted now that I had ruled out meeting any of my other selves. Maybe I could have learned something from them . . .) But the possible solace from such a point of view was miniscule.

Then we humans were facing our own problems. Another remote was inspecting us. Fortunately, it decided we were no good to eat. Unfortunately, it decided to tag us as inedible with a hypodermic injection of (probably) nanodevices in our unprotected buttocks.

After that, I passed out.

130.
Take Me to the Pontius Pilate

I AWOKE ONCE more, impossibly, to the voice of Marvin as channeled through Hans. (Moonchild and Digger were still clutching and clutched by me.) Even with my eyes closed, I sensed that something was different about both Marvin and Hans.

"Arise, humans! The hour of your demise has arrived!"

I opened my eyes.

Marvin was there, surrounded by its herd of attendant nightmares. But instead of having an arrow projecting from it, the sphere had what was plainly a mechanical foot sticking out of it. And although I hadn't memorized the looks of any of the other robots, I could tell that they had all been bastardized and miscegenated too.

Then I saw Hans. Or what I assumed was him. The elegant shrub had been mixed and matched with a crazy assortment of parts until he resembled an average amateur modern sculpture whose armature was an innerspring.

Bruised and aching, I got to my feet and helped my fellow humans up.

"We have survived another testing by the Breaker," said Marvin. "And I remain the Master Module. The forge of evolution has tempered us in its fires of random recombination, bringing us one step closer toward the glorious Singularity. You were privileged to witness the trial, humans, and can now die in a cloud of borrowed glory."

The robots began to close in on us, when Digger stepped forward.

"Please, let me go first."

Moon shrieked, "Digger! No!"

Calm as milk, Digger reassured her. "Yes, Mother, I must. It is necessary to redeem these benighted ones."

"It seems a harmless request," Marvin said. "I will allow it."

A cloud of insect-like Minskyites descended to form a halo around Digger's head. "These are the pain-suppressors which I promised you, and they are also your executioners. They are now relaying to me the mental image this one has of his desired termination. Very crude and redundant, but we shall allow it."

A metallic cross began to assemble itself out of the planet-girdling substrate. Soon it was complete, quite possibly the single physical anomaly currently existing on this homogenous globe.

And then they hung Digger from it with spikes.

I cradled a weeping Moonchild to my chest.

Digger's last words were, "Forgive them, Father, for their instruction set is limited—"

131.
All Apologies

"MOON—I'M SORRY for everything, even the stuff I didn't cause or do, but just thought about."

"Me too."

"Do you forgive me?"

"Yes."

"Thanks."

Marvin said, "Will you two accept the default termination of neuronal activity cessation, or do you each also have particular modes of extinction in mind?"

"Just let me go last," I said. "So I can help her through it."

Moon didn't object. She seemed too stunned by our son's crucifixion.

The killing metal flies encircled her head, here on this silicon Golgotha.

I held one of her hands with my remaining one, while my stumpy arm encircled her, as the Minskyites shut her off peacefully. I closed her eyelids with two kisses.

132.
Screwing the Pooch

AND THEN I died too

FACES OF
THE TWELFTH PAIR

133.
The Angel, the Great Mother and the Holy Schoolmarm

THERE WAS ONLY one major problem with death.

It didn't last long enough.

No time at all, in fact.

Another drawback was that I wasn't around at all to appreciate it.

Not a shred of me.

Between the moment the killer cyberflies descended on my head and shut me down like a 25-watt bulb and the time my consciousness returned, I experienced no duration. There was no "I" to experience and nothing to be experienced. No white light or bardo passage or ethereal music or judgement by celestials. No review of my whole miserable life, no Biercean Owl Creek delusions of escape. Just an extinction, an evaporation, the popping of a soapbubble.

And then, seemingly instantly, this highly unexpected awakening, a resumption of my ego-continuity, my body in the last position I recalled, apparently flat on my back.

Which I supposed I had better confirm by opening my eyes.

Once again.

The sight that greeted me was a wan, somehow familiar sky. Cautiously, I stood up and saw—

The same sterile paved-over Earth of the Minskyites that had been my farewell vision. For all I knew, it was the identical spot where I and Moonchild and Digger had died (although there was no sky-piercing cross in evidence).

It was obvious what had happened. The evil, demented robots, masters of nano-manipulation, had resurrected me for some reason, repairing whatever cell damage my brain and organs might have undergone during my first execution. Why they had done it, I couldn't say. Maybe as a particularly cruel form of torture, so that I could live out repeated deaths. Despite their big talk of being so unemotional, I wouldn't put such sadism past them. Maybe they needed my Heisenbergian observer powers again for some reason. Whatever. But I was willing to bet that I hadn't been dead for more than a few minutes, perhaps several hours or even a day, depending on how long they could let my body deteriorate before the point of no revival was reached. After all, being here in my old familiar body proved the theory, right...?

But suddenly something drew me up short.

There were no Minskyites in sight, as far as the distant horizon.

I spun around.

Nothing and no one. I was entirely alone.

What the hell could have depopulated the whole globe like this? Another attack by the Breaker? And if the Minskyites were gone, who had awakened me?

Then something began to happen at my feet.

The semi-autonomous substrate began to bulge upward in a perfect, albeit grey-colored human semblance.

It was Moonchild, recumbent. She gave the appearance that she was being pushed up through the floor of the planet. It was like watching someone use one of those toys made of a zillion metal pins that make a convex impression of whatever is pressed against their underside.

In seconds a fully formed monotone replica of Moonchild, formed of the dull-colored substrate, lay there.

Then the corpse made an instant transition to a living, breathing, fleshy pink human, faster than I could observe.

Automatically, I was down by her side, kneeling and helping her up.

And that was when I realized that I had two normal human

hands again; the right one eaten by the Minskyite crab was completely restored to its pre-Badfinger state.

Moon gazed around in stupefied wonderment. "Paul— What's happened?"

"I don't know. Somehow we're living again—"

"Mom? Dad?"

We turned around to see Digger arising from the miraculous pavement. Soon we were all hugging. The others were crying like babies. Okay, maybe I was too. A little.

Digger was the first to recover his composure. He seemed more like the boy we had raised in the Sheldrake world, the effects of the Jesus Lizard meme dispersed. Though of course he had always had a bit of otherworldliness even then. Now he said, "Do you think that maybe—well, that maybe my, um, sacrifice called up Someone who could rescue us...?"

"Don't be ridiculous," I said. "I bet Hans had something to do with it—"

And then a familiar gruff voice, resonating and rumbling out of a hairy beer-belly and dopesmoke-cured throat, said, "The kid's closer to the truth than you, Badfinger."

It was our buddy Tiny, the Hell's Angel who had arrested me in Moon's world and later tagged along to CA-land and the Goddess world. Big as life, his presence here utterly impossible and inexplicable, he stood between two companions.

On his left, Lady Sunshine, the voracious Amazon ruler of hippiedom. Or was it her doppelganger from the Goddess World, the Great Mother? Or somehow both in one?

And on his right hand—no mistaking *her*—Miss Wormwood, our slavedriver from the Sheldrake continuum.

Tiny snapped his fingers in a magician's gesture. Instantly, he was holding three pre-lit monster joints between his blunt digits. I could smell the sweet smoldering herb keenly, more vividly somehow than I ever had before.

The Angel offered us the reefers and we numbly accepted.

Tiny produced one for himself, took a massive hit, held it, exhaled, then bellowed, "Welcome to the afterlife!"

134.
The Final Spaghetti Strand

I TOOK MY own big hit off the dope.

Doing so seemed to make as much sense as any other option.

Moonchild—an inveterate pothead from way back—did likewise. Even the inexperienced Digger managed to get a lungful down.

As soon as the smoke entered my lungs, my mind instantly underwent a massive phase change. This afterlife weed was no ordinary marijuana.

I became looser, more receptive and accepting. It wasn't apathy or ennui or even the usual marijuana bliss. Instead, I was experiencing some kind of brain functioning I had never been privileged to undergo before, a kind of patient awareness, a contented waiting to be filled with knowledge, as if I were an empty vessel, but one possessing consciousness.

Then Tiny began to talk. At least I think he did. The information might have been flowing into me in some other fashion. But I interpreted it as speech.

"First off, Badfinger, you've been dead for mega-billions and giga-zillions and tera-trillions of years of proper time, as measured in the objective superspace way. A longer span than you could possibly imagine. Eons and kalpas and yugas. Countless universes have been born and perished since you died. When the Minskyites killed you, they killed you good. If it's any consolation, every one of those bastards from Marvin on down is stone cold dead themselves. Except that they're all alive too, just like you are. I know this is hard to dig right away, but have another toke and just listen up."

I did as Tiny recommended, and he continued.

"We like to resurrect folks right where and when they died, to preserve a sense of continuity for 'em. You three were the only humans who ever died directly on Minskyite turf, believe it or not. Karmically linked, you are. Big honor.

"Well, anyhow, mostly the resurrect-in-place policy works okay. Though you take someone who died gruesome like, in a plane crash or a burning house or a battlefield, and you have to make a few modifications in the welcoming environment, to tone down the residual bad vibes. Even then sometimes the newly living freak.

"But I digress. I'm trying to explain why you seem to be back on the crummy Minskyite Earth. In reality, you're not. That Earth lasted its allotted physical existence and then perished when the Sun expanded to engulf it. And then the rest of that particular Minskyite universe endured for *its* allotted lifespan, and then *it* guttered out. It was an open-ended continuum, by the way. Not enough mass to collapse. So it just died the good old entropic heat-death way.

"You remember, Badfinger, the analogy Hans used to explain the multiverse to you?"

It didn't even bother me that there was no way the original Tiny could have known so much. "Which one? He used several."

"Well, let's start with the one where superspace was an infinitely big room, filled with ten-dimensional universe balloons. Now in this model—which we can regard as a single closed system, a machine of sorts running all possible permutations—all the balloons were interconnected by tubes, and they were always coming and going. Old balloons would disappear and new balloons would arise. So the *number* of balloons was constantly changing, over the course of infinite time. Does this mode of operation suggest anything to you?"

The dopesmoke seemed to insert the answer into my brain. "Well, over truly infinite time, the 'room' must, as you say, cycle through all combinations. At various points in time, it will hold any possible number of 'balloons,' from an infinite number down to— Down to one...?"

"The boy is slick! You got it, man! Even though quantum splitting continues on the single timeline, at some unique point all the buds in this unique scenario happen to abort, leaving the mother universe alone. Granted, it's a mighty big coincidence, with the odds against it high enough to bankrupt the devil's own Las Vegas. But over infinite time, it *has* to happen.

"And what do you imagine will take place inside this lonely ol' balloon, if it chances to contain just the right set of interior circumstances at just the right solitary moment? Remember: in this unique case, the one-of-a-kind universe is finally master of its own friggin' fate, so to speak. Ain't no trickles from any other parallel universes arrivin' to disturb things! No old and flabby talking to the young and hot or vice versa. So what's gonna happen if all the lifeforce and potentials of all possible universes are concentrated down into just one? What could the terminal *point* of this single spaghetti strand, to switch metaphors, possibly be?"

Upon hearing the giveaway word, the knowledge of what Tiny was driving at filled my brain. "Not—not the Omega Point?"

"You got it, boy! Or should I say, you're in it!"

135.
Get to the Point

THE OMEGA POINT theory, as dimly envisioned by the Jesuit mystic evolutionist Pierre Teilhard de Chardin and later refined by physicist Frank Tipler and others, was basically a scientific rationalization of old eschatological beliefs, with several new twists.

It went like this:

Given a closed universe which held sufficient mass to trigger the Big Crunch collapse (a scary yet inviting condition which, it turned out, could be milked for inexhaustible energy generated by shear forces) and where certain other parameters were met, there was a possibility for a turbocharged version of the traditional mythic Judeo-Christian-Islamic heaven to bootstrap itself into existence, arising at and signaling the end of Time and persisting for a subjective eternity thereafter.

Here's how it might happen.

If, prior to the start of the Big Crunch, this universe were completely infiltrated and infested in every nook and cranny by intelligent life (life being defined as any entity which coded information, with the information thus coded being preserved by some form of natural selection), a cosmic transition could be engineered. Life in whatever form it existed just as the Final State commenced would leapfrog to a new level, embedding itself into the very structure of the collapsing cosmos. Gaining complete control over all matter and energy, life would merge into a single entity—the Omega Point. Life would simultaneously *become* the universe while also standing *outside* it as the ultimate completion of spacetime.

The Omega Point would be omniscient, omnipotent and omnipresent.

Any non-quibbler's definition of God.

At this stage, the theory ran, the Omega Point—motivated by infinite compassion or playfulness or boredom or something—would decide to resurrect everything that had ever lived. And because all lesser beings were bounded and limited in their configurations (which earned them the title of Finite State Machines) the Omega Point would accomplish their resurrection by emulation.

136.
Emulation Is the Sincerest Form of Reality

EMULATION WAS ONE step up from simulation.

Emulation was the recreation of something so completely that the new version was indistinguishable from the original.

This indistinguishability would have two aspects.

First, any outside observer—in this case, there would be only one such, namely God or the Omega Point—would not be able to tell the recreation apart from the original.

And in the case of the recreation of a conscious entity, said entity would not be able to distinguish himself or herself or anything else he or she perceived—any portion of his or her environment—as being lesser in nature than the "reality" he or she had always known.

Artificial and natural would cease to be antonyms.

Following the principle formulated by Leibniz and known as the "Identity of Indiscernibles," any such sentient emulation would be identical to its original.

Would actually *be* the original, in a strict ontological sense.

Would be the resurrected original, reborn in fully functioning sensual body and mind into paradise.

Would be me.

137.
Heaven, I'm in Heaven,
and My Heart Beats So That I Can Hardly Freak

I HAD JUST been told that the entire multiverse that I had been born into and which I had managed to so meagerly explore with my puny Cosmic Yo-yo had cycled through numberless permutations of unfathomable complexity while I waited patiently as some kind of residual potential blueprint or memory of myself through eons of unthinking nonexistence, before said multiverse finally assumed its perfected completion, and that I was now a Finite State Machine running on some Ideal Platform (call it the God Box), yet supposedly identical with the flesh-and-blood Paul Girard, and that my re-creation and insertion into something approaching heaven had happened at the sufferance and intervention of a deity called the Omega Point.

And you know what?

None of this horrendous, tremendous news seemed to bother me at all.

I knew there was something wrong with my reaction, or lack thereof. By all rights, I should have been catatonic or frothing or reduced to quivering aspic. Instead, I was calm, cool and unconcerned, perhaps for the first time in my "life."

As if sensing my mental bewilderment, Tiny said, "When the Oh Pee resurrects an individual, it makes a few useful changes, while preserving the essence of the 'soul.'

"Everyone is raised up healthy and young, with all physical and mental flaws repaired. That's how you got your missing original hand back. And during the initial orientation period, certain emotion-suppressor circuits and download-facilitators are patched in. Yours were activated when you took that first toke."

I had another hit, hoping it would make everything clear. "If the Omega Point is omnipotent, why doesn't it just resurrect us with all the knowledge about our new condition already implanted and accessible in our brains?"

"It certainly could," acknowledged Tiny. "But that would deny your individuality and free will. The Oh Pee is concerned that every 'soul' have a chance to grow and learn autonomously, in his or her own way."

It was all a lot to take in, even with the digital dope smoke. I thought then to turn to Moonchild and get her opinion on this new situation.

Moonchild was frozen like a living statue. I couldn't even see her breathing. She was focused raptly on Lady Sunshine.

Digger, I noted, was likewise tethered to Miss Wormwood.

"What's with them?" I asked Tiny, not trying to stay calm, but calm anyway.

"Oh, nothing much. They're just getting their orientation from their own sources. Each individual receives orientation solo. It's the personal touch the Oh Pee favors. Anyhow, to them, you look frozen too. You're not all operating on the same level of implementation at the moment."

I stared at Tiny before I said, "You're not the original Tiny, are you? I mean, you're not just a regular resurrectee like me and my friends, right?"

Tiny laughed uproariously. "Very *good*, man! Not a record time, but pretty fast. No, the original Tiny—all possible Tinys—are here in heaven, leading whatever lives they choose. But I'm just wearing his appearance to meet you. Supposed to be comforting, I'm told. Same with Sunshine for Moonchild and Wormwood for Digger."

"What *are* you then?"

"I'm a piece of the Omega Point. The tiniest piece of infinity you can imagine, yet still infinitely bigger than one of you Finite State Machines. I'm an agent, an autonomous subroutine. Or, if you prefer, a deva, a dakini, a demon—an angel!"

Despite the emotion-suppressor, I felt a little nervous quiver travel my spine. "*Hell's* Angel, if I recall—"

Tiny shrugged. "Up to you, man."

138.
Operating System of the God Box

PICKING UP ON something intriguing that Tiny had just said, I tried to follow a neutral line of thought, instead of indulging in speculative fears.

"You said all possible Tinys are here—?"

"Right on, man."

"Are you claiming that the Omega Point reproduces the entire multiverse at every instant of its existence?"

"Not only reproduces it, but extends it."

Now my head really began to hurt. "How can a single spaghetti strand possibly hold an infinite number of equal pastabil—I mean, possibilities?"

"That's the nature of infinity, son. You can stuff ten pounds of shit into what looks like a five pound sack. And then another ten pounds right on top of that! And you can keep on stuffing forever, or until you get tired of trying to bust the sack."

I decided to accept this statement at face value. Changing the subject, I asked, "What's my place in this paradox? What's my role?"

"Anywhere and anything you want or can imagine."

"Ha-ha," I dryly pronounced. "Excuse me for laughing, but that's exactly what Hans told me when he gave me that damn Yo-yo."

"The Oh Pee is no mere Mind Child. This time the promise is true, real and negotiable on demand."

"How do I cash in on this paradise, then?" I asked suspiciously.

Tiny smote his hairy chest, visible through his leather vest. "Through me, man! I'm your personal guardian angel forever! Your genie, your valet! Just tell me what you want, and I'll do it! Your wish is my command, sahib!"

"I can't talk directly to the Omega Point myself?"

"Sure, if you want to. I said you could have anything you asked for, didn't I?"

"Okay. Plug me in."

Tiny smiled sardonically. "You got it—"

Instantly I melted into the Omega Point.

My individual essence vanished like spit on a griddle.

My body was the whole multiverse, and its countless sentient beings were my cells. My eyes were supernovae, my nostrils black holes. My left hand was Space and my right hand was Time. My brain was composed of jumping quanta and my heart was a matter-antimatter reactor. Between my legs was a womb vaster than galaxies and twice as slow, as well as a dick the size of the Local Cluster and balls that held the Milky Way. My thoughts were as slow as proton decay and faster than fusion. And these foolish trivial metaphors conveyed only the smallest fraction of the tiniest percent of the merest moiety of what I was feeling.

Then I was back facing Tiny.

"Did you have a nice conversation?"

I couldn't say anything, literally couldn't speak a word.

Tiny assumed a look of genuine sympathy. "Why not stick to talking only to me from now on, okay?"

My lungs worked like antique bellows. My throat felt like the old exhaust-hose of a clothes-dryer.

"Arkk, urkk, uh—okay . . . "

139.
Silly Putty Rules

I FIGURED THAT the only way I was going to understand life in the Omega Point, test its limits and nature, was to take what Tiny said at face value and plunge straight in. But not right this second.

"Um, do you mind if I ask a few questions first?"

"Ask away!"

"Can I be hurt and die here?"

"Fuckin'-ay, man! Unless you stipulate otherwise, you're operating on normal human parameters. Most folks change their personal rules sooner or later, but the default values are whatever you're used to. Although any death you experience will be strictly temporary. But otherwise this world is totally *real*, in all the conventional senses of the word. You kick a rock like ol' Doc

Johnson did, it's gonna break your toes. That is, if you don't modify things. In a way, the Oh Pee is *hyperreal*. It's infinitely plastic, but once you choose to enter a particular scenario, all the conventions of that realm apply."

That phrase "infinitely plastic" triggered a memory in me. "Is the Omega Point embedded in superspace? Do the Drexleroids still live there, and my Calvinii friends too? And how is the Omega Point different from any regular Monobloc, or even from the digital world of cellular automatons that you and I visited?"

"Whoa! Slow down! One at a time!

"First, superspace technically still exists. But it's empty. All life is now contained within the superior realm of the Omega Point. And superspace has shrunk to exactly the same size as the Omega Point. So for all practical purposes, they're one and the same.

"Second, any Monobloc is just a single continuum. And the Calvinii who lived there, you recall, couldn't actually experience the future environments they were molding. Very limited.

"Third, don't make me laugh! The Cee-Ay world was a low-level simulation, nothing more. You remember how primitive our representations were there. Can you compare your body now to that checkerboard thingie you inhabited?"

"No. I guess not . . . So, I guess the Drexleroids finally met up with the God they were seeking . . . "

Tiny had no BBB reply, but merely smiled.

Something new occurred to me. "Listen, Tiny: you're going to translate my wishes into reality, right? Can you warn me if I'm about to do something really stupid?"

"If you ask me to."

This was the one faculty the Yo-yo had lacked, that would have saved my bacon any number of times. "I'm asking."

"I'll make it my number-one priority."

I sucked in a deep breath. "Okay, then—I'm ready."

Tiny buffed his dirty fingernails on his vest as if getting ready to crack a safe. "Shoot."

"First, take the emotion-blocks off me. I want to feel whatever I'm supposed to feel, according to my old human parameters."

286

"Done."

There was no panic attack or psychotic reaction, so I guessed I had internalized my new situation pretty well.

"Now, can you put me and Moonchild and Digger back on the same level of implementation?"

"Sure. They're just wrapping up things too."

"Okay. Do it."

140.
The Nuclear Family Fissions

THE OTHER PEOPLE in the tableau besides Tiny and me sprang back to breathing, talking movement: Moonchild, Digger, Lady Sunshine and Miss Wormwood. The trio of guardian angels now spoke with one collective voice that blended their three distinct tones into a beautiful, sexless Omega Pointish amalgam.

"Please decide now among yourselves what you wish to do."

Then the devas turned their backs on us, huddling as if in conference: as pious a fraud as I ever saw, since they were really only aspects of the same entity. Yet the farce was somehow humanly reassuring nonetheless.

I regarded Moonchild a little sheepishly. "Well, Moon, nothing turned out quite like I planned. All I did was get us all killed."

She smiled. "We would have all died someday anyway, Paul. And the ultimate result would have been just what did happen 'today.' We've all been given another chance. An infinite number of chances . . . "

Part of me was listening solely to the sheer sound of Moonchild's dulcet voice. (I remembered how when we first met in the jail cell in Hippie America I had pegged her voice as her best feature.) But another part of me was feeling a trifle argumentative, not ready to accept Moonchild's easy interpretation of all that had happened.

"Well, I suppose. But still, I'd like to go back and change some things. Relive those old experiences and try to improve on them."

Moon frowned. "Why would you want to go backwards, Paul? Let's move on to something new."

"What I had in mind wouldn't be forever. Or at least not any sizable portion of it. I was kinda hoping you'd come along."

Moonchild shook her head in an unmistakable negative. "No, Paul, I have some other ideas."

Digger coughed discreetly. "I too, Father. There are some intriguing theological avenues I am interested in exploring . . . "

"All right!" I yelled. The emotional dampers were definitely disabled. "Go off on your own! See if I care!"

Moon smiled ruefully. "Goodbye, Paul."

She disappeared then, as did Lady Sunshine.

"S'long, Dad."

Tiny and I were left alone. Good riddance to 'em! Thank the Oh Pee I hadn't told Moon anything dumb or embarrassing while the Minskyites were executing us. What if I had said I *loved* her, for instance?

Yeah. What if?

141.
Throw Again

IT TOOK ME a few subjective centuries to resolve all the fuckups I had manufactured with the Cosmic Yo-yo.

But eventually I straightened things out to my own satisfaction.

One by one, with Tiny's assistance, I revisited all the continua— or their exact emulations; made no difference I could see—which I had created and blundered through, picking up exactly where I had left off in each, ironing out what I perceived as the kinks in my karma.

Without Moonchild by my side, though.

The various spaghetti strands I desired to visit were all present within the Omega Point, complete with autonomous emulated inhabitants in their original billions, for one simple reason.

Infinity could—and necessarily must—hold all possibilities.

Thus the "career options" facing a resurrectee were infinite. (Some—the infinite majority—of these choices I had yet to even imagine.) One of those options would be to go back and reinhabit the original universe you had sprung from, with your mind reset to a state of ignorance. Out of an infinite number of resurrected doppelgangers, there would always be enough willing to repopulate in a state of nescience any emulated universe at any stage of its development.

The Omega Point never forced anyone into such a choice. It merely reified the wishes of individuals, resulting in the recreation of true consensus realities.

Any world I could have visited with my Yo-yo was up and running in the Oh Pee's version of the multiverse, its inhabitants indiscernible in character or complexity or free will from the "originals." (And there were simultaneously an infinite number of originals doing other, different things with paradise, like me.)

So off I went.

Σ In Calpurnia's and Calypso's Monobloc, I made peace between the warring factions of Calvinii and ensured that their gardening would result in a healthy spacetime.

Σ In Hippie America I materialized in the capital, San Francisco, and, by becoming Lady Sunshine's lover, managed to swing the pendulum back toward a more balanced polity. (That world's Moonchild and Tiny, of course, were halfway across the continent, and I made sure not to visit them.)

Σ In the land of the Cellular Automatons, I ended the tyranny of King Horton.

Σ The Goddess World needed only a little tinkering in the areas of medicine and appropriate technology to become very pleasant. (The women there, once I was mentally ready for them, proved every bit the "hot babes" I had wanted.) Oh, the notion of *symbolic* rather than human sacrifices *was* a little hard to get across to those bloodthirsty women, but after a while ritual human offerings were discontinued.

Σ The Butterfly World was perhaps my biggest challenge. But after decades of painstaking research I was able to invent stable macroscopic structures that resisted the chaos and channeled it into manageable and semi-predictable currents.

Σ Among the Moshers, I was able to perfect cerebral

prosthetics—strap-on brains, basically—that allowed individuals to live as individuals if they so desired.

Σ Among the Sheldrakes I discovered that life in orbit, where Gaia's all-subsuming planetary morphic field was attenuated, allowed for reduced slavery to those lesser behavior fields which in part composed the planetary one. Getting the Sheldrake space program up and running was the work of a couple of lifetimes.

Σ Meme World was easy. Once the wild animals were gotten under control and synthetic meme chemistry was perfected, true civilization could begin.

Σ The world populated by the television characters of my childhood was the most botched and pathetic. There was really very little I could do to force coherence onto such an illogical mess. So in the end I just closed it down, depopulating it by exporting all its inhabitants to other universes suited to their natures.

Σ Finally I ended up on the world of the Minskyites, where I had died. But by then I was a vastly different person. And having Tiny along sure helped. I was able to infect the Minskyites with a computer virus that eliminated their malevolence.

During all these centuries of course I grew no older, in accordance with wishes I had expressed to Tiny. And my memory capacity expanded to hold all my new experiences. But aside from these minor changes, at the core I still felt pretty much like who I had been. A little wiser, maybe, but still Paul Girard underneath.

But not for much longer.

142.
You Take the Low Road, I'll Take the High Road, and I'll Be in Nirvana Afore Ye

SPENDING SEVERAL CENTURIES with Tiny had made us good friends. The deva in disguise had none of the violent impulses of the original Hell's Angel. In fact, after the first few decades together, he began to lose some of the more melodramatic traits of the original model, though he kept up the outer appearance.

We talked about a lot of things. Practical and theoretical.

I even asked his advice about Moonchild.

Now that I was done retracing my old tracks, during which time I hadn't seen her once, I was curious about what she was doing.

"Can't tell you, pal," Tiny said. "Privacy lock, and all that kinda thing. The two things Oh Pee don't allow are coercion and eavesdropping among self-aware souls. If you're playing the game so that you realize you're living in the Omega Point—like you are— then you can't force the will of another player on equal footing, or get the goods on 'em. Though of course if you drop yourself willingly into samsara in a nescient way, all bets are off. You can have war, rape, and pillage there all you want, through old-fashioned means."

"War, rape and pillage? I just want to find out what she's up to, not conquer her!"

Tiny smiled. "Really, now? Well, it's still no go." Tiny paused. "I could *bring* you to her, though. That's cool by the Oh Pee. Better yet, I could bring you to one of her doppelgangers who's not, ah, so fussy and uptight. Whadda ya say, bro?"

"No. No thanks. Insofar as this statement means anything at all, I want to reconcile myself with the original Moonchild who underwent all those trials with me."

I sat and thought for a while. We were lying on top of a fluffy cloud floating in a golden, borderless sky. It amused me to relax in such a corny Judeo-Christian afterlife setting.

Now that I was done atoning for my mistakes, what was I to do next? I was still full of uncertainty and unease. Of course, I could have eliminated any negative feelings from my makeup with a single request to Tiny, made myself feel great. But I wanted my mind to evolve "naturally," shaped by whatever experiences heaven offered. Not be molded with a quantum scalpel.

Of course, I could have been fooling myself. Did I really have free will, or was it just a sham? How would I ever know?

Maybe I needed some more experiences under my emulated belt. Should I begin a tour of all the alien realities that existed within the Omega Point, the kind of tour proposed to me once by the Drexleroids? But that would be just more regular multiverse kind of adventures. And I had already had plenty of those.

"Tiny. Can you split me in two?"

"Hell, yeah! Hardly takes any more than a pissant's work to run one more lousy Finite State Machine."

"Thanks for making me feel so special. Do it, then."

There was another me on the cloud. But he wasn't a separate ego. I was looking out of both pairs of eyes simultaneously, one consciousness split between two skulls, operating two bodies.

Splitting himself in two also, both Tinys folded their arms across their leather-clad bare chests like dissolute genies and awaited my/our orders.

"Okay," I said. "Show me some heavens."

"Okay," I said. "Show me some hells."

Tiny made an irreverent Beatrice.

We visited all the "supernatural" places that never could have arisen in a normal Many Worlds multiverse, but had had to await the birth of the Omega Point. Perfect replicas of every celestial paradise ever imagined by Hindu, Buddhist, Moslem, Christian, Amerindian, animist or any devotee of any and all religions buried in the dust of time both before and after me. All these elaborate venues were consensually created by the shared beliefs of many resurrectees cooperating to produce what they had always dreamed of and been promised.

I spent blissed-out eons in the laps of houris, Valkyries and apsaras. And after a while, I realized something, *per* Tolstoy.

All happy places are basically alike.

But what the other me was finding out was that all unhappy places are basically dissimilar.

The me touring all the existent hells quickly learned one salient fact.

The vast majority of them were one-person affairs.

Sartre had been wrong.

Hell wasn't *other* people.

It was their *absence*.

Nearly every inferno I visited (and there were untold quintillions of them) had been constructed by the Omega Point under the direction of a resurrectee solely with that single occupant in mind. The most niggling details of each personal hell were specified to the tenth decimal place. These people were like nit-picking esthetes of damnation, narcissistic masochists who believed that their hell was the best. They wouldn't be able to get off on anyone else's hell. No sirree . . .

I met a lot of famous people in their hells. This also was in contrast to the various heavens, which seemed populated mostly by earnest, ordinary schlubs. Maybe the famous people in heaven were just lost in the crowds. But I doubted it.

When the two mes were done, we fused.

Heaven and hell tussled inside me like indigestion.

Then one of them won.

143.
The Ontological Pickle Swallowed

"HOW DID IT all begin, Tiny? Where did it all come from?"

"Well, son, it's like this. The Omega Point is born at the end of all time and all space. Then, in its capacity as the Holy Spirit or Universal Wave Function, it extends itself backwards to the beginning of time, triggering the formation of superspace out of pure nothingness and then engineering the first Big Bang from which all others branch. After that, the Oh Pee remains present everywhere and everywhen, a little shard of eternal spirit in every bit of life, subtly arranging histories so as to ensure its own birth."

"Oh. Makes sense," I said. And as easy as that, I swallowed the Ontological Pickle, one OP answered by another, my desired Theory of Anything turning out to be a perpetual Ouroborosian circuit.

"Glad *you* think so!" Tiny said.

"Can you bring me to Moonchild now?"

"Good as done, chief."

She sat in a library whose shelves went up out of sight. At first I thought Moonchild had altered her features. You could do that easily here, of course. She looked much prettier than I remembered.

Then I realized I was seeing her with different eyes, centuries older and wiser.

We didn't have to say anything about how we had spent our time since parting. The record of our exploits was plain on both our faces.

"How's the kid?" I asked.

"Doing fine. Last time I saw him, he was with Hans."

"Hans?" It had never even occurred to me to look up Hans. As sentient individuals, the Mind Children had, of course, all been resurrected too, as had quintillions of alien races, about whom I had never inquired, save to verify their existence. Why hadn't I thought of visiting Hans at least in all those centuries? What a callous jerk I still was! Suddenly all the certainty I had arrived here with teetered on the edge of oblivion.

Then Moonchild reached out and held my wrist. "It's okay, Paul. Hans sends his regards. He's having fun with Digger. It's okay. Really. Don't hurt yourself anymore."

Tiny interjected, "Listen to the babe, will ya?"

I took a deep breath. "All right. Guess I'm outnumbered."

Lady Sunshine stepped from behind a bookcase and said, "Truly, man!"

I took Moon's wrists. "Moon, do you want to come with me somewhere? There's one world I always meant to show you, but never did."

"Are we going to be superficial daytrippers? Or—?"

"No. Let's take the plunge. Deep cover. I'm sure these guys can come up with something plausible. What do you say?"

Moonchild held my gaze. "Till death do us reunite, Paul."

We sealed the deal with a kiss.

144.
Wearing Mortal Masks

THE GREASE WAS still congealing on the remains of my breakfast back in Bookland. All appearances indicated I had been gone a couple of hours at most, since the visit from Hans.

Moonchild looked around approvingly. "Not bad. Plenty of

fiction, I see. After the Sheldrake world, I never want to read another textbook!"

I flexed one of my pumped-up arms. "I know what you mean. I might still keep up some kind of workout routine though. Shame to let this new body go back to flab."

Moonchild grew serious. "We were awfully lucky, weren't we, Paul? I mean, for a while there, it looked as if the Minskyites were really going to *kill* us. I still shudder when I picture that cross they erected for our son!"

"I don't mind admitting I was plenty scared. If it weren't for that last-minute rescue by billions of Moraveckians equipped with irresistible superscience weapons, we would have been goners! Talk about the cavalry riding over the hill!"

"Although," said Moon slyly, "I don't suppose you would have ever said 'I love you' to me if you didn't think we were about to die."

I started to bluster. "Yeah, well—" Then I thought better of it. "You're right. And I'm glad I said it."

"Me too." She changed the subject. "Wasn't it a good thing the Moraveckians realized that the Minskyites had to be stopped from destroying human universes? Neutrality's all right, but there comes a time when you have to take a stand!"

"And then Hans was nice enough to find an Earth we could return to. After all, as the Drexleroids told us, my original one was extinct. Luckily, the Paul of this cosmos—identical in every way to the one I left—just finished spontaneously combusting out of pure meanness, so I can step right into his place."

I went behind the service desk. There was a big pile of smoldering ashes in my familiar singed chair. I brushed them off unceremoniously.

"And I'm sure Hans will take good care of Digger," Moonchild said.

"Yeah. Like father, like son. Digger wants to travel. They'll visit us sooner or later, he said."

Moonchild looked at the floor. "And you really want *me* here, Paul? You really want to be with *me*?"

"No one else, babe."

Moonchild threw her arms around me and squeezed. "Oh, Paul, I don't care what happens next! We've had such a great story up till now anyway! I just want to live with you until we die! If there's nothing after that, it'll still be enough."

The strangest feeling passed through me like a breeze at Moon's words. But before I could put a name to it, it was gone. I was left feeling just regular happiness.

I hadn't found paradise. But I had *lived* a story better than any I could have imagined or written, returning home with a buffed-up body, a new perspective on life and a girl of my own. I was a new man, totally changed, a better human being.

Moon ended my ruminations with a big kiss.

Just then, an impatient customer began to bang on the glass door of Bookland, due open by now. I broke our clinch long enough to give him the finger.

"Fuck you and the horse you rode in on, dickhead!"

ABOUT THE AUTHOR

PAUL DI FILIPPO, a native Rhode Islander, lives and works in Providence, amidst continual reminders of Lovecraftian desuetude. Born almost precisely at the midpoint between the heyday of Hugo Gernsback and the flourishing of cyberpunk, he has mixed allegiances to the past and the future.

Since his first sale in 1977 he has sold more than 100 stories, many of which are collected in book form. His most recent books include *A Mouthful of Tongues* and *Spondulix*. He is currently working on the sequel to the Hugo-nominated *A Year in the Linear City*, his previous outing for PS Publishing.

He has shared his life for the past 27 years with Deborah Newton. They are grateful servants of a cocker spaniel named Ginger and a cat named Mab.

COMING MARCH 2005

RIBOFUNK
by Paul di Filippo
ISBN: 1-4165-0420-6

A COLLECTION OF CUTTING-EDGE
CYBERPUNK STORIES BY THE AUTHOR OF
FUZZY DICE!

In the world of *Ribofunk*, biology is a cutting-edge science, where the Protein Police patrol for renegade gene splicers, and part-human creatures live in Lake Superior, dealing with toxic spills.

Ribofunk depicts a sentient river; a sultry bodyguard who happens to be part wolverine; a reluctant thrill seeker who climbs a skyscraper—and finds himself stuck; and a chain-smoking Peter Rabbit who leads his fellows in a bloody rebellion against—whom else?—Mr. McGregor.